RAVES FOR RITA NOMINEE
SHANNON DONNELLY!

A MUCH COMPROMISED LADY

". . . a scintillating tale filled with charismatic characters and plenty of intrigue."

—Teresa Roebuck, *Romantic Times Magazine,*
4½ Stars and a Top Pick

". . . well-done and very witty . . . a wonderful hero, who will out-duke any duke you've ever read about."

—Kelly Ferjutz, *The Word on Romance*

UNDER THE KISSING BOUGH

"[Donnelly's] tale of individual growth, slowly advancing trust, realization and acceptance of self, and the blossoming of a love destined to last forever proves compelling, heartwarming, and not to be missed."

—Judith Lansdowne, best-selling author of *The Mystery Kiss*

A DANGEROUS COMPROMISE

"This second Regency by talented newcomer Shannon Donnelly is a clever romp with two utterly charming protagonists who are clearly meant for each other."

—Teresa Roebuck, *Romantic Times*

"Delicious, delightful, and devilishly good reading . . ."
—Emily Hendrickson, author of *The Rake's Revenge*

A COMPROMISING SITUATION

"Enjoy *A Compromising Situation,* a lively Regency romance that touches the heart."

—Jo Beverley, best-selling author of *The Dragon's Bride*

"A delightful read! A warm and tender love story with appealing characters. An impressive debut novel."

—Mary Balogh, best-selling author of *No Man's Mistress*

BOOK YOUR PLACE ON OUR WEBSITE AND MAKE THE READING CONNECTION!

We've created a customized website just for our very special readers, where you can get the inside scoop on everything that's going on with Zebra, Pinnacle and Kensington books.

When you come online, you'll have the exciting opportunity to:

- View covers of upcoming books
- Read sample chapters
- Learn about our future publishing schedule (listed by publication month *and author*)
- Find out when your favorite authors will be visiting a city near you
- Search for and order backlist books from our online catalog
- Check out author bios and background information
- Send e-mail to your favorite authors
- Meet the Kensington staff online
- Join us in weekly chats with authors, readers and other guests
- Get writing guidelines
- AND MUCH MORE!

**Visit our website at
http://www.kensingtonbooks.com**

PROPER CONDUCT

Shannon Donnelly

ZEBRA BOOKS
Kensington Publishing Corp.
http://www.kensingtonbooks.com

For Dad and Ole
and fathers everywhere

One

Oh, heavens, what has he done now? Penelope thought, an uneasy prickle dancing down her spine. She stared out the window to the front paddocks, where her father stood with Squire Winslow, and the certainty crept into her that despite all her efforts, her father had found yet another folly into which he could toss the last of their money. And this time, perhaps even Harwood itself would be lost to them.

Frowning at herself, Penelope tried to focus only on the reality before her and not on her own dark thoughts.

Sunlight kissed with the last breath of summer slanted through the windows that stretched nearly from floor to ceiling in the tidy study. Outside, a brisk wind stirred the row of tall elms that marked the far boundary of Harwood Manor. It was only a day spent with the household account books that had left her gloomy. Columns of numbers that refused to tally often did.

But the disorder in the books on her desk could no more be ignored than could the black horse who now stood in the drive.

Frowning, she glanced at the horse again.

A shrill whinny—sharp with demand and fury—had pulled her attention from the household books and drawn her to the window. She had glimpsed her father at once, hatless, his sandy hair tugged into disordered wisps by the wind, standing in front of the white post-and-rail fencing that enclosed the paddocks.

He was a good figure of a man still, and Penelope had her own height from him. He rode and walked enough that age had but thickened his figure, and in his loose brown coat and buff breeches, yellow waistcoat, and cravat tied in a simple mailcoach style, he looked like the country gentleman he was.

He ought—with his patrician nose, pale, soft blue eyes, and comfortably craggy face—be a father for whom a daughter could have fond affection. A father to be proud of. Instead, that too familiar disillusionment had crept into Penelope.

Oh, why could he not at least drink it away, or stake it at cards, or do something I could honestly despise?

But there were no vices to task him over. Just unwise decision after ill-advised blunder.

Uncomfortable with such undutiful feelings, she had turned her attention to the man next to her father.

Squire Winslow's stocky figure, ancient black frock coat, and black slouch hat had made him instantly recognizable. Under the brim of his hat, his face glowed ruddy, and not from the bite of an autumn wind. All Halsage knew that the squire loved a well-set table as much as he did his brandy. And few blamed him, for as a widower he had no one to look after him, and he had sons with devil enough in them as could drive any man from sobriety.

The squire had been gesturing, as if waving to someone to hurry, and Penelope had glanced down the drive to where two grooms led a horse up the graveled drive, with its patches of bare dirt that showed their inability to afford its maintenance.

Large and dark, with grooms dangling from the long lead lines like puppets, the horse had seemed to survey the men as if selecting a target. Rearing, he had struck out at one groom, then come down on all fours and balked, planting his hoofs in rebellious defiance.

From the arched, heavy neck and its size, Penelope knew he must be a stallion—and an unpleasant one at that.

Then realization had struck like a hammer against her chest.

He had to be Squire Winslow's stallion, the one she had heard about. As the grooms struggled to get the horse to move forward, toward the gate her father had opened, she could only guess that her father had bought the animal.

Warmth drained from her face now as the stallion squealed again, then lashed out with a vicious kick. The groom dodged, and his fellow on the opposite side jerked on the lead. Swirling that direction, the horse lunged, and the man ducked into the paddock, the horse bounding after him. Instead of turning to break free, as would most horses, the animal spun around to attack again, rearing up on powerful haunches to lash out with his forelegs.

Scrambling over the railing, losing his hat, the groom struggled out of reach just as the other man swung the gate closed. Even so, the horse slammed his massive, dark body into the railing, and then raged along the fence, as if seeking some means to come after the men again.

"Oh, heavens," she muttered to herself, rubbing her arms with her hands.

All Halsage had heard the stories: One of Winslow's stable boys nearly killed. A mare meant for breeding so savaged that she was a month laid up in her stall. Penelope's stomach tightened. What did her father plan now? Raising race horses? As if anyone would breed to such a mad animal, despite the famous Eclipse bloodlines the squire had bragged of the horse possessing.

And how much had he paid for that dangerous renegade?

She glanced back at the estate books, uneasy. Local talk had it that the squire had paid nearly eight hundred pounds for that stallion. A ridiculous sum. And he was a man notoriously tight of purse as well as short of temper. He would not have parted with that horse for anything less than what he paid.

That thought terrified her. The estate had produced just a hundred and sixty-two pounds that year. If those funds—and more—had gone to the horse, would they now have to live on credit? Or had Father mortgaged the house itself to pay for this new venture?

The squire and her father started down the drive, the grooms following, and Penelope straightened. Heavens, if the squire himself—a man noted for having mounts and dogs as bad tempered as himself—did not care to face this stallion, what hope had anyone at Harwood? Which mean that the horse must be returned. Yes. That was the answer. Of course the squire would be reluctant to have back such a devil, but if she convinced her father that he must be sensible about this, then he could, in turn, be adamant with the squire.

He would have to be.

Turning, she started for the door, her mind searching for arguments. How could she make Father see sense? Her conscience pricked at her. Oh, heavens, would she sound too like a nursemaid following an errant charge rather than an obedient daughter? Well, she would have to manage. After all, she had not only her sisters to think of, but her mother as well, and she could not imagine what might become of them if circumstances became any more strained.

"But that has not happened yet," she muttered to herself.

Striding down the stairs, she sorted through different approaches, discarding each idea that came to mind.

Though they lived in the largest manor in Halsage, it was now a house half-closed to save costs, and starting to show neglect in odd corners. The lead roof really did require more than another set of patches, but harvests had been so very slim.

And if this horse had cost them . . . no, she would not think about that.

Oh, heavens, if only she could take complete control of matters. However, she was but a daughter. And to date it had been almost enough that she had convinced Father to allow her to help with the accounting, since they could no longer afford a steward or any sort of man of business. She had been able to ensure that payments to the local tradesmen came before any other expenditure, but her efforts to convince her father there was not the money for any more schemes seemed to meet only with failure.

Penelope scowled. If only he had not started with that first ruinous investment. Every venture since had started with him assuring both herself and her mother that it would at last put them on firm ground. Or if only she had a financial independence with which she could look after her mother and her sisters.

Oh, heavens, she might as well wish to be nineteen again, and short and vastly pretty as well, for all the good that did anyone.

As she reached the main hall, which lay in the older part of the house, paneled and dark, a distant, high-pitched screech echoed from the library, startling her from her thoughts.

Heavens, what now? she thought, a frazzled edge tearing lose inside her.

Muffled voices, one of them far too low to be mistaken

for either of her sisters, echoed from the library that lay just off the hall.

Her frown tightened. Of course, it might be Bridges, their butler, but she rather doubted that. Not if Cecila was also in the library.

Hesitating, she glanced at the front door. Her first duty ought to be to go after her father, but he might still be with the squire, and she could not, as a respectful daughter, make demands in front of their neighbor and his grooms.

And what odds that Cecila entertained another Winslow?

That thought decided her. Cecila was drifting perilously close to ruining herself with one of those wild Winslow lads, and that Penelope could not allow.

Besides, it would take but a moment to sort out Cecila. It would take a bit longer, she rather thought, to convince her father he really must get rid of that rogue of a horse.

With that in mind, she strode across the hall to the library and pushed open the half-ajar door. Her sisters turned toward her at once, and Penelope's mouth thinned with disapproval.

Cecila had been bending over to look up the chimney of the fireplace, and she straightened now with a guilty start. Large enough to hold a roasting ox, the hearth—built as part of the medieval hall before the stairs and main entrance had been added—lay empty and dark. Soot streaked Cecila's cheek, emphasizing its soft curve, and a dusting of ash lay over her best bronze velvet gown and her golden-brown hair.

Taking in the gown, and the care Cecila had taken to tie up her curls, Penelope's glance swept the room for the masculine presence that must accompany such efforts. However, she noted only Sylvain, their youngest sister, who stood near the windows and the heavy burgundy drapes, her chin down and a similar guilty look upon her face.

With her red-gold wispy hair and her vague blue-gray eyes, Sylvain seemed a younger copy of their father. At eighteen, she actually ought to rival Cecila, but she was too thin, too quiet, and too removed from the world, Penelope knew. She frowned now at Sylvain, whose high-necked and high-waisted dark green gown was torn at the hem and mud-stained and whose faded shawl looked more fitted for a kitchen rag.

A flutter of white wings revealed the cause of the commotion—an owl, with one white wing still drooping from an injury, perched on the drapery rod above Sylvain. Its eyes huge and dark in its flat, heart-shaped face, it swiveled its head as if seeking an escape.

Penelope let out a long breath.

Thankfully, at least, it seemed Cecila had not decided to flout convention by entertaining one of the Winslows with no better a chaperone than Sylvain and her owl. She must have been mistaken about having heard a man's voice.

Her hands relaxed and she put a smile in place, even though it felt tired on her face. "Really, Sylvain. Has not Father said that you must not bring Mr. Feathers into the house?"

Sylvain's wide mouth pulled into a mulish line as a muttering of words slipped out. Penelope caught only a few of them: "Mrs. Merritt . . . mice . . . pantry."

She almost shook her head. Mrs. Merritt would no doubt take a broom to any owl brought into her kitchen. However, she did not have the heart to tell Sylvain that, so she said, "Yes, dear, but you really must allow Mrs. Merritt to deal with that. Now, do take Mr. Feathers outside."

"I cannot. He scared him."

"He?" Penelope asked.

Sylvain gestured with her shawl to the fireplace. Then a man's muffled cursing and a fall of ash pulled Penelope's full attention back to the barren hearth and Cecila.

The girl's cheeks pinked, but she merely folded her hands before her and focused her eyes on the bookcase, as if one of the worn leather-bound volumes had just become of inordinate interest.

Penelope folded her arms. "Cecila, who is in the chimney?"

"Theo's stuck," Sylvain muttered.

Cecila shot a glare at her younger sister, but Penelope remained focused. "Really, Cecila! You are quite as bad as Sylvain, but you are two years older and ought to have a better sense of decorum!"

Her cheeks pinked brighter, but Cecila's chin lifted. "As if I have done anything wrong! Mr. Winslow has been helping me find the Harwood treasure." She shot another glare at Sylvain. "And he is not stuck."

Another muffled curse and a scattering of ash from the chimney made a lie of Cecila's defiant words. She at least had the grace to blush deeper, Penelope noted, so that her ears reddened.

However, this just would not do.

Theo might be the younger of the Winslow brothers, but that did not seem to slow him in following his brother's wild lead. If even a quarter of the neighborhood gossip had it right, neither man was a fit acquaintance for any lady. But more than that, Penelope disliked that he seemed willing to encourage Cecila's childish belief in the Harwood treasure. Such rubbishing tales only led to disappointment and heartache, and that was not the future she had planned for her sister.

Well, I am yet again to be cast as persecutor, Penelope guessed, as she watched her sister's blue-green eyes darken with rebellion. But it had to be done.

At another dusting of ash, Penelope unfolded her arms and strode toward the chimney. "For a man who is not stuck, he seems none too pleased with his predicament. Perhaps he is simply too absorbed and needs the distraction of a tug on his boots?"

Cecila looked ready to argue this, as if to deny the slightest of flaws in her Theo, but another muffled curse made her hesitate. As Penelope stepped into the wide, tall hearth, Cecila reluctantly joined her.

"He was only trying to help search the places where we have never looked," she muttered, then sneezed at the soot which floated around them.

Penelope let that comment pass. It seemed too obvious to point out that no one had climbed up the chimney for a good reason—as in what could possibly be there? And after a hundred and sixty years, the treasure said to have been hidden from the Roundheads had likely never existed. Either that or some other Harwood had long ago unearthed and spent it—a far more probable occurrence.

For now, however, Penelope simply wanted Theo Winslow out of the chimney and gone from the house. If only she could ban him forever. But as their lands marched with the Winslows', that would only tempt Cecila to meet him in secret in the woods, the pastures, or some equally unsuitable location.

A puff of soot trickled from the chimney, making Penelope wrinkle her nose and draw back. "Mr. Winslow, please stop wiggling until we have hold of you. Then you may push on the count of three."

The boots that dangled in the darkness of the inner hearth stilled. Penelope took hold of the left and glanced over to see that Cecila, her face grimaced in distaste, had done the same with the right.

With a silent prayer that Theodore Winslow wore his

boots cut too tight to easily slip off, Penelope counted to three, squinted her eyes closed, and pulled.

For a moment, it seemed as if the boots moved in her hands. She vowed to herself that if his boots were all they succeeded in removing, she would send to the stables for Mrs. Merritt's son, Peter, who also served as their groom, to come and tug on Winslow's stockinged legs.

Soot began to crumble loose around her. Then, with a choking billow, Theo tumbled down, knocking Penelope backward and off her feet. He fell into the empty hearth, swearing in a colorful stream of rude curses.

Waving her hand before her face, Penelope coughed. The ash of ancient fires swirled around her as she opened her eyes to glare at him. "Mr. Winslow, kindly watch your language. There are ladies present!"

White teeth flashed in a grin, and Penelope wished to heaven he had as much sense as he had charm. Black-faced, as filthy as a sweep, he sat in the hearth, his dark hair made lanky and spiked by soot and twigs, and his clothing a ruined mess. Soot slashed across his straight nose and his high cheekbones, making him look far too much the dashing ruffian.

"Damn . . . beg pardon, I mean dash, but I could swear my fingers almost touched something," he said.

An instant's hope flared in Penelope. She crushed it at once, knowing it for the poison it was. Ever since they had heard the story of the Harwood treasure as girls, she and her sisters had spent hours searching the house. An amusing task for childhood.

Of course, they had found not so much as a glimpse of gold, nothing more than discarded, broken furniture in the attic, rooms of dust, and stored books in forgotten rooms. The most exotic items found had been the hideous porcelain Chinese figurines of lions, which had recently gone off to auction. But she was not going to start believing in such tales again. No, she was far too pragmatic for that these days, thank heavens.

Conscious that she must look nearly as ragged as Theo Winslow—Cecila certainly did—Penelope rose with an impatient dusting of her own sensible dark-brown gown.

"Mr. Winslow, what you no doubt felt was the bird's nest which now decorates your hair. Thank you so much for dislodging it. Cecila, you had best go and change. Mr. Winslow, I am certain, can find the front door on his own."

Now on her feet, Cecila turned a blazing glare on her sister. "Really, now! At least I know better than to leave a gentleman to find his own way out."

Penelope kept her tone even as she regarded Theo Winslow with disdain. "As do I, my dear. But we are speaking of Mr. Winslow."

Under the soot, Theo's cheeks reddened, and his blue eyes darkened. He came to his feet, sputtering a protest about her inference that he was no gentleman at the same time Cecila did, and he turned on her. "I can fight my own battles, damn it."

Cecila stiffened. "Can you? And you could also slip up that chimney and down in a trice, as well. She is my sister, and I will sort this out."

"You will not!"

With that, the squabble began in earnest, and as voices rose, Mr. Feathers resumed his whistling screech and Penelope resisted the urge to put her hands over her ears and flee.

She disapproved of Theo Winslow's language, but she could bear it for the sake of seeing Cecila treat him more like a sibling than a lover. She waited for a moment in which to interrupt.

Oddly enough, both Cecila and Theo cut off their words on their own, and their stares widened and shifted as one to the doorway behind Penelope.

An uneasy chill settled across Penelope's shoulders, and she swung around at once. Someone had entered, and she could only hope it was not Mrs. Graves, the worst gossip in the neighborhood. She would be bound to spread a tale about this that did no one at Harwood any credit.

But two gentlemen stood in the doorway, strangers both. Penelope could only stare at them and blink in surprise.

Two

Dark haired, with the quality of London apparent in the smooth fit of their heavy greatcoats and the close cut of their buckskin breeches, they seemed a rather imposing pair. Mud spattered their white-topped riding boots, and each carried a tall black beaver hat.

The taller of the two, a gentleman with brown hair and eyes, smiled. He dressed with casual indifference, and his even features and straight nose might have been called handsome, but pockmarks cragged his cheeks.

The other gentleman, black haired and black eyed, was more than handsome by anyone's standard. But something, perhaps the unsettling intensity in his black eyes, stirred an uneasy awareness in Penelope. He had a strong jaw and a strong nose that matched the long, lean face. Black brows flared over his dark eyes, and his skin held the tones of strange lands in its gold hue. Next to his companion, he seemed the more compact of the two, looking naturally graceful and far more at ease than did the other gentleman. But it struck Penelope that with his dark exotic looks, he seemed almost as out of place in this room as Sylvain's owl.

He gestured with his left hand and hat back toward the hall, his greatcoat opening to show a glimpse of blue coat and a richly embroidered waistcoat. "Pardon for intruding, but your manservant seems to have abandoned us. Is this not Harwood?"

Penelope's cheeks warmed. Something really would have to be done about Bridges, despite Father's insistence that what he lacked in experience he made up for with a strong back and a willingness to double as a valet. He might cost only two pounds a year, a fraction of what a butler ought to command, but after a month of service, Bridges still seemed to have no idea how to deal with visitors. Perhaps because they had so few.

However, he really must learn not to leave guests standing in the hall.

Striding forward, all too aware of her own disheveled state and wishing she had at least heard the knocking on the front door so that she might have had some warning, Penelope forced a smile. "I beg your pardon. Bridges must have gone in search of my father, but he is not at home. And yes, this is Harwood. I am Miss Harwood, in fact."

She had extended her hand to the gentleman, and he took it, his own hand encased in the softest leather she had ever felt. *Oh, he must be very rich to afford such luxuries,* she thought, and then she chided herself for being mercenary enough to notice and shallow enough to be envious.

His grip closed tight and warm over hers, and his mouth curved into an enticing smile. "How do you do?"

Her mind blanked as that broad hand enveloped hers and a male scent, spicy with a touch of musk, wrapped around her like a spell. Her lips parted and her pulse quickened. She stared into eyes so black that they seemed endless.

With a start, she realized she ought not to stare like a child, and she glanced down at his gloved hand, which still held hers.

Stop being such a goose! He no doubt smiles at everyone just so.

And then she went utterly cold as he said, his voice as rich and dark as the rest of him, "I'm Nevin, and this is my cousin, Bryn Dawes."

She forgot that he held her hand clasped in his. She forgot the presence of others. She forgot everything except that it was a Dawes who had first led her father and her family into the start of financial ruin with that canal scheme.

Pulling away, her mouth thinned, and she tried to stifle the instant antipathy that swept into her. She ought not judge this man by his predecessor, but she would be a fool not to be cautious. Blood will out, after all. And the one time she had met the previous Lord Nevin six years ago, he had seemed affable. Then he had proven himself a man who bettered his own fortune at the cost of others. That seemed a family trait.

Or so rumor told.

Over a year ago, she had heard that the title had passed from the previous Lord Nevin to this one, and gossip of unscrupulous dealings in the matter had reached even this corner of Somerset. Penelope had not listened closely to the whispers—she really wanted nothing more to do with any Dawes. But she had hoped at the time that the Daweses might keep to cheating each other instead of involving others in their schemes.

However, here was the current Lord Nevin, looking arrogant, prosperous, and entirely unsettling. What did he want with her father? Oh, why had she not paid more heed to the talk of last year so she would better know what sort of man stood before her? And why did this fellow not at least pretend enough manners to have waited in the hall, even if he had overheard their voices coming from the library?

He glanced around the room, his expression aloof. "I

have business with your father. Do you know when he might return?"

Business! Shock settled cold in Penelope's stomach. And then she had to bite back the impolite remark that her family could not afford any more business with his.

Instead, she lifted her eyebrows and gave him a cool glance, one calculated to show complete indifference. "I doubt he will be home for some time. You had best write if you wish to make an appointment to see him."

"I have written. Repeatedly. Which is why I am here to settle matters in person."

Settle matters? Oh, heavens, this did not sound good at all. "My father keeps an erratic schedule. I doubt you will be comfortable waiting. Mr. Winslow was just le—"

A shriek from Sylvain's owl cut across her words and Penelope startled, then shot a glare at her sister, but Sylvain's attention remained focused on her owl, which had started to inch away from the girl's attempts to net it with her shawl.

Penelope let out a frustrated breath, and then Nevin's voice pitched low, his tone sarcastic, reached her. "Doesn't she have a lure?"

She turned, ready to blister him for presuming to comment on her sister's allure, or rather its lack. But as her gaze locked with his, she realized her mistake and her cheeks tingled. A *lure*. For the owl to chase. Of course. How stupid of her.

Embarrassed, and in even less charity with him because of it, she said, her tone sharp, "Well, of course she does. My sister is quite accomplished with . . . with owls."

The owl screeched again, making a liar of her. She ignored it and stared at his lordship, silently defying him to voice another criticism. Heavens, did Sylvain have lures?

Nevin glanced at her, and a flicker of amusement

flashed in those dark eyes, further disconcerting Penelope. She did not want him laughing at her family.

"Then she should train her friend to come when he is called," he said. Pursing his lips, he let out a shrill whistle.

The owl stopped its retreat and swiveled its head toward the sound, which Nevin repeated.

Penelope stared at him, her lips parted. What sort of lord was he, that he could imitate owls? And remarkably well at that.

With a slow, easy gesture, he pulled a white handkerchief from the pocket of his greatcoat, wadded it in his fist and tossed it out in a low arc. The owl watched the fabric, then swooped down to pin its 'kill' to the carpet.

Sylvain moved at once to capture her wayward pet. The owl hopped away from her, but it had not the strength in its injured wing to fly upward, and she scooped up the bird in her faded, torn shawl.

She offered Penelope an apologetic glance, gave Cecila a scornful one, then ducked a hasty curtsy to the London gentlemen before muttering a good day and fleeing the room with her struggling, screeching owl.

One trouble gone, but too many more remaining, Penelope thought, scowling at Lord Nevin. If only she could bundle him and this other Dawes out so easily.

Nevin turned back to her from having watched Sylvain leave, his eyes still bright. As his gaze met hers, his lip curved and she realized that he seemed to be enjoying making her uncomfortable. A proper gentleman would hardly do such a thing, and it confirmed her instant dislike of him. It also confirmed that if she did nothing else this day, she would drill into Bridges's mind that he must never again leave any visitor standing in the hall, but should show them into an unoccupied room—any unoccupied room.

With a thin smile, she folded her hands. "If you would

rather wait, I can show you to the drawing room." *And you may stay there until you are heartily sick of the place,* she thought, her smile widening as she thought of the dank room, with its unlit fireplace and its north exposure.

If they were lucky enough, these Dawes men would grow impatient and leave. She could not imagine a greater blessing.

Nevin had been staring at her, his dark eyes assessing, as if taking her measure. She gave him back his stare with one she hoped seemed as assured, though in truth she had to wiggle her toes in her slippers to keep from further fidgets.

"We will wait," he said, his tone curt.

She nodded. With a word to excuse herself to Theo Winslow—and a warning glare at Cecila to behave—she turned and swept past the Dawes men to lead the way to the drawing room, which lay across the hall from the library. She made no offer of refreshments, for she wanted them to know full well how unwelcome they were.

Once in the drawing room, she hesitated. With its heavy red brocade drapery and its formal furnishings from the last century, the room seemed altogether too depressing. Its high, ornate plaster ceiling and its impressive length had once held upward of a hundred guests. Now there were not even candles in the wall sconces, and her slippers echoed hollow against the parquet floor.

She could not do it. She could not leave them in such bleakness. Striding to the windows, she drew back the drapery. The weak light barely reached the corners of the cavernous room, but it was better than nothing. At least they would not be able to see the dust, nor the faded spots on the wall where paintings, now sold, had once hung.

She dropped a stiff curtsy. "Do excuse me, Lord Nevin, Mr. Bryn. I have other duties to attend."

She hoped she sounded suitably daunting. Heavens knew Nevin looked that way, his expression dark and unreadable. It irritated her no end that she looked a charwoman with the soot in her hair and on her gown, while he looked . . . well, never mind how he looked, she told herself, all too aware of his graceful attraction. Besides, she had no need to impress a Dawes.

Now if only they would grow bored or cold, or both, and leave.

And with that thought, she shut the door on them and strode back to the library to ensure that the other bothersome man in the house was shown out.

"A distinct chill to our reception," Nevin said, eyeing the gilt-edged door Miss Harwood had closed behind her. He did not strip off his gloves or remove his greatcoat. Judging from the cold air on his face, he would do better to keep them. His hat had not been taken by the boyish butler who had admitted them to the house, so he set it down on a rosewood drum table. "How long do you think we shall be forgotten?"

With an absent smile, Bryn threw himself onto a brocade couch and sprawled there, his booted legs stretched before him. "'And yet a spirit still, and bright, With something of angelic light.'"

"Angelic? Did we meet the same Miss Harwood?"

Bryn glanced up. "The same? Oh, not that one. 'A maid whom there were none to praise, And very few to love.' The other miss, not the one with the owl, but the one intent on her argument with that gentleman-chimneysweep. But perhaps the 'maid whom there were none to praise' found our intrusion unforgivable?"

Nevin's mouth twisted. "None to praise? Oh, I should think her regarded as a paragon in her community. No doubt a lady of great virtue and standing, and quite willing to tell you so—her displeasure came in response to our names, cousin, not to the form of our arrival."

"Did it?" Bryn said, his voice drifting and his stare already distant.

With a shake of his head, Nevin turned away to study the view from the window. He knew his cousin well enough by now to know that look. Poems—his own and lines penned by others—must be swirling in Bryn's mind, and there would be nothing sensible from him until his muse quieted.

Folding his hands behind his back, Nevin stared absently at a tidy garden, its rosebushes already cut back and its flower beds as carefully contained as had been Miss Harwood.

He ought to have expected her reaction. By now, he ought to know that his name always brought those stares. The kind ones offered condescension. The proud ones, like the starchy Miss Harwood, treated him to contempt. The rest attempted to ignore his existence, just as his uncle had once tried to obliterate him.

Poshrat. That was the Romany word for him. Half Gypsy, and as much an outcast to his mother's people as he was with his father's kind. But he would change that.

He was Baron Nevin now, a man with title and position. He had fought and gained his rightful inheritance, and his sister had married a lord. And now he would remake what the world thought of him.

By God he would.

A frown tugged at his mouth. The proud Miss Hardwood was just the sort of female he had met most often in London, disdainful ladies whose smiles chilled and who pulled their skirts aside when his identity became known. But how did she justify such lofty contempt when she kept such a ramshackle house—an owl loose, some fellow who looked a well-dressed sweep dripping soot on the carpet, and a butler who did not look old enough to shave?

Yet, with all that, she had folded her hands primly before her and had done her best to stare him down.

A smiled tugged at his mouth.

Ah, but that one knew her worth.

She also had a figure for a man to admire, with generous curves, and a spark of something interesting which had kindled in her eyes when he had taken her hand. She had seemed not to care that she looked more scullery maid than lady, with her worn dress, her brown hair soot-darkened, and a dusting of ash across her cheek. And he liked how she had leapt to her sister's defense. Accomplished with owls, indeed!

But then he had said his name, and he had felt the cold sweep into her, more chilling than this room.

Turning away from the garden, he glanced around the room she had left them in—another indication how little she thought of him, to have left him in this unused corner of the house. Not even candles to light, and not so much as a splinter of wood in the grate.

Well, this might be an insult to Lord Nevin, but to a half Gypsy who had grown up traveling the road, this seemed quite comfortable. She would have to do better than this if she thought to make him turn tail and run.

His smile widened at the thought.

He had forced more than a few in London's select circles to overlook the sin of his birth in favor of the title he had fought to regain. It helped, of course, that his sister had become countess to the Earl of St. Albans—not that anyone called St. Albans respectable. But an earl's influence still carried weight, even if that earl had a black reputation. And Nevin had used St. Albans's influence, as he used whatever tool he needed, to recover what had been stolen from him after his father's death.

Still, it had not been enough. Not yet.

His uncle had taken more than a title. And he had done harm not just to his own family, but to others. However, those days were done. Whatever it took, Nevin would make the world see that his title and name held something of honor again.

And the Harwoods would be the tools he used to do that.

Bryn sat up suddenly and turned to him. "Winslow! Of course! 'And I am black, as if bereav'd of light.' That fellow by the hearth must be Terrance Winslow's brother. The family resemblance for getting into trouble is far too strong to be a coincidence."

Nevin smiled. He had no idea what Bryn quoted now, but they had time to pass. He came closer and sat down on the arm of the couch, leaving one booted foot swinging. "Who is this Terrance Winslow?"

"Terror Winslow, they called him. He was a few years older than I, and ran with a far different set at Winchester, but I do remember the scandal when he was sent down. Something to do with the headmaster's daughter."

"Daughter? What, as a mere schoolboy?" Nevin asked. He had never seen the inside of a school himself. At that age, he had been barefoot and learning to read Gypsy signs left upon the road as to which great houses tolerated a camp in their woods and their rabbits snared for dinners. But he knew enough of the polite world to know the ages at which a boy from a good family went to public school, and that would have put Terrance Winslow in his early teens at the most.

"Oh, he was a terror even in short pants," Bryn said,

and then embarked into his stories. Nevin listened, amused, but that slight thread of unease slipped into him as Bryn talked. His cousin had the ability to make friends easily, and as he spoke with affection for school days past, Nevin felt that otherness in himself grow stronger.

His own youthful stories would be of broken-down horses, bought for little and then fattened and sold as younger than they were. Or of how he had distracted farmers at fairs while his sister cut bulging purses. Not exactly the sort of tales meant to endear one—not even to family.

So he listened to Bryn, and smiled and tried not to feel the gulf that lay between them. His past had made him old already, with one life already lived as a Gypsy.

But that life no longer owned him. The wandering, the struggle to survive, even the tight bonds between him and his sister and mother and with the faithful Bado, who had traveled with them, were things of the past.

A pang for what had been lost surged in him, but he let it lay, knowing it would pass, no more than a cloud across his mind. A lord could not sleep under the stars and travel the road. Not if what he wanted was his place in Society.

Besides, his mother had finally married Bado this past summer, and the two of them roamed the road yet, comfortable in that life as he had never been. And his sister had a home, as well, and a family of her own on the way.

So he listened to Bryn's stories and immersed himself in his cousin's past.

An hour later, Bryn's voice had worn thin and finally even he ran out of scandal to remember. Nevin's temper had shortened as his fingers chilled. He had expected to wait, but this had become intolerable.

Pulling his watch from his waistcoat pocket, he flipped open the gold lid and noted the time. He pocketed the watch again and began pacing, his long strides taking him down the wall to the empty fireplace and then back again to where Bryn sat. At least it kept him warm.

Ten laps of the room later—more than enough time to study the three age-darkened portraits on the wall— he glanced at his watch again.

Quarter to three. Dark in another hour and a half, he judged. And his resolution to have done with this task as soon as he could was fading with the daylight.

Pocketing his watch, he started for the door, stopping only long enough to take up his hat. "Come along, cousin."

"Ah, salvation is at hand. I had begun to think you meant to wait 'till Judgment Day. 'A dog starved at his master's gate.' That's what we'd be by morning's light. And parched as well. I could do with a mug of ale, or something more warming."

"Oh, we shall come back well fortified," Nevin said, leading the way into the empty hall. He glanced around, but not so much as a footman waited. Ramshackle, in-deed!

"Back?" Bryn asked, wincing. "Not back to London? I sense a crusade in the making. Only what will you do if Mr. Harwood should prove as starched as his daughter and just as determined not to have any dealings with the likes of us?"

Nevin's mouth curved. How like Bryn to make this his battle as well. 'Us,' he said, when he knew full well that his reception would have been far different had he ar-rived on his own. He had no Gypsy blood in him. But Bryn had honor. He had given up his claim to the title, after all. *How could he be so unlike his father?* Nevin wondered. But, then, how could two brothers be any more unlike than his own father and Bryn's?

In the hall, he turned to offer some light comment to Bryn, but the swinging open of the heavy oak front door interrupted, and he turned to face the older man who had paused on the threshold.

Harwood, Nevin thought, noting the resemblance to the daughters of the house—the same height and shape of face as the eldest and the same coloring as that child with the owl.

"Harwood?" he asked to confirm his assumption.

Hatless, his sandy hair windblown and face ruddy, Harwood's glance sharpened. "You have the advantage of me." Then worry tightened his forehead. "This isn't about a bill of some sorts? In my day, a tradesman looked a tradesman, but millers dress like lords these days. But I won't be dunned on my own doorstep. No, sir. I simply will not have that."

Nevin's mouth tightened. First to be put aside, and now to be accused of being in trade. These Harwoods seemed determined to drive him away. However, he had his task to remember, so he forced a polite tone. "I am Nevin. This is my cousin, Bryn Dawes. And this has nothing to do with bills."

Harwood's expression softened, though his pale eyes still seemed wary. "Nevin? Oh, yes, I had your letters about some new scheme you wanted to put forward to me. Do forgive me, but you've wasted a trip, you know. I've done with such investments. No head for it. But where's my manners? I've not even offered my condolences on your father's passing, and I should have written you that much at least."

"That would be my father you mean," Bryn said, his tone hollow.

Nevin sent a sharp glance at his cousin. Bryn had not

been close with his father. Even now, he shied away from speaking about the man, which told Nevin far more about Bryn's confused feelings than Bryn would ever want known. Nevin thought of the painful gap in his own life. He had never even known his father. But how much worse to have known and despised one's own blood?

Ah, but such thoughts had no place in the lightness of civil conversation, so Nevin turned back to Harwood with a smile and a ready answer. "Thank you, but could we not speak to you in a more comfortable setting than the hall?"

"But of course, of course. Do forgive me," Harwood said, coming forward to shake their hands and then usher them up the stairs. He looked perplexed at the odd line of inheritance, from uncle to nephew, instead of father to son, but Nevin did not want to go into his family's shameful history, and he guessed that Harwood would be too much the gentleman to ask.

He was right.

With a strained smile, Harwood led them up the stairs and into a snug, book-lined study. Ringing for a servant to come and take their coats and hats, he offered refreshments, adding, "I believe there might be a spot of brandy yet in the cellars."

Nevin declined the brandy, but accepted the offer of wine, and Bryn moved at once to the books that lined one wall of the room, drawn to them like a hound to scent. The youthful butler, Bridges, responded to the summons and managed to take their coats as Harwood maintained a polite flow of chatter, asking about their journey and how long they stopped in Somerset.

Such trivialities wore at Nevin's already tired patience, but he accepted a glass of burgundy and gave back conventional answers. Then Bryn joined them, asking

Harwood if he had actually read William Cobbett's *The Parliamentary History of England*.

That set them off.

Not only had Harwood read Cobbett, but he had strong views on that gentleman's suggestions for far too revolutionary reforms. Nevin listened as Harwood and his cousin swapped names and book titles, long and short, and he knew himself to be out of his depth.

It is not as if I have never read anything, he told himself, frowning. But they might as well be speaking French or Latin or any number of other languages that a gentleman ought to know.

And which he knew nothing about.

The gulf of difference began to widen, and he tried to hold on to his scorn for such things. Books and words, after all, could be used by any gentleman as justification for every sin in the world—as his uncle, a learned man, had done.

Actions showed better a man's true character. And all this talk left him restless and eager to have done with his errand.

He waited until he had finished his wine, then decided good manners could ask for no more.

Trying to keep his tone even and not too abrupt, he interrupted at the next pause in their discussion, saying, "Mr. Harwood, I actually came to see you because of old business between our families. And I think it's time we discussed that."

Three

Harwood's forehead bunched into well-worn lines. He blinked, as if unable to adjust to this sudden change in topics. "Old business?"

"The canal venture that my uncle brought you into," Nevin said.

Harwood sat down heavily in a leather chair, his face sagging, his gaze losing focus. He did not want to dredge up such painful memories. His age settled in him, sapping his strength. How had he become this old man? How had youthful dreams and energy gone so quickly?

His words came out heavy and slow. "Oh, that business."

Then the old rancor began to rise, and with it came the despair. Such folly. Such waste. Useless, of course, to blame anyone but himself. He had been the one who had gambled his family's security. He had to face that fact. He had to keep remembering, for how else could he keep from repeating that mistake yet once more?

He had promised Matilda, after all. And Penelope as well. After that last venture, he really could not put them through any more.

Still, the urge stirred in him. That wonderful tingling anticipation and start of excitement at the thought of a new endeavor. That proof that youth could still fire in his veins.

Perhaps this time . . .

Don't be a bloody, damn fool, you old, silly man!

Did he not think the very same thoughts every time? Did he not succumb to the lure of his own good intentions? And had not every enterprise turned sour?

Past time he learned caution. Yes, indeed. He ought to have kept his interests firmly fixed in the country. That is exactly what he would do. Yes, indeed. He had made a new start already in that direction with the purchase of this stallion—a son of the great Whalebone, with an ancestry that boasted Herod, Matchem, and the peerless Eclipse. Yes, by God, now in that he had done something solid and real, for the horse now stood in his own paddock. So he had no need to listen to this temptation of other speculations.

Straightening, he glanced at Nevin. "Your uncle was a lucky man to get out when he did. Damn lucky. I wish to heavens I had, but what is it they say about wishes and horses and beggars riding? I never did have a mind for business, I fear. No, never did."

Nevin put on a polite smile, but he had to clench his back teeth at Harwood's praise for his uncle.

Luck had had nothing to do with the late Lord Nevin's slipping out of that financial disaster—or several others. His uncle had known when he came to Harwood that the canal scheme was near to failing, and he had sold out at a profit, leaving Harwood to bear the losses. The papers Nevin had inherited along with his title had told the story clear enough.

Of course, no actual law had been broken. The deceit had been a sin of omission, a lack of truth, rather than any open falsehood. While this had not been the only shameful secret in his uncle's legacy, it rankled most, for it was a betrayal of friendship. Nevin found that appalling. A Gypsy—even a *poshrat*—knew better than to steal from his own kind. But his uncle had never made that distinction. Not even with his own blood.

However, this was no simple matter. Even his cousin had cautioned him, saying, "If Harwood's a man of pride, he won't want charity, and you'll only insult him if you offer it."

Nevin had seen the truth of that. He would feel the same were the situation reversed. But he had found another way.

Or so he had thought.

Setting down his wine glass, he began again. "Sir, I must tell you that things were not what you thought. In fact, you—"

"No, no, my lord," Harwood interrupted, holding up his hand to stop Nevin's words. "I am too aware I made bad judgments."

"Yes, but my uncle did—"

"He did what he thought best for himself, sir. And that is enough said on it. I shall not hear anything more. Spilt milk and barn doors and all that. Your uncle is dead, and it is best not to speak ill of him now, and that failed business is best left buried with him and the past."

"But he left you—"

"I know exactly in what state I was left, my lord," Harwood said, his tone louder and his face reddening. The look in his eyes sharpened. Then he said, his voice quieting, "There is nothing to mend it. I hold the responsibility for my own past actions."

Nevin heard the unspoken message in Harwood's words. Harwood knew that he had been duped. He knew, but he saw himself as the one to blame, for he had been the one to trust. Well, Harwood might stubbornly wish to avoid this, but Nevin had his own certainty of his duty.

"Very well, if you do not wish to talk of the past, what of the future? There is an opportunity in London that . . ."

"Yes, yes. You wrote me of it. And I set your letter aside, meaning to write you that I no longer deal in such matters. You have made your trip for nothing."

Frustrated, Nevin glanced at his cousin, who offered a sympathetic shrug. The plan had seemed so simple. Since Harwood would not answer his letters, Nevin had intended to see him in person. He had taken pains to find a fail-proof venture that would recoup a good deal of what Harwood had lost. All it required was Harwood to invest his funds, and he would have ten times his investment returned, at the least.

He had not counted, however, on Harwood being so . . . so obstinate.

Eyes narrowing, Nevin set his jaw. Harwood might be making this difficult, but Nevin had grown up with a far more arduous life than this. And he would not add to the disgrace his uncle had created by turning away from the task of restitution.

"Mr. Harwood," he began again, trying to keep his voice reasonable, "I quite understand that you must be reluctant to enter into any enterprise put forward by my family. However, if I could explain the details, you would see that this is an opportunity that cannot do anything but succeed."

Harwood's shoulders sagged and he shook his head. "My lord, they all seem so to me when they are explained."

Nevin met the man's stare and saw battered pride in those faded eyes. He understood now why Harwood had not answered his letters. The man looked haunted by too many past failures, and terrified of yet another one.

Still, there was a flicker of interest. He could swear it. Only how could Harwood be convinced into agreement?

An angry heat stirred inside Nevin, and he sent a few curses that his uncle's soul might now be paying for what he had left behind in this world. The man had robbed far more than this man's pockets. And he saw now that he had set himself a more difficult task than he had anticipated. After all, what man wants to be burned twice by the same fire?

Abandoning his plans, he started making new ones. If he had learned nothing else in life, he had learned how to adapt.

"I quite understand, sir. It takes a wise man to know his limits."

Harwood's face softened and his body relaxed. "Just so, my lord. But if I cannot give you the satisfaction of having won an investor, let me at least offer you dinner. We're quite informal, so no need to worry that you haven't a change of clothes, but Bridges can show you to a room where you may wash the dirt from you. And we'll speak of more pleasant matters, shall we?"

Nevin hesitated, half tempted to decline. He had a fair idea that Harwood's notion of pleasant matters meant more talk of books he had not read. Only there stood Bryn, eyes alight, his face more alive than Nevin could ever recall seeing. And Harwood gazed at him with expectation, obviously pleased to offer his hospitality.

Then Nevin thought of the too proud Miss Harwood and her likely reaction at having to sit down to dinner with him.

His mouth quirked. Would she claim a headache to avoid his company, or had she enough spirit to face him? And what would she look like without the soot?

Well, if he did not stay to dinner, how could he find a way to change Harwood's opinion in his matter? And how could he possibly turn away from the chance to taunt Miss Harwood with his presence?

He gave Harwood a smile and the low bow that his

brother-in-law, the earl, had spent months criticizing until Nevin had gotten right. "We should be delighted."

She cleaned up well, Nevin decided.

The high color on her cheeks and the militant spark in her eyes gave her something more intriguing than the conventional beauty of her younger sister. So did her height, for when they met in the drawing room, her eyes were almost level with his own and her stare as haughty as a duchess's. He now knew exactly how a duchess looked, for he had met two of them this past year, only to be shunned by one and accepted by the other after charming the pack of dogs that followed her about. All that had been excellent training for Miss Harwood's icy stares.

He also suspected she had dressed for battle—or at least to impress him. No, not to impress, he decided, looking again at her, appreciation for that lush figure of hers stirring. Rather, she meant to show him she cared nothing for his opinion, he decided.

The dress, something the color of autumn leaves, suited her, pulling flashes of red from her loose brown curls, hugging the curve of her breasts and hinting at an alluring swell of hips. But the gown lacked the flounces and ribbons he had seen this past season on the most fashionable London ladies. No doubt he and his cousin did not deserve her finest wardrobe.

In fact, Penelope had agonized over her appearance once she had gotten over her displeasure that two Daweses had been invited to dine, and after she had settled poor Mrs. Merritt's agitation at what to serve a lord on such short notice.

Sorting out Mrs. Merritt had been the easier task, for Penelope had simply told the housekeeper to toss away the menus for the week and serve most everything tonight. She would not have these Dawes men thinking Harwood too poor a house to set a proper table.

Then she sent Cecila to help Sylvain into some suitable garb, and finally she faced the task of sorting out her own dress.

Anything in silk seemed too formal—and far too much as if she wanted to show herself to advantage. But a sensible, high-necked morning gown might look as if she could not afford anything better. That would not do at all. Which led her back to evening gowns. After pulling out three and discarding them all as too revealing, too ornate, or too much for a country dinner, she decided on a russet gown in merino wool, four years old and quite out of the current mode. However, trimmed with gold braid and with a black and gold shawl over her shoulders, it set the tone of elegance she wanted.

She had sorted through her jewelry before deciding to do without. She did not want *him* to think that she dressed to honor his presence, after all.

Oh, what in heavens had Father been thinking to invite a Dawes to dine!

If she had found out about the invitation before it had been offered, she might have pointed out how awkward this must be. And with all the fuss it caused, it meant she still had not had a chance to bring up the issue of Squire Winslow's stallion.

Well, that would hold until after dinner, when their guests departed. In fact, she would see Father then and would both insist he send back the horse as well as inform him that Theodore Winslow was spending far too much time with Cecila. Yes, everything could be sorted out then.

For now, she had to smile as her father formally introduced her and her sisters. Then she had to think up polite chatter to fill this awkward time before they went in to dine.

Cecila, thank heavens, seemed inclined to follow her lead in giving Lord Nevin and his cousin a chilly reception, though Penelope suspected that was due in part to Cecila's mortification at their having seen her covered in ash. And while Sylvain, in blue-dotted muslin, looked more her eighteen years of age and less the schoolgirl hoyden, Penelope trusted her to keep her distance. Shy as her owl, Sylvain always kept her gaze down and never spoke to company unless compelled to do so. Ordinarily, Penelope would have done all she could to encourage her youngest sister to participate, but tonight she was quite happy to allow Sylvain to keep her reserve.

Now, if only she could make her father see that was how he ought to treat these Daweses as well.

But he and Mr. Dawes had taken up what seemed an ongoing conversation over the intentional symbolism within Coleridge's *Kubla Khan,* a subject on which Penelope had no opinion, having read very little by the poet. And so it was either talk to Lord Nevin or allow her sisters to speak to him. She would as soon permit them to talk to the devil, for at least they would know to be wary of Lucifer's brimstone charm.

So, with a bland smile in place, she turned to Nevin. "Fine weather we have been having, is it not?"

He stared back at her, his eyes glittering with some secret amusement and his lips—the bottom one full and sensual, the top slim and ascetic—curved at the corners. *Contrasts and conflicts,* she thought, even in the shape of his mouth. He wore elegant clothes, but a hint of something uncivilized lay in those dark, exotic looks. He moved with controlled grace, but there seemed gathered about that well-shaped figure an unsettling restlessness. And for all that he was a lord, his manners did nothing to set others at their ease, but almost seemed too over-bearing.

He wanted the world on his own terms, she decided, as she waited for his reply.

When he merely gazed at her, she tried another conventional topic, thinking he must have decided her question unworthy of an answer.

"Do you stop long in Somerset?" she asked, her smile still in place, although it now felt stiff.

One eyebrow, black as a demon's heart, lifted a fraction. Again he made no answer.

Her own temper fired, and she pressed her lips tight to keep from saying something utterly rude. Was he deaf? Or did he wish to stare her out of countenance? Well, she was no schoolgirl to be easily ruffled.

She widened her smile. "Perhaps, my lord, we ought to continue to stare at each other like mute savages?"

His lips curved even more, and then he said, his voice rough velvet, "Is that not what you already think me?"

Heat rose to her cheeks and her irritation mounted. She had not been made to blush in years, and it frustrated her that he could bring the color to her cheeks with only a few words. Well, two could be so blunt.

"Do you honestly care what I think?" she asked. "Your lack of answers would indicate that you do not."

"I think it goes the other way around—do you care what I would answer to such inane questions?"

She bit her lower lip, and Nevin wondered if she had just bitten off an honest answer. Honest, but quite improper, he guessed. Would she retreat back into mouthing courteous nothings? He hoped not.

The color had deepened on her cheeks, an attractive rose that highlighted the delicate bones of her face and left her eyes shining. She had darker brown lines in the irises of her eyes, he noted, like the facets of a gem. And he liked her better this way, with her temper—and her poise—near to lost, instead of so chilly and civil.

Gathering her dignity about her, she lifted her chin. "I care, sir, to make polite discourse. That requires an answer to a question, and questions meant to elicit a pleasant exchange of wit."

"What wit is required for the weather? I must state the obvious, or invent something other than what can be seen out any window. As to my stopping in Somerset, I suspect the answer you wish is that I stop not at all."

"Is that the answer you would give me?"

He smiled. "It is if you would have a lie."

"I would rather the truth."

His dark eyes danced. "Ah, but I thought you wanted polite discourse?"

"What, can you manage only one or the other?"

"Can anyone manage both?"

Penelope frowned. "So you imply that I am not honest if I am polite? Well, I will tell you that it is possible to balance the two."

"Is it? Are you honest and polite when you make conversation with me, asking questions that interest neither of us?"

"Oh, I am greatly interested in how long you stop in Somerset, my lord," she said, her jaw tight.

Something flashed in those black eyes—something hot and not the least bit domesticated. Then he said, his voice silky, "How flattering that I interest you."

Oh, she had known it. These Lord Nevins were not to be trusted. They had more charm than anyone deserved. And he had taken her words and twisted them to his own meaning.

She tried to form a polite answer that would remove any illusions he held about the nature of her interest, but only childish denials sprang to mind.

Thankfully, Bridges entered to announce dinner.

Smiling, Nevin offered his arm as if they had indeed been talking of nothing but the weather. Manners demanded she accept, so she placed her hand on his arm while wishing him to perdition.

They dined at country hours, and in the old-fashioned style, with dishes already laid upon the table when they came in to the square, high-ceilinged room. Still tense next to Lord Nevin, Penelope glanced at the table, and then her shoulders loosened one knot. Against the white damask tablecloth, silver sparkled, china gleamed soft— its pattern of strawberries wound around the edge of the dishes—and crystal goblets glistened in the candlelight.

Mrs. Merritt had done the house proud, with a joint of beef, a dish of leeks, white mushroom fricassee, what looked like a trout on a platter, the pair of wild ducks meant for Sunday next, two sauces, and a cream soup in a tureen. Penelope could only hope the housekeeper had kept something for the second course, and that there had been time to bake cakes for dessert. They would at least have the apples from Mr. Holloway's orchard, for Sylvain had come home just yesterday with her dress hiked up to carry the pilfered fruit.

Father continued to talk of books and authors—he and Mr. Dawes had moved onto comparisons of translations of Plato—but when the talk moved to the recent novel by Miss Austen, Cecila joined the conversation, quite ready to speak of such lighter works.

That left Lord Nevin, seated between Penelope and Sylvain, to think of something for them to discuss, other than to ask for dishes to be passed his way. Penelope decided that if he addressed one word to her, she would answer with cold monosyllables that would show him he did not intimidate her, nor did he interest her.

However, she had not the opportunity.

He turned to Sylvain and, bending his head close to hers, said something that actually lifted her stare from her soup and then pulled a quiet reply.

Wary, ready to jump in to protect her sister, Penelope strained to hear the low conversation. But the literary discussion ranged far louder on the opposite side of the table. She sent a frown at Cecila, hoping her sister would quiet, but she was far too intent on expressing her preference for a novel with at least one foundling or orphan, a ghost, shameful family secrets, and more adventure than just ordinary people talking at each other.

Penelope glanced again at Lord Nevin and Sylvain, and she nearly dropped her soup spoon.

Sylvain was actually smiling. Then Nevin leaned closer to say something and Sylvain covered a small giggle.

Alarms rang though Penelope like church bells. She tried to remain calm. How much harm, after all, could Nevin do in one evening? But worry ate at her peace. How little had it taken for her to succumb to Jonathan's charm? He had not had the advantage of Nevin's dark, enticing looks, and look what damage he had done.

She tried to taste her soup, but memories tightened her stomach. She had promised herself to do everything possible to keep Sylvain and Cecila from ever having a Jonathan. Which meant that something ought to be done about Lord Nevin now, before anything could come of anything.

As soon as Bridges came in to remove the first course and lay out the second, helped by Mrs. Merritt's gangly son, who seemed wide-eyed at being able to glimpse a real lord, Penelope took up the opportunity presented.

Turning to Lord Nevin, she asked, "And what brings you to see my father, my lord?"

The pulse beat rapid in her throat. She ought not to ask such a direct question, but Nevin had already stated his preference earlier for such impolite plain speaking. Now she would see if he had meant it.

He turned to her, his black eyebrows lifted as if she had surprised him. He hesitated but a moment before he answered, "I came to offer him an investment opportunity."

The bite of grouse pie in Penelope's mouth turned to dust. Heavens, exactly what she had feared. Business. The chance to lose the rest of their fortune.

All too aware of his stare on her, she had to take a long drink of wine before she could swallow. "Really?" she asked. Her voice sounded too bright and she drank another sip of wine.

"Yes, but he would not discuss the matter."

Penelope glanced at her father, who sat smiling as Cecila argued her preference for Sir Walter Scott's novels rather than his poetry. The tightness in her chest loosened. He had remembered his promise, after all. *Oh, bless you, Father.*

She glanced back at Lord Nevin. Well, he must know that he wasted his time here, and he would soon enough leave Harwood.

And then inspiration struck.

Of course. How simple to deflect Nevin's attention away from Sylvain. And it was not entirely fraudulent, she told herself as she thought of her earlier argument that manners could also be honest. No, she was interested in hearing his answers on this. And she would say nothing to him other than the truth.

Yes, that would do nicely.

Putting on a brilliant smile, she fixed her full attention on him. "Why do you not tell me about this venture, for I should be happy to speak to my father of it?"

Four

Nevin frowned even as his pulse lifted. Where had this dazzling smile come from? And why had the glacial lady of a moment ago suddenly become a soft woman? This one, she tempted like fine brandy—all sharpness at first, and then she loosed a mellow fire that set the senses to burning. The warm smile better matched those generous curves of hers, but the change left him suspicious. Why so interested now?

Then he saw through her trick.

Polite honesty, she had called it—a balance of both that would offer neither, in fact. What had been her exact words? Ah, yes, she had said she would speak to her father. *Speak*. A balanced blade that if ever he had seen one, with no mention of which way her words would cut, either for or against him.

Which meant she must have another reason to ask, other than casual curiosity. Did she perhaps wish to interfere in the matter? Her earlier reluctance to have him stay had been obvious, as had her disapproval that he had actually met with her father. And when he had spoken to her sister—a scamp of a girl really, with her owl and her shy smile—that had brought more frowns to Miss Penelope Harwood's lips.

But the intensity of her dislike left him wondering if something more than scorn for a half Gypsy lay behind it. Perhaps the tarnish of his uncle also clouded her view. That seemed both possible and probable.

If that was the case, he should at least be able to convince her that while he might share a name and blood with his late uncle, the likeness went no further.

And if he could convince her it was in her family's best interest to take up this investment, perhaps she would sway her father. Or perhaps she would simply offer more freezing stares and continue to think him a lying thief of a Gypsy.

His smile twisted, and he said, "I did not think business affairs ever interested a lady."

Irritation flashed in her eyes and her lips tightened. That had nettled her. He wondered which would she choose—being a lady, or pursuing her business questions?

Then her mouth softened with that warm smile again, and Nevin's skin tingled as it once had when he was about to get the bad end of a horse trade.

Her words came out sweet as water from a snow-fed spring, and just as frosty. "Actually, my lord, whatever affects my family is my concern. But if this is such a shaky venture that you would rather it kept in the dark, I am happy to oblige."

She gave her attention to her meal, glancing at the dishes laid out as if to make a selection.

Nevin frowned. He knew a challenge when he heard it. And he was not going to have her telling her father he came with such a *shaky venture* that he would not discuss it with her.

He waited until she had selected a portion from a dish of curried potato. When she turned to offer it to him, he set it aside, saying, "I keep nothing in the dark, Miss Harwood. Ask your questions."

She glanced at him, her head tilted. "Well, as a lady, I do know so little of these matters, as you pointed out. However, it seems to me that if this investment really is such a splendid opportunity, why not use your own funds? Is it not common sense to seek money from others only if the venture is too dangerous to risk one's own wealth?"

"Perhaps. But I never ask others to take a risk in my place."

"How noble of you," she said, her tone dry.

His mouth twisted. "Is it? But if I enjoy such risk, then my motives seem more selfish than anything. The same mountain looks different when viewed from the top instead of the bottom, does it not?"

Penelope lifted her brows and regarded him. She had to admit he was clever. And she could almost believe him about his enjoying risk. He looked as if he would. "So this safe business venture is too boring for you? That still does not say why you bring it here. Do try the white sauce on the rabbit. It is a specialty of Mrs. Merritt's."

"Thank you, but I prefer my meat without embellishment."

"Like your conversation," she muttered to herself.

That wicked light gleamed in his black eyes, and she knew he had overheard. Warmth rose to her cheeks, but she tried to ignore that—and him. Only then the corner of his mouth lifted with a smile, and she stared at him, wary and trying hard to remember that he was a Dawes and therefore not to be trusted. Not even if he did have such a disarming smile.

"To be direct about it, Miss Harwood, it seemed to me that my family owed yours the favor of a sound scheme."

Surprised, she drew back. That almost sounded an apology. If so, she would have to credit him with having both a consideration for her family's pride as well as a sense of honor. She was not certain she could believe a Dawes capable of such things.

Cautious still, she asked, "You have yet to mention any specifics. I assume there are specifics?"

"Have you been to London in recent years?" he asked.

"We do not travel much," she said, and she hoped she kept any trace of bitterness from her tone. She loved Harwood, and the only pang it cost her in staying was that Cecila and Sylvain had no opportunities to meet many gentlemen.

He seemed not to hear anything in her tone, for he went on, his own voice quite casual. "The city has grown—vastly—and property is becoming ever more valuable. Of course, it is in the development of property that profit can be realized, and my men of business have drawn up plans to build an arcade of shops, with the lane covered over in glass."

"An arcade? Do forgive me, but I do not see where the profit lies? In the shop rents? What if no one wishes to house their shop in this . . . this arcade? The war, after all, has left many in rather dire circumstances."

Nevin's smile twisted, and he had to stop himself from shaking his head. This one would doubt that the sun rose unless she saw it with her own eyes. "The war also left London hungry for luxury. There is one such arcade already, the Royal Opera, with eighteen shops. And I know that Lord Cavendish plans to build yet another such next to Burlington House. What could be better than a third, with an address off Regent Street, and with the finest fittings to be had? I have already consulted an architect as to costs, which are within reason. Long-term leases will offset the initial investment and can provide far more security than year-to-year rents."

He went on describing details for her, laying out how his agents had secured the property, acting quietly so as not to drive up costs, talking plans of how to best build.

His black eyes gleamed, and his face lost that edge of

harshness, leaving his features warmly handsome. She could discern no evasion in him, just open information about what sounded quite viable.

As she stared at him, a quiver of interest grew into fascination. An exclusive set of shops under a glass roof. She could just picture elegant society ladies strolling there. Why, he made it sound so very possible.

Heavens above, this must be how it is for Father, she realized, reining in such unfounded hopes. It must all seem so attractive, so simple. All that needs be done is to give over the rest of their fortune—and trust a Dawes again.

That sobered her, as if she had dipped her face into the morning water from the pitcher on her nightstand. And dislike for Nevin—strong and bitter—rose in her again.

Oh, perhaps he meant well, but she knew better than anyone in this house—possibly even better than her father—just how little money the family had. Why, to even think of investing in this venture would require hundreds, if not thousands, of pounds! He was a devil to suggest a tempting vision of riches that could cost them far, far too much. For despite Nevin's glowing description, she could see at least a half dozen dangers, from fire that might destroy the structure and leave them with debt and only land to be resold to the possibility that the shops might still fail and leave the family destitute.

They could not risk that.

But part of her gave a wistful sigh as the wish chased past that perhaps just once something could be as good as it seemed.

Reality never worked that way, she reminded herself. And she said, as politely as she could, "My lord, all this sounds . . . well, it sounds a most excellent opportunity."

He stared at her, one eyebrow lifted in skeptical resignation, and then he said, "I hear a hesitation coming."

Her irritation deepened. Why must he be so . . . so

brusque about everything? "Very well, since you like your words unvarnished, I shall tell you that while you say this opportunity comes without any risk, I can recall that your uncle said exactly the same when he sat at this table some years ago."

Fire kindled in those black eyes, and Penelope had to swallow the sudden tightness in her throat. Her pulse jumped, and she knew that he could be a dangerous man to cross.

Almost she could wish her words back as she thought how unkind they must sound. She ought not to have implied that he lied, just as his uncle had. Only she could see no other way to state the truth. And he had wanted honesty, had he not? She shifted in her chair, the wood squeaking beneath her.

Quietly, he said, "There is no risk to your father, for I plan to guarantee the entire venture."

For a moment, she could not believe what she had heard. Then indignation on her father's behalf rose in her. "My lord, you mistake my father's character if you think he would accept that to which he has no entitlement. Your guarantee is no more than an offer of charity should we find ourselves made destitute!"

His eyes flashed, and a dull red flared across his high cheekbones. "My guarantee, Miss Harwood, is the assurance I have that this venture cannot do anything but succeed beyond every forecast."

Penelope bit her lower lip. She wished she could turn away and end this now, but manners compelled her to utter a muffled apology for her assumption.

Then she turned from him, unable to meet his gaze any longer, quite certain she had offended him, and mortified that she had had to accept the blame for her too hasty words. Heavens, but she hated to be in the wrong. She took great effort never to be placed there.

However, this man seemed to bring out the worst in her manners and her tongue. Well, she could remedy that.

Turning to her father, she asked if she should ring for the course to be cleared and the covers removed. And then she focused her attention for the rest of the meal on what her father was discussing.

The pears and apples, the almonds and spice cake, the walnuts and the raisins came and went, and Penelope could at last rise to lead the ladies from the room so the gentlemen could enjoy their port. Sylvain rose at once as well, but Penelope had to clear her throat to capture Cecila's attention, and she looked unhappy to leave the gentlemen.

Customarily, Penelope visited her mother after dinner. This evening, however, she sent word with Bridges that company delayed her. She did not want Cecila and Sylvain to be without a chaperon.

"That," Cecila said, slumping onto the couch next to the fireplace, "must rank as one of the worst evenings of my life! Can you imagine, he thinks the most unknown of poets—other than Byron, of course, but everyone knows of him—to be genius, and he will not allow any real author of inspired stories to be anything more than . . . what was it? . . . ah, yes, hackneyed scribblers, he called them. As if he knew anything!"

Penelope paused beside the fire, her embroidery basket in hand, and a slight smile in place. "I rather thought you seemed to be enjoying yourself."

"Oh, yes, I enjoy arguing with such a thick-headed gentleman as that. Mr. Dawes is quite the dullest person I have ever met. I wish I had chosen a seat next to Lord Nevin."

Penelope smoothed her skirts as she sat in the chair opposite the couch, close enough to the fire to keep her fingers warm and nimble. She hoped to finish the handwork on a pillow for her mother's bed. "I doubt you would have had much better conversation," she said, starting to sort her threads.

"I liked him."

Looking up, Penelope gave Sylvain a level stare. "You liked him?"

Cecila straightened. "Do not be absurd. You never like any gentleman."

Sylvain folded her arms and sank onto the couch. "He said he would teach me how to make a call like Mr. Feathers."

"Do not slouch," Cecila said, automatically correcting her sister. "And that is just what every young lady should know—how to screech like an owl. Really, you are getting too old for such antics!"

Sylvain made a face at her sister. Penelope only shook her head and bent over her stitching. "He most likely said that to be polite, dear. It is wise to ignore such easily offered promises, and let a gentleman's actions speak for him instead."

Sylvain and Cecila exchanged a glance over their sister's head, Sylvain's expression pained and Cecila's worried.

She is still not over that dratted Jonathan, Cecila thought, with a hope that that gentleman had suffered torments of regret every day of the past six years. She still did not quite understand what exactly had happened between Penelope and her once-intended. Penelope never spoke of it. But she could faintly recall his presence—and how happy Penelope had once been.

Penelope had not really been happy since.

And something had to be done just now to cheer her before this silence went on too long. There were times, of course, that she could be the most overbearing of sisters, but Cecila could not forget that Penelope always found time to stitch her a new gown of such elegance that she never felt ashamed. And she always tried to at least make Sylvain look a lady, even though Sylvain forever ended up with her hem torn or with leaves in her hair or dirt under her fingernails.

How could he not love her enough? Cecila thought, her temper fierce. Then she forced a smile and offered to play something on the harp. Like their mother, Penelope enjoyed music, even though she had no talent. So Cecila offered to play. And later tonight, when the house lay quiet, she would find time for her own plans.

The gentlemen left their port far too soon for Penelope's liking. But not long after, their father took Lord Nevin and Mr. Dawes off to his library with the comment that he must show Mr. Dawes some of the volumes of herbal prints still housed at Harwood.

"Yes, indeed, the Harwood catalog once listed over sixty thousand books. Most remarkable. Why, I do believe it even included a Gospel lectionary illuminated in the eleventh . . ."

Penelope listened to her father's voice trail off as he and the other gentlemen left for the library. The Harwood collection had indeed been remarkable—in Queen Elizabeth's time. That Harwood ancestor, Joshua Harwood, had made the family fortune as one of the queen's sea hawks, preying on Spanish galleons. From a life of piracy, he settled in Somerset, building Harwood House on the site of a twelfth century manor.

His son had amassed the library, his grandson had expanded it, and then it all went to pieces with Cromwell's attempt to do away with the crown. Charles II's return gave back the Harwoods their property, and it had passed through male descendants for the past hundred and fifty years. The house itself would pass to an unmet cousin when her father died—such was the rule of male inheritance. And Penelope did not mind, for at least it meant a Harwood would still be in residence. But what would become of them if they had to sell any more of the unentailed land? Or, worse, if they had to give up the house in lease to someone because they could no longer afford its upkeep?

Heavens, I am acting as if Harwood is already lost, and that will not do, she thought as she finished setting the last stitch of the leaves.

She glanced up to find Cecila asleep over a book, one of those novels at which Mr. Dawes would no doubt turn up his nose. Sylvain had slipped away, most likely to pay a visit to Mr. Feathers in the stables—which reminded Penelope that she must caution Sylvain to avoid Squire Winslow's stallion.

Setting aside her embroidery, she rose, stretched her back, and then woke Cecila and sent her—grumbling all the while that she was not the least bit sleepy—to her bed.

Then she went to say good night to her father, and good-bye to the Daweses.

She found them, as she had hoped, in the hall, and she paused on the stairs as she took in the sight of Bridges handing them their hats and greatcoats. She allowed herself a relieved sigh. Then, smiling, she came down the stairs. She stopped, however, as Bridges opened the front door.

Rain gusted across the threshold, bringing with it a swirl of dead leaves. In the darkness framed by the oak door, light split across the sky, and thunder rumbled an instant later.

Penelope shivered. Well, the Daweses would certainly earn a soaking for having delayed their departure.

Bridges closed the front door at once, putting his shoulder against the heavy oak to shut it against the invasive wind, which seemed almost as if it were a living thing which crowded in, seeking entrance.

She started down the stairs again, and at the sound of

her steps on the stone of the hall, her father turned and smiled. "Ah, my dear, just the very person. Will you have Mrs. Merritt see that two rooms are readied? Lord Nevin and Mr. Dawes are staying the night."

For a moment, she could say nothing. And then the urge to drop a dutiful curtsy and go and ask Mrs. Merritt to prepare two rooms up in the attic, where the second footman and undergardener had once slept, almost overcame her.

But there was Lord Nevin, eyebrows arched with interest and those black eyes gleaming as if he anticipated the pleasure of seeing her provoked into forgetting herself.

Well, she would not give him such satisfaction.

And she certainly could not, with a Christian conscience, send anyone out on such a beastly night. Not even a Dawes, unfortunately.

She gave the merest nod and said, "Of course, Father."

And what a pity she could not put Lord Nevin in the east blue room where the chimney smoked quite dreadfully. But that just would not do. No, she wanted his lordship to have the best hospitality of Harwood. If he had any conscience at all, he would feel a sense of obligation to the family for having provided him shelter. And he would leave.

She dropped a prim curtsy, then turned on her heel to seek out Mrs. Merritt in her rooms just off the kitchen.

Small as she was wide, Mrs. Merritt had been with the Harwoods for as long as Penelope could remember. She had a pleasant disposition, but at the mention of needing two rooms ready with no notice at all for those London gentlemen, Mrs. Merritt's gray eyes lit with excitement.

Then her round face paled and she shifted from one foot to the other. "Oh, but, Miss, wherever do we put them? There's that chimney what smokes, the wall coverings are peeling in the gold room, and the west blue room has the most terrible rattle in the windows when the wind gets up as it has."

"They are a . . . I mean, it is a nuisance, I know. And I am so sorry to bother you so late, but we must improvise. Why do you not put Lord Nevin in Mother's old bedroom? I think the covers will have to come off the furniture, and it is rather pink, but he certainly will not be able to complain it is a mean room, not with its size."

"And the other one, Miss? Wherever does he go?"

"Oh, heavens, where, indeed?" Penelope folded her arms and dropped her chin to think as Mrs. Merritt waited, one hand turning the rings on her plump hands.

Short of using the attic—and since she had the suspicion that Sylvain might be right about rats being in the house, and if there were, they would be there—she had little choice.

"I shall have to sleep with Mother. The cot is still in her room, is it not? And we shall put Mr. Dawes in my room."

Mrs. Merritt frowned, her mouth pulling down and her forehead bunching under the blond curls that peeked from her lace cap. "Oh, but, Miss, it don't seem proper to have a gentleman in your rooms."

"Why ever not? I shall not be there. I shall, however, take a change of dress with me, and since he has no clothes to put in the wardrobe, all should be fit and proper."

Mrs. Merritt's face pinked. "Oh, but Miss!"

"Yes, well, I shall be mortified later at the thought of male clothing. And speaking of such, Mary shall have to press out their garments first thing on the morrow, before they leave. For now, let us see what we can do about those rooms."

Half an hour later, candles had been set into wall sconces, covers had been removed, sheets found—unmended ones, even—and Bridges had laid and lit fires.

It cost Penelope a pang to glance around her mother's room, with its pink silk damask wall covering and its gold and pink drapery, and think of a stranger here. However, she could only hope that perhaps he disliked pink.

Her own room needed no such attention, so Penelope merely took the first morning gown that came to hand in her wardrobe, then piled on a nightshift, her dressing gown, walking boots, stockings, her brushes, and a fresh shift to change into.

That done, she glanced around her room and hesitated. How odd to have someone stay in her room. But she saw nothing to embarrass herself. A painting of the garden done by her mother hung on the wall, and a selection of books—a rather dull work on the sights of Somerset, a history of England, and a copy of Shakespeare's sonnets—lay on the table beside the bed.

She had put away any other girlish folly.

The letters and sketches Jonathan had given her long ago had made their way onto the fire. The pressed flowers he had sent had gone onto the kitchen compost heap. And her childish scribblings of love and barren dreams lay buried in a hatbox beneath her bed.

The room looked quite suitable for anyone, she thought with a touch of satisfaction.

And so she turned and left.

She had no wish to see any more of the Daweses tonight. And she had the most absurd notion that their visit seemed to extend itself every time she glimpsed them, so she sent Bridges to lead them to their rooms. Then, carrying her clothes, she slipped down the stairs and headed to the back of the house.

After her mother's collapse six years ago, the doctor had cautioned against any exertion. A weak heart, he had explained, required quiet. Her mother had been in tears at the thought of giving up so much of her life, even her garden. So Father had done over the music room, moving a bed downstairs, remaking it so that what had once been a room used only occasionally by Cecila was now their mother's haven. The depth of caring shown by her father, a man not given to elaborate expression of feeling, in taking such action still amazed Penelope.

If only he had proven so attentive to financial matters, she thought, and then chided herself for such an uncharitable attitude.

Besides, she had to give him credit for turning aside Lord Nevin's offer. Perhaps he had learned something from that last disaster. And that meant perhaps it would not be so difficult to convince him to return the squire's dreadful horse.

And perhaps I simply ought to give up such optimism, she told herself.

With a sigh of fatigue and her shoulders slumping, she knocked softly on her mother's door, in case her mother should be asleep. Then she slipped into the room.

Her mother sat up in her bed, her eyes alert and her lace cap tilted to the left. An oil lamp burned on a table beside her, casting a halo of light into the room. Its glow revealed a glimpse of the brocade day couch beside the long windows, the easel and paints in the far corner, and the cot made up near the banked and glowing embers of the fire. The room smelled faintly of turpentine and roses—an odd combination, but one Penelope found comforting for its association with her mother.

Penelope made her usual inventory.

Illness had thinned and lined her mother's face, but tonight the skin did not seem stretched taut over her delicate bones. A good sign. The aged skin, now almost like parchment, seemed neither too pale nor too bright with color. And her mother's lips widened in a smile with no trace of that ghastly blue which denoted an attack.

Her eyes also seemed a clear, mossy green, not the dull gray that showed fatigue. She must have slept a little today. That always made her evenings easier. A lace cap with pink ribbons perched on her silver-streaked hair, which she wore cut short so that the thinning strands had some curl. Penelope smiled to see the cap and the pink satin bed jacket. Those days when her mother, always so meticulous, could not be bothered with her appearance left Penelope fretting.

Lowering the book in her hands so it lay open on her lap, her mother glanced up. "So you are to sleep with me tonight? How like old times, only much more pleasant these days without my gasping for every breath. Now, come and tell me all about our guests, and how you have enjoyed them."

Penelope fought to keep her composure in place as she had all evening. *I am not going to trouble Mother,* she told herself, the voice in her head stern. *I shall simply say they were nothing out of the ordinary, and I will not tell her how absolutely horrid everything became.*

But then her mother's smile widened and she stretched out her hands. The years seemed to tumble away, and the words spilled out in a rush. "Oh, Mother, he is just awful—and I have been even more so!"

Five

With either of her other daughters, Matilda would have expected an immediate dash across the room following these distressed words, so as to claim a comforting embrace. But Penelope came toward the bed with a dignified stride. She put down her clothes in a neat pile, and offered only a quick grasp of her hands before pulling away.

Matilda's forehead tightened.

Her poor, sweet Ella. She had always been the most independent child, determined to do everything for herself. And oh, so stubborn, ever since she had struggled away from her nurse to take her first steps—and first fall—when she was just under a year old. Now . . . oh, she wished she knew how Ella carried on in the world, and not just in this one small room. Was she convinced she must manage everything? Or did she at least allow her father and sisters to help her—just a little?

"Who is so awful?" she asked, and then a suspicion troubled her. Laying a hand on her chest, she told her heart to slow. If nothing else, the years confined to her bed had taught her how to regulate herself.

Then, voice calm, she asked, "Not your father again?"

That last disagreement between Penelope and Stephen had been quite frightful. Of course, Stephen had deserved some of the blame for being so careless with their funds—again. But Penelope really ought not to task him so hard with his faults. He meant well.

However, Penelope only shook her head. She sat primly on the edge of the bed, her hands in her lap. "No. Not really. And now I have disturbed you when I meant to come in with smiles and gossip." She offered up a strained smile as proof of her intent.

Matilda reached up to smooth her daughter's face. Such a strong face, so like her grandmother, with that broad forehead and that square, determined chin. "So you meant to bore me into slumber, did you?"

The smile gained some faint humor, lifting the corners of Penelope's mouth and softening her face. "You and myself."

"Well, I insist that you tell me what troubles you instead. Sharing them will make them lighter."

"But I do not wish . . ."

"To disturb me. I know. And I promise I shall not be so in the least. I am quite clever at listening without doing anything else, you know. Besides, you have a lovely voice, and I never tire of hearing it."

Penelope took her mother's hand to squeeze it again. She ought not to say anything, and she tried to resist the urge to unburden herself. But when she began to talk about the arrival of Lord Nevin and his cousin, it all came out. Her distrust of them. Nevin's smug, superior ways. Father's dinner invitation. Nevin's investment proposition. The only thing she managed to keep hidden was any mention of Squire Winslow's stallion. The beast should be gone tomorrow, so her mother need never know.

As she spoke, the tension slipped from her shoulders. She could even make light of having put Lord Nevin into her mother's old bedchamber, and confess her wish that so much feminine decor might encourage him to leave all the earlier.

Thankfully, her mother seemed not the least upset that Lord Nevin had come to see them, saying only, "It does him credit that he seems interested in making matters right between our families, but it is just that his methods are not what we would desire. However, you really ought to leave such matters to your father."

Penelope bit down on her cheek to keep from mentioning just how close a thing it had been the last time she had left the family's well-being to her father's care. He had thrown their money into a patent for a steam engine, which had exploded two days later, killing its inventor.

Instead, she said, "Yes, well, I supposed if it had been up to me I would have sent the Daweses back out in the cold tonight."

"That does sound rather harsh. And, you know, this Lord Nevin really may be nothing like his uncle."

"Yes, I know. But there is something about him . . . something not quite honest. Something . . ."

Penelope's words trailed off as she struggled to put that unsettling feeling into words. He disturbed her.

As she searched for a reason why, her mother asked, her tone gentle, "Does he perhaps remind you of Jonathan?"

She almost flinched. Forcing herself to remain still, her face blank, Penelope asked, her voice only a little higher than usual, "Jonathan? Why I have not thought of him in ages!"

And may God forgive me for such a lie as that, but I will not worry Mother over the likes of him.

"However, now that you remark it, perhaps there is a . . . well, a similar charm. Why God ever cursed this earth with charming men, I shall never know."

And then she smiled and began to talk of how nice a table Mrs. Merritt had managed to set.

The echoes of Jonathan's memory lingered. Oh, heavens, did Nevin remind her too much of a man she had once loved and now hated? Did that color her feelings? She did not mind judging him by his own kin, but to judge him by chance resemblance would be too unfair.

And then she made herself admit the truth of it.

Nevin did have for her a fascination—an attraction. And Jonathan had exerted just such a pull, drawing her to him from the first moment she had glimpsed him at the Wells Assemblies. She had allowed that allure to blind her to his faults, and she had not discovered his true character until the cost of it was the shattering of her dreams.

Well, she would avoid repeating that mistake. She knew better now than to trust anyone without a good, long hesitation.

Her mother's hand over hers made Penelope look up, and she noted the slight dulling in her mother's eyes. Smiling, she covered her mother's hand. "I've worn you out with my chatter. But you were right—I do feel better."

"I hope so. And do try to remember, my sweet, that the past hardly ever repeats itself unless we make it do so by refining upon it too much."

Leaning down, Penelope kissed her mother's cheeks. "I shall remember."

Though much good it shall do me, she thought as she rose to turn down the lamp and dress for bed. For she seemed to be cursed to remember everything, including the ache of loneliness and regret for a love that had only been an illusion anyway.

Bryn woke from hazy dreams to a scrabbling sound of nails on wood. His first blurry thoughts went to mice in the wainscoting. But then door hinges creaked and a light voice whispered into the darkness, "Ella, are you awake?"

The hinges creaked again as the door shut, and then bare feet slapped on the wood between the door and the carpet that lay under the bed.

His voice still thick, he struggled upright, muttering, "'Dear child! dear girl! That walkest with me here'—but I suppose that ought to be 'wakest me here'—only that is not Wordsworth."

A white figure, indistinct in the darkness, paused beside the bed. Then a voice, quivering with outrage, announced, "Mr. Dawes, what are you doing in my sister's room?" A short pause fell, then the voice added, still outraged, but tinged with curiosity, "And just what sort of word is *wakest*?"

Bryn squinted into the darkness. He could just glimpse moonlight that outlined a tumble of curls and a white, wraithlike figure which ought, he supposed, to elicit either dread or desire. He could summon only a grumpy wish to go back to sleep. He had been having the nicest dreams—or at least he rather thought, from the wistful tatters that remained, he had.

"I was sleeping," he grumbled. "And you may take the outrage from your tone, thank you. Your sister found repose elsewhere. Rather more restful ease, I should think. And wakest seems a very good sort of word . . . Miss Cecila, is it?"

"It is. And I should thank you not to refer to me as a dear anything—most certainly not a 'dear child'!"

"I shall make you a bargain, for 'the night is a-cold.' I shall cease to refer to you in any fashion if you but cease to disturb my dreams."

"Oh—I . . . I beg your pardon. Good night."

The figure drifted toward the door and footfalls padded across the floor again, but then paused, and her voice, quite as wistful as his dreams, asked, "You do not happen to know where Penelope might be sleeping, do you?"

He ought, he knew, insist she leave. She had no business being in his room at this hour—or at any hour. But he knew the sound of a troubled soul. God, did he know that sound. And who else walked at night, unless to seek solace?

Since he could not very well send her to her sister—for he had no idea where she laid her head—he had to do something else.

'A sadder and a wiser man, He rose the morrow morn.' Well, Coleridge had that right. But neither sadness nor wisdom could keep him from helping another.

Rubbing a hand over his face, he sat up, then dragged the covers to his chin. That youth of a butler, Bridges, had lent him one of Mr. Harwood's nightshirts, which had pinched at his shoulders, so he had left it off to sleep in nothing more than his skin. The night's chill had already brought the gooseflesh to his back.

"I wish I could refer you to your sister, but since I cannot, I shall have to ask the obvious: can I be of any assistance?"

"No, no. I should not have troubled you. Good night."

"Are you certain? You've already woken me, and you could sit on the bottom of the bed here and picture me as your sister—it's dark enough I could pass for that—and I shall make sympathetic noises at you as she might."

Cecila almost loosed a rude snort, except young ladies of breeding never uttered such a sound. So she choked it back and stood on one foot so she could warm the other against her calf. This was quite dreadfully awkward, but the amazing part of it was that mortification had not flushed hot across her cheeks. And his voice held such kindness that she very nearly did as he asked.

Only she simply could not. She hardly knew the gentleman. Besides, Penelope would blister her ears with the worst dressing down if she ever heard about this improper meeting.

"Thank you, Mr. Dawes, but . . . well, thank you. It is very kind of you to offer. Good night." She opened the door and then hesitated again, glancing back at the dark shape on the bed, seeing little more than a lump of bedclothes. The feeling that she ought to say something more held her still.

What could she say? She had come here after tossing and turning, her thoughts tangled and fretful. Only she could say nothing to a stranger such as Mr. Dawes, no matter how inviting and kind his voice sounded.

"Good night," she said again. He had seemed so pompous at dinner, but he did not seem so now. And she knew she must sound an utter goose, uttering the same words over again. So she left, shutting the door quietly behind her, and then muttering the entire time as she hurried back to her room about what a ninny he now must think her.

Bryn heard the door close and then he listened to the silence. The rain seemed to have stopped, for it no longer rattled against the window, but wind blew a faint, mournful dirge down the chimney.

With a sigh, he lay back, staring up at the bed canopy and seeing only darkness.

What made the fair Cecila walk at night? Why did he now feel compelled to lie awake thinking about her? And might it have been rather nice if she had decided to stay and sit with him in these dark hours when souls walked the world?

Lying in his bed, hands clasped together under his pillow, Nevin watched dawn filter into his room, transforming darkness into gray-hued shapes. No matter that he now was a lord and could sleep as late as he liked, his body insisted on habits trained into him by too many years when the sun woke him.

Once a bed such as this, with its thick feather mattress and its soft lavender-scented linen, would have seemed a luxury. A room of his own, paneled in wood, painted in white and gold, had been a dream. Now he judged critically that it seemed smaller than his chamber in Nevin House. It smelled also of musty roses and ash from the burnt-out fire, and he did not welcome the sun's changing grays into an overabundance of pink.

Despite the air of disuse to the room, however, he could not complain of his comfort. Not with a soft bed, warm covers, and a lark beginning its morning song outside.

But he also could not laze about like a lord. He still had not learned that trick of gentility.

Sitting up, he swung his legs out from the warmth of rumpled coverings. He could see well enough to dress, for he had pulled aside the drapery last night. He could not sleep in a room that did not give him a view of sky— another habit of the Rom he had not been able to shed.

Breeches went on over his drawers. Then he dragged on silk stockings and stamped his feet into his boots one at a time. He pulled his lawn shirt on over his head, leaving it open at the neck, then shrugged into his greatcoat. Who would even be awake to notice his disheveled state? A milkmaid, perhaps? Later would do for a proper cravat tight around his neck, and his waistcoat and coat.

And that is another gentleman's habit yet unlearned, he thought with a twist to his mouth. He did not yet know how to be comfortable in too many clothes.

He eased open his own door, keeping it silent on its hinges, as if he still needed to slip from a house without anyone knowing. With his step light on the worn carpet, he made for the stair. A clock's ticking echoed, measured and loud against the lack of other sounds.

He found the front door unbolted—a trusting sort these country folk—and let himself into the dawn air.

Cold stung his cheeks and neck, and his breath clouded before his face in a warm mist. The sun still hid behind the eastern trees, showing only as a pale half circle of advancing brightness. The day smelled of wet from last night's rain, and heavy drops glistened like tears from the branches of the trees, dripping from the autumn-aged leaves.

Making for the stables, he strode toward the side of the house. Gravel crunched under his boots. The drive, he noted, showed muddy pools in some spots, but perhaps Mr. Harwood was not the sort to care—or even notice—such casual neglect. He seemed the type to perhaps be more caught up in his books—like Bryn, who could go for days without so much as shaving when the fever gripped him to write down the rhymes in his head.

At the side of the house, Nevin glimpsed an iron-gated archway that led into a garden. A kitchen garden, he decided, glimpsing the plants there. He turned his steps to that path. A few carrots stolen would no doubt be blamed on rabbits, and his pockets needed some treats for Cinder.

The garden impressed him. Neat rows of carrots, turnips, and other root vegetables for winter had already sprung up from the dark earth. A few now straggling vines of beans had not yet given up their last crop before the cold, and other bare plots told of seeds yet to be sown.

Was it Miss Harwood who tended this spot with such care? He doubted that. Her hands seemed far too white, too soft.

Ah, but he did not want thoughts of her and her scorn with him this morning. No, the morning seemed cold enough.

Instead he focused on sparrows that had begun their chattering and on distant cowbells. The milkmaids of the neighborhood must be awake and afoot, even though the moon had not set. Ah, but this morn had the promise of warmth rising that set his blood singing. Almost, he could long for the . . .

With a frown, he broke off those thoughts. The road no longer called him, he reminded himself. And if he found the air as potent as fine wine and the land beckoning to him, well, that did not mean a lord such as he had to answer.

Letting himself out by the gate, still frowning at where his thoughts had taken him, he headed for the stables, a low-roofed building that gave off the unmistakable odor of hay and horse.

Gravel changed to brick as he stepped into the building, still half-hidden in night's shadows, and he put aside his dark mood. It would only make his horse nervous.

A low whistle drew Cinder's answering nicker. And then he stopped where he stood.

Miss Penelope Harwood, her hair pulled up into a disorder of loose curls and a cloak thrown back from a dark green gown, stood beside his horse, one hand resting on the gelding's black neck.

Six

She looked as shocked to see him as he was to find her in the stables at dawn. Her eyes had widened, and the glance she shot toward the doorway betrayed her desire to leave. However, her lush form stiffened, back bracing and elegant chin lifting. Ah, but of course—this one would not give ground to anyone. He had to smile at that. Despite their shared antipathy, he admired courage. And there was more to admire in her than that.

From a window set high to draw the light, a golden finger of dawn slanted down to touch her curls, adding fire to the rich brown. She did not look the too proper lady this morning, he thought, with some satisfaction. In fact, with her lack of bonnet and her disordered curls, she only lacked bare feet under her skirts to look the complete Gypsy.

Unable to resist the impulse, he glanced down. The tips of scuffed brown walking boots showed under the ankle-high hem of her skirt. So she was a *gadji* through and through.

A touch of disappointment feathered through him, but he shrugged it off. He had no reason to feel anything for this one, not when she served him only her disdain. But he could hardly turn on his heel now. That would only prove he knew nothing of manners, and he would not have her thinking he could not act the gentleman.

So he came forward to the black gelding's stall and bade her good morning.

Her hand dropped from the horse's neck. She offered back a polite nod, and then said, her voice almost as chilly as the air, "My lord."

Nevin's mouth twisted even more. They sounded as if they had met at a London ball, not in a dawn-flushed stable, both of them looking like urchins instead of a lord and a lady.

She shifted on her feet, and again glanced past him toward the doorway. Was she inventing some excuse to leave? Or would obstinacy keep her from yielding anything to him, even the stables?

Cinder pushed against his arm, as if to remind him that a better greeting than mere words had not yet been offered. Turning to the gelding, Nevin dipped his hand into his pocket and broke off a chunk of carrot.

Penelope remained where she was, hands folded before her as she watched Nevin feed his horse. What now? She had not expected company, particularly from Nevin, and words fled her mind.

He unnerved her, just as he had yesterday. How did the man manage to move without seeming to make the least noise? And he really ought not to have come downstairs so . . . well, so half-dressed, as if he were a farmer.

But, somehow, she liked him better this way. He looked far less the too fashionable London gentleman, and far more approachable without that barricade of fine clothes. He looked . . .

Oh, for heavens sake, just admit it—he looks impossibly attractive!

His black hair no longer lay in careful order, but stood every which way, as if he had only bothered to drag his fingers though its thickness. Underneath his open great-coat, which swept to his ankles and whose capes made his shoulders seem even broader, his shirt lay open at the neck. Skin darker than any gentleman ought to possess lay framed by white fabric in an intriguing contrast. Any woman, she decided, would admire that strongly corded neck and a fine glimpse of muscle.

Her taking notice of such a thing indicated nothing more than that she was human, she thought, only her cheeks still felt warm for having noticed so very much.

Oh, heavens, what do I say now?

She could, of course, note her surprise at his having risen so early, but it seemed fatuous to state the obvious. And their conversation at dinner, in which he had ignored her repertoire of polite nothings, left her unwilling to try a remark on how pleasant a morning the rain had left behind.

She scowled at herself.

Stop gaping and think!

Embarrassed to be so lack-witted, she dropped her gaze to his boots, but then that low voice of his pulled her stare up again.

"You met Cinder?"

With relief, she turned her attention to the gelding. "Not a proper introduction. However, he would not allow a visit to my Juno without receiving some notice."

"You mean he shamelessly begged. Did he convince you he is a horse starved to weakness?"

A smile tugged at her mouth, for the horse had whickered at her in the most plaintive fashion, just as if he had not the energy to do more. Now, the large black head and neck leaned over the bottom door to the stall as the gelding searched Lord Nevin's pockets with energy.

"Well, he did ask for a handful of oats," she admitted.

"Ah, but then he should offer his thanks to you."

He reached for the latch to the stall, and Penelope stepped back. She ought to find some excuse to go on her way. She had certainly stayed long enough to be civil. But she wanted to know just how this horse of his—Cinder, he had named him—would thank her.

And something else had stirred her curiosity.

Nevin did more than look different this morning. There seemed to be a . . . a relaxation in him, a . . . a difference. Only why should a disheveled state make him seem so much more approachable? She could almost forget he was a Dawes.

However, the change also left her wary. How could one trust any man whose character shifted so drastically, particularly when he *was* a Dawes? Which side should she now take as his true character—this gentleman so at ease, or the aloof lord of yesterday?

After unlatching the stall, he swung the bottom door out, settling it against the wall and its mated top half. The gelding stood alert in the fetlock deep straw, his neck arched high, his ears pricked.

He knows something is towards, Penelope thought, watching the horse and wondering what Lord Nevin intended.

The gelding butted his nose against Nevin's chest again. With a smile, Nevin stroked the horse's face, his long fingers offering gentle caresses as he muttered foreign-sounding words. His voice flowed into the morning, soft as spring mist, and something knotted in Penelope's chest.

Lips parting, she watched, unable to look away from those elegant hands, transfixed by that low voice. Heat flowed into her, like the warmth of sunlight through a glass.

And then she realized what was happening.

Heart pounding, she forced her stare away. *No, no, no!*

I will not do this again, she thought, already bottling the emotions that had started to swirl inside her.

She would not allow feeling to sweep away her judgment. It had cost too much to learn that lesson. And she had her father's excellent example of the continuing disaster caused by ignoring reason.

Stiffening, she scolded herself for her weakness.

So the man cared for his horse. That did not make him a paragon. It meant less than nothing. It did not make him a man to be trusted—or liked.

And she simply would not think about the ache that had opened inside her at the glimpse she had had of such tenderness.

I have done very well without that in my life, she told herself.

Still, her glance stole back to him.

The whole of his attention seemed focused on his horse as he dug in his pocket again. He continued muttering. Then he stepped back, saying, "Make your bow, Cinder."

The black horse bent one knee, tucked his left foreleg back and stretched downward to bow his head, his black forelock lifting with a flourish as his head nodded.

Penelope gave a startled gasp, one hand lifting to her chest. "Oh, my word!" A quivering laugh of delight slipped out.

Nevin glanced at her, amazed she could be startled into such an expression, and he found himself more astonished than she must have been.

Her face glowed. Amusement had lightened her eyes to the color of fine toffee. He suddenly wondered if she was younger than he had first thought. *Devla,* but this one could fill the eye. Not with beauty, but with this vibrancy of life that she kept hidden under those sharp edges.

But why did she hide this, like a treasure she must

guard? He knew well enough, as did any Rom, how not to trust the *Gadje,* but what had taught this lady to be so wary? She and her kind owned this world. So who had stolen that birthright from her?

Wanting to see if she had more smiles, he put Cinder through his tricks, asking his questions and giving the subtle hand signals he had taught the black gelding.

They were few enough—bow, count his age, shake his head for no and nod for yes. Then the carrots had been eaten, and he could think of nothing else to ask the gelding.

Still, the tricks had thawed Miss Penelope Harwood. They lured her into stepping close enough to run her fingers under Cinder's back forelock. Close enough that the faint scent of lilac on her skin teased Nevin. Close enough that he glimpsed a tempting beauty mark just under her left earlobe where the sensual curve of her neck met the line of that stubborn jaw.

She smiled wider as the gelding nosed her skirts. "What a clever fellow you are—and you are also quite the glutton."

Nevin leaned against the edge of the stall doorway. "Ah, but that only makes him easier to teach. And he would not be mine now if I had not found out his weakness."

"What, did you lure him to your stables with a bucket of oats?"

For a moment, Nevin held still, his eyes narrowed. Then he forced himself to relax. He had heard no sly insult in her words as to a Gypsy's reputation for thieving. No, she only smiled and stroked the gelding's face as she spoke, as if unaware how close her words came to the truth of his past.

"I did not have to lure him," he said. "He came as a gift from the Earl of St. Albans who . . . well, let us say only that my brother-in-law did not appreciate Cinder's talents."

She gave him a sideways glance, her eyebrows arched. "What, did Cinder make his bow at the wrong moment, perhaps?"

Nevin could not stop an answering grin. The memory was too sweet. "In Hyde Park—at the fashionable hour."

She choked back a laugh, then said, "How mortifying for an earl. I can see why he might be displeased."

"Displeased? My skin would now be decorating his study if he had been able to find me that day. But I have a sister who knows how to get her way with her husband, and she talked him into giving me the horse if I promised to stay away from the rest of his stable."

"Well, your sister's husband sounds rather stuffy if he cannot appreciate such a rare trick."

Nevin almost laughed. He could hardly wait to see the Earl of St. Albans's face when he told that devil this story. *Stuffy?* St. Albans would be appalled that these provincial Harwoods did not know enough to tremble at the mere mention of the worst rogue in England. Or perhaps St. Albans would not care in the least. Nevin had never met a man so utterly unconcerned with anything but his own world.

Then he glanced at Miss Harwood. She ought to be like that, certain of herself and assured. He had thought her so yesterday, but today he found himself remaking his opinion of her.

"Would you care for me to teach you how to make him bow?" he asked.

Her face brightened, but then she pressed her lips together and shook her head, looking like a child who did not dare impose herself. "I should not trouble you."

"Come, it is not that difficult."

"Well, I . . ."

"Just fold your little finger back—like so," he said, demonstrating with his own hand. "Hold your other fingers straight."

With her lower lip between her teeth, she tried to copy his gesture. She had not worn gloves, and he was glad to see it. Perhaps she was not so much the too proud lady as she pretended.

"No, no, the other fingers must not move, for that means something else," he said, taking her cold hand.

At his touch, her fingers stiffened, and a stronger awareness of her swept into him.

The softness of her skin, the delicate bones—all of it fascinated him. He wanted to circle her wrists with his fingers just to see if he could. A tremble shivered in her, and he wished he could hold her hands closer and warm them between his rougher ones.

Instead, he slid his thumb across the inside of her wrist, where the skin was softest. Her pulse fluttered, so he stepped closer, lured by the gleaming lights in her hair, by the warmth of her, which wound around him like smoke from a fire.

Suddenly, she got it right and Cinder stretched down to make his bow. She gave a laugh. "Oh, heavens! I did it. My word, but I shall have to teach Juno this trick, if she is not too old. Oh, I do wish Father had half your skill with a horse, and then it would be no bother that he bought that devil from Squire Winslow."

She glanced up at him, her eyes bright and her face still animated from her chatter.

He met her gaze and held it.

She went still, her smile fading, her eyes widening.

I have only to lean down and I could kiss her, he thought. He could slip an arm around her in an instant, pulling those lush curves against him. And what would that feel like?

He ached for an answer.

But he was a lord now.

A lord and a gentleman, and he had no plans to take his brother-in-law, the rakish earl, as his model.

Releasing her hands, he stepped back and gave Cinder the reward of a pat on the neck instead of a carrot. "Does your Father need help with a horse?"

She looked away, her cheeks flushed, one hand rising to fuss with the curls that had started to slip from the ribbon that held them before she forced her hand down again. "He . . . well . . . I beg your pardon, I should not have mentioned it."

She glanced up at him again, and for a moment he glimpsed the emotions flicker across her face—the uncertainty, the tug of interest, the distrust that began to shadow the pleasure of a moment ago.

He wanted to reach out and somehow stop her from banking that fire, but it vanished too fast as she pulled away from Cinder—and from him. And there she stood again, the proper lady with her too sharp smile and her walls.

She had forgotten herself while he made Cinder perform, but now she had remembered. And he had to clench his hands to keep from reaching for her to make her forget herself again.

Ah, but it was nothing to him if she chose to hide herself. He had to remember that. He had to act like a *gaujo* now and pretend nothing had happened between them, even though they both knew better.

"I really ought to return to the house. Good day, my lord." With a fleeting façade of a smile, she left, back straight, step firm, head high.

Leaning against the black gelding, he watched her go, his eyes narrowed. He had no business to be thinking the thoughts that now stirred in his head and in his veins. He had come to give back to the Harwoods what his uncle had taken and, in doing so, to finish the job of reclaiming his family's honor. That was all he wanted here.

Cinder blew deeply through his nose, and Nevin smoothed his palm down the gelding's sleek neck. "You have that right, my friend."

And then his thoughts began to turn. What had she said about her father and a horse?

He began to smile. Had she perhaps dealt him a new card to play in this game between himself and her father?

Cecila heard footsteps on the stairs and glanced up to see her sister ascending, her boots falling heavily on the worn carpet. A tentative smile curved Cecila's mouth. Last night's doubts still hovered close, made worse by a dream she had had that she had been trapped in the chimney and it had started to close in upon her. Suffocating, she had fought herself awake only to find herself so tangled in her bedding that she could hardly move.

A shiver slid down her back. That dreadful, trapped feeling lingered. And she did so want a talk with her sister, for Penelope's brisk words could be a tonic at times.

It was Penelope who had gotten them all through Mother's illness when it had seemed as if she would not last another day. And it was Penelope who somehow managed to make life seem not so desperate when they had had to sell more than half the acreage around Harwood.

Only just now the tight, cross expression on Penelope's face made Cecila wonder if her sister's words might be as brisk today as a copper-bristle brush on her skin.

Hovering in the hallway, Cecila pretended to straighten her hem. She did so wish Ella would banish her midnight doubts. Was she really doing the right thing? Ella certainly did not seem to think so, but someone must find the Harwood treasure someday, must they not? And they certainly needed it now—desperately, she feared.

She never had had any head for figures, but she had eyes to see the dwindling number of servants, the neglect in the gardens and house, and the economy that had left trips to anywhere except nearby Wells or Taunton for the dances held once every quarter. And while Cecila had her own future settled and Penelope certainly seemed happy at Harwood, the question of Sylvain remained. More than any of them, that child needed a season in London to give her some decorum—and to remind her she was a lady, not a woodland creature.

But her worries over their future had been made worse by the fact that Theo had told her that his father had sold a stallion to her father—for nine hundred and fifty pounds.

The sum boggled Cecila's mind. Why, poplin for a gown was only four and seven a yard, and silk shoes could be had for ten shillings—just half a pound. Nine hundred and fifty could dress them all in the grandest style and still leave money for the household accounts for a goodly time.

She could not help but wonder if Father really could afford such a sum just now.

He was not miserly, thank heavens. But that only meant the conditions at Harwood had to be due to a lack of funds rather than a reluctance to spend them.

No wonder she had dreamed of being closed in and suffocated.

She glanced up as Penelope came toward her. Well, one could but try the waters. And so she put on a cheerful smile. "Hullo, Ella."

Her sister gave her a critical glance. "Your best blue gown? In hopes of seeing Theo Winslow today? Really, Cecila, you ought to realize by now that he is quite as irresponsible as his brother and is most certainly trifling with you."

The hairs on the back of Cecila's neck rose. Honestly, Ella was growing more prickly than one of Sylvain's hedgehogs! Chin lifted, she looked Penelope up and down, taking in the curls falling loose and the straw on her gown. "Well, I should rather be trifled with than make myself so disagreeable in looks and manners that no man will have me!"

She regretted the words at once, for Penelope's cheeks had paled and a look of pain flashed in her eyes. *Oh, but I did not mean to remind her that she had been jilted.* Only she had meant just that. Penelope's harsh judgment had goaded her to it.

It was just too unfair, for Theo Winslow was not really irresponsible. He simply needed stability in his life. He needed someone to look after him. In short, he needed her. And she only needed time enough to make him realize it. She also needed to see him more than once in a month if she was going to make him realize anything in less than a dozen years.

Why must Penelope make everything so difficult?

Of course Theo was a touch wild. His brother's influence, Cecila knew, for there could be no man as uncivilized in the neighborhood as Terrance Winslow. He boasted of having kissed every girl in the district, and he had indeed stolen a kiss from Cecila, which she had reluctantly given at the last May Day fair. He might have taken more had not Theo come along. Yes, Terrance was another problem, for he drank too much, rode too hard, could be seen in public with tavern wenches hanging on his arms, would bet on anything, and Theo worshiped him.

But that would end when she and Theo married.

Cecila would make certain of it.

So she gave her sister a defiant stare. There was not a thing Penelope could do to stop her from seeing Theo. And while Father loathed any disagreement, particularly with his eldest daughter, Cecila knew he would not ban Theo from the house. Squire Winslow was their neighbor, after all.

Eyebrows lifting, Penelope returned Cecila's stare, and then she said, her voice quiet, "Well, if you wish to follow my path, then by all means continue to court Winslow's attention."

She walked past Cecila, leaving her struggling for an answer that would show Penelope just how little Cecila cared for her sister's opinions.

However, all she could manage was an insulted, "Well!" For the emotions churned inside her, making it impossible to think.

Turning away, she started down the stairs, muttering about interfering sisters, and crushing all desire to ever confide in Penelope again.

"As if I ever really needed her help with anything!" Cecila muttered. Then she stepped into the breakfast room and stopped, her face hot.

Bryn Dawes sat at the round table, his hands wrapped around a cup of steaming, dark liquid. He had been staring out the window, but he turned toward her, his expression questioning, and she wondered if he had overheard her talking to herself. Oh, she could just die.

But he only smiled and said, "Good morning, Miss Cecila. I trust you slept well?"

Seven

Cecila shot a frown at him. In his brown riding coat and buff breeches, his cravat carelessly tied, he looked quite unpresuming. He had even buttoned his waistcoat one button off, and her fingers twitched to correct it. However, his question sounded far too like an offer to discuss their accidental midnight meeting. And she disliked how a knowing look lay in those warm brown eyes, as if they shared some secret.

The best course seemed to be to act as if nothing had occurred, so she closed the door behind her, and offered a polite, "Yes, thank you." Then she turned to the sideboard and took up a plate to make her selections.

That soft voice rose again. " 'I had a dream, which was not all a dream.' You know, I had a friend at Cambridge who used to walk in his sleep."

Mouth pressed tight, she swung around, her empty plate held before her, gripped hard in her fingers. "Mr. Dawes, do you plan to continue making allusions to an incident which gives neither of our reputations any credit?"

He glanced up to the plasterwork ceiling as if seeking his answer. Cecila's temper heightened as she waited, and she had to fight the urge to tap her slipper in impatience against the wooden flooring.

Then he looked at her again, his smile widening into something quite charming. "Yes, I expect I do."

She glared at him, flustered. Even Theo Winslow had never been so . . . so unaccommodating. "Well, I ought to have expected as much from a Dawes!"

"'Now the hungry lion roars . . .'"

She had been about to turn back to the silver trays of food upon the sideboard, but she could hardly allow such a remark to pass. She had been compared to many things, but this did not sound the least favorable.

"And what is that to mean?" she demanded.

He rose and was at her side in two strides to take her plate, which he began to fill with eggs and rashers of bacon. "You sound cross, so I expect you are hungry. I am always so when starved—or when woken, and I must beg your pardon, for I seem to recall being out of temper with you last night. The coffee, I believe, is still hot. Or do you take tea?"

"I take hot chocolate, thank you very much. And you have now given me enough to feed myself as well as another person."

"That was the general plan." He took her plate to the table and held out the chair next to his. "Come, now, lady, and be kind. This time, note, I am not even quoting at you, which shows how seriously I take this. But you must tend to my affliction."

Eyeing him warily, she followed him to the table and sat down. She still had no intention of humoring him. However, she was curious. "What affliction? Your quoting?"

"No, that is an affectation. My affliction is what renders me unable to refrain from poking into matters that are none of my concern. You had a reason to walk last night. You must. That fellow I mentioned whom I knew at Cambridge walked the moon-decked halls because of a tragic love affair. He kept insisting that someone take a poke at his face—I assume a broken nose would have taken his mind off his broken heart. I do hope you are not caught in a similar fate."

She had picked up her knife and fork, but now she put them down again. He touched a little too close to the truth, for part of her worries last night had had to do with Theo Winslow.

However, she only said, her voice prim, "Mr. Dawes, you presume too much on too little acquaintance."

Bryn smiled at her. She ruffled up like an angry tabby, all bristling fur and very much on her dignity. But not terribly frightening. And he still wanted to know just what disturbed the fair Cecila's dreams. Only she did not seem inclined to answer him.

"Very well, if it is not your heart we are to speak of, won't you at least grant me some ease from this sin of excessive curiosity? I vow, I only wish to help in some fashion. It's my vice, you see. Some men drink. For others it's cards. For me, it's an inescapable urge to act the knight errant."

She glanced at him from the corner of her eyes. Rather fetching eyes, Bryn decided. An intriguing cross between green and blue that reminded him of the waters off the rugged Cornish coast where ancient castles lay and legends lived.

Then she said, her eyebrows lifting into two attractive arches over those eyes, "Why?"

He blinked at her, roused from metaphors for her eyes that had begun to spin in his mind. "Why what?"

"Why is being a knight your vice? Or your affliction? I certainly could understand a vicar feeling he must always aid others. It is his profession, after all. But if you only wish to feel superior to me because you—"

"Oh, but that's not it at all."

"Then why?"

He stared at her, the tips of his ears warming. He had not expected her to question his motives, and he found himself reluctant to explain them. It meant hauling out too much of his past—and far too many sins of omission. And he would have to think of his father.

As always, the guilt cut into him like a whip across his soul. Could he have stopped . . .

Well, there he was again, swamped by hopeless desires to change choices made in the past and therefore beyond mending. And it seemed to him that the future before him, terrifying in its emptiness, held as few choices. What did a man do, after all, when he had given up his inheritance to his cousin?

But none of this could have much interest to a lady only just met. A lady who had her own problems, it seemed.

So he returned her stare and said, keeping his answer as honest as possible, "I wish it had something of superiority to it. The truth is that I seem unable to do anything to right my own world, so why not at least try to help others?"

Cecila bit her lower lip. She ought not to have been so direct, but she thought he would give her back more fanciful quips. Instead, she saw the shadow in his eyes, darkening them.

Oh, the wretched man! She had thought him and his titled cousin quite horrid, only it seemed he was not. And it was not she who needed aid—not really. But if he found some measure of satisfaction in offering his services to others, she would be heartless to deny him.

"I am not certain there is very much you can do. I have been looking for the Harwood treasure, and if I am to own the truth as well, then I have to say I am not at all certain I shall be able to find it."

He began to smile again. "Treasure hunting? In your sister's rooms?"

Picking up her knife, she began to butter her toast with more vigor that she ought. It began to crumble on the plate, but she kept buttering. "No, not in her rooms. I was . . . well, I wanted Penelope's . . .well, her reassurance on that and on some other matters."

She stopped buttering. Her toast lay in crumbs, as did her appetite.

He said nothing, but one eyebrow had lifted and she saw the skepticism in his glance. Irritated, she put down her knife. "You need not look so disbelieving! I know your opinions of the sort of books that do have treasures in them, and you look as if you expect me to claim a ghost here as well! Only Harwood is not the least haunted, and the treasure is quite factual. I can even show you!"

With that Cecila rose, pushing her chair back from the table. Bryn had no choice but to stand as well, and he had curiosity enough to follow as she led him upstairs and to a room at the back of the house.

The door squeaked with lack of use as she pushed it open. Then they stepped into a room lined with bookcases.

It looked a workroom of sorts. The bottom parts of the age-darkened cases held wide, shallow drawers, and dim light filtered in from a single window set opposite the door. An unlit fireplace huddled against one wall, its grate barren even of ashes, and the wall sconces on either side stood empty of candles. Dust dulled the crowded shelves, which seemed crammed with papers, books, tarnished vases even, and bits of ugly porcelain statues.

Bryn plucked one of the leather covered volumes from its place—a copy of Lucian's *Dialogues*. The leather had begun to crack, but he noted with relief as he thumbed through the Greek text that the pages turned free of mildew. He hated to think of these poor books so neglected.

The squeak of wood on wood drew his attention and he glanced up to see Cecila pulling open one of the drawers. She had lit a half-gutted candle that stood on the long, dusty table in the center of the room. That and a high-backed wooden chair constructed with the stiff austerity of ages long past were the only furnishings.

After pulling out a bundle of vellum sheets tied with string, Cecila turned to the table.

Bryn stepped closer, intrigued at the glimpse of ink now aged to dull red. It pleased him to find he still had a scholar's quickening of interest. "Letters?" he asked.

"We Harwoods have not been noted for much, but we do have some rather outstandingly zealous correspondents in our family, though I think this Harwood outdid them all."

She placed the letters on the table, unknotted the string, and bent over them to sort through them. Bryn admired the play of candlelight on her hair, watching how gold and brown contrasted in the curls.

Then she straightened, pulling out one sheet from the rest to hand it to him with an air of righteous vindication. "There! Read that. Oh, not the first bits—that's just the usual flourishes one must put in for royalty."

He glanced at her, then took the letter to the window and began to read. Immediately, he glanced up. "Why, this is to Charles II."

"Oh, that is nothing. We have letters dating back another two hundred years prior to that—several to Elizabeth, even. I did tell you that we Harwoods do like writing. But I think this is most interesting of the lot. It's from Cecil Harwood. But do go on. The bit about the Harwood treasure is halfway down."

Scanning the letter, he found the paragraph, and read aloud, "*The gold plate has been sent with due care, and should cross the Channel this month. Not having heard of the ship* Highlander, *I lost no time in writing to convey that Captain Alexander will seek you out to deliver his precious cargo. Know also that Harwood's true wealth lies now hidden, and with God's grace will not be found by those who have so grievously plotted against your person, their true king and sovereign. . .*"

Bryn paused and glanced up, and Cecila came over to take the letter from him. "He means, of course, that they hid everything that could be taken. Poor Cecil lost his own life, but his widow did at least have the house and lands returned to her after Charles got his crown back. Only Cecil never told her where he had tucked anything. There are more letters from her, writing to practically everyone about it."

"But she never found anything?"

"No one seems to have—or if anyone did, it has not been mentioned in any of these." She gestured to the letters.

Bryn glanced around the room, then thought of the rambling house with its centuries of renovations and additions. There could be a dozen hiding places—double walls, with newer plaster covering stone, rooms shut off by builders, concealed staircases, or simply unused rooms such as this one.

The excitement kindled in him.

If their gold had been sent to help the Royalist cause, what other treasures had been tucked away? Jewels pried from the gold? The family silver? Paintings or tapestries—or perhaps something else?

Lord, what a challenge. And an opportunity. Why, he could make better restitution to these Harwoods than his cousin. Of course, that assumed a treasure still lay waiting.

He glanced at Cecila. She looked ridiculously young, her golden-brown curls tumbling forward as she concentrated on making a tidy bow of the string around the letters.

How likely was this belief of hers that in nearly two hundred years the wealth hidden by Cecil Harwood had not been discovered and spent?

Turning away, Cecila tucked the letters back in the drawer and closed it, then came back to him. She had folded her hands before her, but Bryn noted the anxious look in her eyes, as if she had trusted something of value to his care and did not yet know if he would handle it gently.

He understood that. He knew how easily dreams could be broken by harsh words. He had seen that happen to his mother.

So he only asked, "Where have you searched already?"

A smile, luminous with relief, rewarded him.

He stared at her, his mouth drying and his pulse quickening, and he knew himself caught. A smile such as that would catch any man.

Well, at least if lost causes were to be his only inheritance, he could not imagine a better one to joust at. But already he dreaded the disillusion that must someday come to her when they failed.

If they failed.

"Father, I must speak with you."

Stephen Harwood's hand jerked, and the ink on his quill spread across the cream parchment in a black splotch. He looked up at his eldest daughter. She stood in the doorway to his study, her brown curls tidy, her dark blue dress neat as a nun's habit, and with that look in her eyes.

Lord, how he hated that look. Reproach touched by disappointment. He could bear the reproach—he deserved it for the poor choices he had made—but the other was hard to endure. He could still recall teaching her to ride her first pony, and the unrestrained adoration that had shone from laughing eyes.

How long had it been since he had last seen such a look on her face? Too long, he feared. Instead, it was that look, with her mouth prim and her tone sharp. And each year that look seemed to grow harder. He swallowed the knot lodged in his throat. If she ended her days a shrewish spinster, he would have that on his head as well—and he had only wanted the ability to give them what they most wanted.

Ah, my Ella, he thought. *I've not done well by you.* But he laid down his pen and rose without mention of his worries. She would get over her fretting. She always did. And surely she could not object that much to their guests—could she?

Coming around the desk, he took her hands. "My dear, it's only for a few weeks. There is nothing for you to fuss over."

Confusion tightened her brow, and then a hesitant smile hovered on her lips. "What, do you mean to say that you are only stabling the squire's stallion for a short time for him?"

He let go her hands and began to twist the bottom brass button on his waistcoat. "Stabling? No, no, my dear, that splendid animal is ours to keep. He is going to be the remaking of our fortune. I know it. Why, Nevin has already offered—"

"Nevin? What has he to do with that beast?"

"Well, nothing, really . . . or at least very little. But he quite admires him. He's a man who sees quality in a horse,

I must own. Made me a splendid offer, but we shall do far better with the stud fee, but he is going to be . . ."

His words drifted off as Penelope's expression became more blank and baffled. Tentatively, he asked, "Did you not come to complain about Nevin and his cousin staying with us?"

The corner of her mouth pulled down, and he knew he had said the wrong thing. *Oh, dear.*

Taking her hand, he gave it a pat, as he had once when she was but sixteen and had returned home from her first assembly, where she had not once been asked to dance because of her height. She had not cried then, but here she was again with that muted distress which she struggled so hard to conceal.

"My dear, it really shall be no bother to you at all. I have already spoken to Mrs. Merritt, and she is to have the rooms ready by this afternoon when they return. They've gone off to bring back their servants and things from Halsage, don't you know? And I plan to take them out shooting, you know, so we shall have grouse and pheasant, and Mrs. Merritt's boy can bring in eels and trout from the river."

Penelope pulled her hand free to rub her forehead, as if to ease the lines that had formed.

He kept smiling, but a leaden weight formed in his stomach. "My dear, I know you do not care overly for Nevin, but his cousin offered most generously to look through the library. He thinks there actually may be a few volumes of some value. Would that not be a godsend? And it has been too long since we last entertained. Will that not be a delight?"

He forced his smile wider, but her mouth turned down an answering degree. Then she looked away, her stare dropping so he could no longer see the expression in her eyes. Worry tightened in his chest.

In truth, he did not know how the invitation had slipped out. And he could not blame her for her concern. It would be a bit of a stretch for the household to entertain two guests, particularly such fashionable gentlemen. However, when they had been taking their leave—expressing a polite regret and remarking on how Harwood must be proud of his daughters—the notion arrived that here stood two eligible gentlemen, and he was watching them leave.

The words seemed to come out all on their own.

Afterward, he had given himself a dozen reasons for it. The gentlemen would provide better escorts to the local assembly than had been available since well before Waterloo. And while doubt troubled him that Penelope had not exactly expressed any warmth to Nevin, he had been certain she would not learn about it until this evening. By then, she would have all of dinner to see what a pleasure it would be to have new conversation at the table.

She looked up at last, and his shoulders relaxed. She did not have that look back in her eyes, simply the more customary irritation.

There was hope, after all. She was only concerned. Yes, merely concerned, as befitted a girl who had taken on too much responsibility of late. He really never should have allowed her to take on the household accounts, as well as its management. It was all wearing her down dreadfully—and why would it not? Numbers always made his head ache.

"Father, it is just that . . . well . . . Father, I do not trust this Lord Nevin. What if he turns out to be a copy of his uncle—charm on the surface, and deceit underneath? There is something . . . changeable in his character that one cannot like."

"But, my dear, it is only a short visit. And if he can help with that stallion . . ."

"Help? Father, you did not encourage him to have anything to do with that . . . that wretched beast, did you? It is one thing for that horse to have savaged a groom, but it just will not do if he now attacks a peer of the realm—a gentleman who is supposed to be our guest."

"But Nevin insists that the horse has simply been mishandled. And if he thinks he can help, why not allow him the chance, eh? Now do stop fretting. With Mrs. Merritt to see to all, you may have the next few weeks to entertain and enjoy."

He gave his daughter a warm smile, then sent up a silent prayer that for once, God willing, things would go as he hoped.

Penelope's lips remained pressed tight as she stared at her father. She ached to pour out a dozen excuses to make to the Daweses as to why they might not stay, only she could not think of even one reason that sounded polite—or true.

And then she began to reconsider. Heavens, yes, she ought to have seen the opportunity at once. Of course. Her shoulders eased, and in turn she saw her father's face relax.

Slowly, testing the idea, she said, "Well, Lord Nevin does seem rather skilled with horses. He has taught his own mount the most wonderful tricks."

"Capital ones, I am certain."

"And I suppose if he cannot do something with that stallion, who could?"

"Exactly my point, my dear."

"Then you really must allow Lord Nevin a chance. And if he cannot help, why then you have the perfect opportunity to insist that the squire takes back that hopeless beast."

His face fell. "Take back? But I—"

"Father, do you not have utter confidence in Lord Nevin?"

"Well, he says—"

"Then let us allow him to prove as good as his words."

"But I don't think—"

She put her hand on his and tried for her softest smile. "Please, Father? Won't you put my mind at ease by promising that if the unlikely possibility comes about and he fails, you shall send this animal back?"

He stared into her face, his forehead knotted.

She did not have Cecila's coaxing ways, so she added the words she knew would weigh heaviest on him. "If not for me, then for the sake of the family?"

He seemed to struggle for a moment, but then his shoulders slumped. With a sigh, he smiled at her and lifted his other hand to pat hers. "Very well, my dear. Of course, I am certain he will succeed."

Relief flooded into Penelope, and she almost threw her arms around her father. But shyness held her still—that and uncertainty. Her father might still choose not to remember this conversation when the time came to send that horse back. He did so hate confrontations, and she expected the squire to be quite difficult in this matter. However, in the end, things would be put right. She would see to it.

And by means of thanking Lord Nevin for having provided this opportunity, she really would have to do all she could to keep the squire's stallion from killing him.

Penelope enjoyed dinner. She had her own room in which to dress, for Mr. Dawes had been settled in the blue room after a slip of paper had been found to wedge into the window to stop its rattle. And a visit from the sweep, as well as the addition of paintings from other rooms, had made the gold room respectable enough for Lord Nevin. So with their guests and their menservants settled, Penelope found herself able to relax, and to entertain everyone with every horrible story she could recall about the squire's stallion.

Besides his having savaged a groom and another horse, there was the stall he had destroyed. He had also bitten the squire and Terrance Winslow. And she made the most of the horse's unruly arrival at Harwood and how he still wore his headcollar due to the fact that no one dared get close enough to his teeth and hooves to remove it.

Lord Nevin listened to these stories without comment, his face revealing nothing of his thoughts, but she felt certain she had given him cause to think twice about approaching that animal. It would be ideal if he failed through the simple act of not even attempting to go near the stallion.

She also noted with a touch of pride that both Cecila and Sylvain carried themselves well throughout the evening. After dinner, Cecila entertained with a few songs from her harp. She had a pretty voice, and Penelope could only wish she could coax Sylvain into a duet. But Sylvain would probably rather die than sing for anyone but herself or her animals.

As Cecila played, Penelope glanced over at Sylvain. Lord Nevin stood close to her, his head bent to say something that pulled a shy smile from Sylvain. A shock flashed through Penelope, but did not stay long enough to resolve itself into a thought. Just worry, she told herself. Concern that Sylvain had no idea how to deal with a gentleman of Nevin's obvious sophistication. Nothing more could lie behind that twist of emotion, which had already vanished.

Still, it bothered her.

However, when Cecila finished her song, Penelope rose and excused herself and her sisters to visit their mother for tea. Within a quarter hour of being settled with their mother, both her sisters seemed to have forgotten their guests, and the knot in Penelope's shoulders eased.

Fatigue soon began to dull her mother's eyes, so Penelope rose to shepherd the girls to bed.

She stopped to give her mother a kiss, and her mother smiled and said in a low voice, "How nice that Cecila has the distraction of gentlemen who are not Winslows."

Penelope's mouth curved. She could not agree more. But she glanced at her sisters, who were already halfway out the door, then looked back at her mother. "Yes, well, so long as it also does them no harm. I . . . well, perhaps Sylvain could be . . . a little too vulnerable to a gentleman's flattery?"

Her mother's eyebrows rose with a question, but Penelope found herself reluctant to say more. Now that she had started to speak of them, her complaints about Nevin's attentions to her sister seemed petty. Heavens, could she actually be in danger of preventing Sylvain from making a lasting connection?

Her stomach churned at the thought. She did not begrudge her sisters their happiness, but Sylvain deserved far better than a Dawes, did she not?

The touch of her mother's hand drew Penelope's attention, and she glanced down to see her mother's frown, so she said, "I suppose if this visit pulls Sylvain from her shyness, that must be counted a blessing."

"Yes, dear. And you need not worry. I think your sisters have a good enough watch on their own hearts, you know."

Agreeing in order to comfort her mother, Penelope

bent to kiss her mother's soft, dry cheek. She turned down the lamp, then left, calling a final good night from the doorway.

But she doubted her sisters could look after themselves. Cecila had shown her poor judgment in forming an affection for Theo Winslow, and Sylvain had not a clue in the world about anything outside of the home wood. However, Penelope would do her best to see this visit would work out well enough.

And when Nevin failed with the squire's stallion, he would leave and so would the stallion.

With all that settled in her own mind, she undressed for bed and expected a good night's sleep. But when her head touched her pillow, the troubling image came back of Nevin and Sylvain, their heads together, one so dark, the other so fair. Such an attractive contrast. She pushed the thought away only to have it return, stubborn as a stray cat.

Propping herself up on one elbow, she pounded her pillow into a different shape. "And what if he does smile at her?" she muttered, then threw herself down again.

Sylvain deserved smiles from more than one gentleman. So why did this one disturb her? It must be because she did not trust him. Yes, that accounted for it nicely.

At last her mind began to drift as she found a worried path to sleep, but the night came troubled by visions of Nevin being savaged by that stallion.

She woke with an abrupt start, the stories she had told at dinner now a vivid jumble. Only in her mind she had seen Nevin cornered against the wood of a stall by that hulking dark form.

She shivered.

Dawn drifted into her room, reassuring her that it had only been a dream, and she let out an unsteady breath as she pushed the stray curls from her sweat-dampened forehead.

Then she heard the stallion's angry squeal.

Not all of it a dream, it seemed. Or perhaps that had been the cause of her nightmare, what with him raging about, and her own tales too fresh for comfort. That shrill bellow echoed again.

Heavens, had he cornered one of the dogs?

Throwing off the bedcovers, she rose and hurried to the window, her feet bare and cold. Pushing back the velvet drapery, she glimpsed only a corner of the paddock and the peaceful view of sun glistening on dew-drenched grass, half-bare trees with leaves still turning, and fleecy clouds turned pink on the edges by the dawn.

For a moment, she worried her lower lip with her teeth. Then she made a hasty decision. It took but a moment to attend to her body's needs and splash cold water on her face and a moment more to slip into a brown woolen dress and walking boots. Then she was running down the stairs.

The house lay quiet around her, and the night's air hung chill in the hallway. Her boots clicked across the stone flooring of the front hall, and the brass knob of the front door cooled her fingers as she twisted it open. Then sunlight and brisk air bathed her face.

But the sight before her froze her still.

It was not one of the dogs who had dared venture into the stallion's territory.

Nevin, in riding breeches and boots, his coat off so that his white shirt billowed in the breeze, stood in the paddock, his feet braced apart as he confronted the black-coated horse who stood not six feet in front of him, neck arched and ears pinned backward in anger.

Eight

The stallion's breath misted before it in small puffs, like smoke from a dragon's nostrils. The lead lines, now ragged from where the horse had stepped on them and snapped the ends, still dangled from the leather head-collar. The animal's ears swiveled forward, then pinned back as the stallion tossed its head and again bellowed a warning.

Heavens, that man must be mad!

Anger with his foolishness surged in Penelope, hurrying her down the front steps, her hands fisted at her sides and her heart pounding. "Come out at once, before he harms you!"

At her words, Nevin half turned, and the horse used that moment to lunge.

Teeth bared, the stallion's neck snaked out. And then a slap echoed as Nevin's hand connected with the horse's muzzle.

The horse swung its head away, its eyes wide and startled. Nevin gave him no chance to regroup, but went after the horse, waving his coat to drive the stallion away, shouting in a language Penelope did not recognize, although she could not mistake that tone of utter confidence and command.

Spinning around, the stallion let off a frustrated kick and galloped away, bucking and squealing.

Penelope let out a breath and realized she could move again. The sick knot in her throat loosened, and she lowered the hand that had risen to her chest when the horse had attacked.

Her anger flamed even hotter, and she strode to the fence, determined to make this fool see some sense. "Are you mad? Did you hear nothing I said last night?"

He turned from watching the horse, his eyes narrowed, and the hard look he gave her checked Penelope's temper with a moment's doubt as to the wisdom of having interrupted. But then she thought of her dream and how much damage an iron-shod hoof could do to a man's head or shoulder. Chin lifting, she gave him back a steady stare.

Slowly, he came toward her, his coat dangling from his fingers. The breeze fluttered his shirt, left open at the neck, and she glanced there, drawn by the play of white against darker skin. A glimpse of the ragged tear in the shirt fabric drew her thoughts back to what had almost happened.

She looked up into those black eyes of his. "I think you may account yourself lucky, my lord, that you walk away this morning with no more than a torn shirt."

He paused at the white post-and-rail fence, laid his coat over the top rail, and then settled his palms on either side of it. The hard, flat look in his eyes had not changed, but now the corner of his mouth quirked, as if he were amused.

"The question here is, do you wish to see me dead?" Without waiting for an answer, he vaulted over the fence, landing light on his feet.

Penelope tried to hold her stern glare. With him standing before her, so agile, and those broad shoulders rather daunting, it began to seem absurd that she had worried for him. Still, no man's strength could match the power of a rogue stallion.

She folded her arms. "I think you have an obvious answer in that—"

"You interrupted, Miss Harwood. And your distraction caused this." He lifted his shirt, pulling wide the tear left behind by the horse's nipping teeth. Her stomach contracted as she noted the faint red marks also left on his skin, which showed through the tear.

She looked away for a moment, the fast beat of the pulse in her throat making her a little ill, unable to meet his gaze. But then she took a breath and looked up again. She had never lacked for courage, thank heavens.

"I am sorry you were hurt, but you were foolish enough to venture near that horse. I did warn you."

The corner of his mouth lifted higher, and the smug assurance in his expression irritated her no end.

"Miss Harwood, I cannot recall the last time a horse has been quicker than I, but then I know to listen. A horse never lies, not even for polite reasons. He will tell you what he plans, and this one is no different. He has learned not to trust because all he has been given is distrust. And he has learned to strike before he is struck.

"You told me all that last night, and he told me as much this morning. But if he is to have any hope, then he must decide to trust again. It is his choice. But I intend to challenge him again and again until he makes that choice, because I know his secret."

"And what, pray, is that?" she asked, her voice sharp.

Nevin glanced toward the dark figure in the paddock. The stallion now stood at the far end, his head high and defiant, but shifting uncertainly on his feet, pacing as if he did not know what else to do. Then Nevin looked back to the woman before him. Her posture matched the stallion's in willful hostility, and Nevin could almost imagine he glimpsed the same puzzled hesitation in her eyes.

Ah, but this one would never admit to her own doubts.

And so he said, his tone blunt, "He wants to belong, Miss Harwood. It is in his blood and his bone to be part of a herd, and that longing will make him choose to join with someone or something. For to be alone is to die a little each day. And any animal knows the wisdom of choosing life."

Her cheeks had paled as he spoke, and he frowned at her now, wondering what thoughts wound through that mind of hers. A horse's language he could read, but this lady with her mix of sharp edges and fortress walls confounded him.

She seemed not to care for him, yet she had come out to save him from a danger she perceived. And she looked now as if he had spoken of her, not of the stallion behind them.

Why did she make this so personal? Why did she seem ready to fight not just him, but her own family and even the world? Something drove her, he realized, but he understood far more about that too proud, rebellious horse than he did about this prickly *gadji*.

Then, her tone cool, she said, "Very well, if you have no intention of listening to reason, I shall not interfere again."

She spun on her heel and started away, the gravel crunching under her step. Then she paused and turned back. "Mrs. Merritt can mend your shirt if you wish, but the local doctor will be far less skilled with any broken bones, so you may wish to be ready to send to London for a better physician."

Turning away, she strode into the house.

Nevin watched her, then shivered as the morning breeze slipped under his shirt to brush his skin. Leaning against the railing, he took some comfort from the wood, hard on his back. *Devla!* He knew the ways to coax a horse into trusting him, but how did one do that with a lady? And why did he even want to make the effort?

But he knew the answer—he knew it as he knew the hot rush of blood in his own veins.

He wanted to belong as badly as did that rogue of a horse. And the proud Miss Harwood was fast becoming the personification of all the world for which he sought entrance.

What in blazes am I looking for? Bryn wondered as he wandered the house.

Like many old houses, Harwood carried generations of alterations overlaid upon each other—hallways added, stairs rerouted, wings built onto the older structure and rooms done over to change their size and proportions. He had been through the house once with Mrs. Merritt as his guide, but now he wanted to see it on his own, without her to distract him with historic details and tales of past Harwoods.

What he saw left him wishing he had the sense to mind his own business.

A hundred possibilities suggested themselves for hiding a room—or even a small crevice with a ransom of jewels. Ought he knock on walls to determine if they were but concealed, hollow-sounding doorways? Or perhaps he should press the carved wood along the wainscoting to see if something might turn. Only he feared he might easily twist a rosette loose or break off a carved leaf. Besides, either notion seemed faintly absurd. And the memory of how ridiculous young Winslow had looked, covered in soot from what must have been a similar search, kept Bryn to an uncommitted amble.

He had seen the picture gallery, though the lighter spots on the wall had told their own story of paintings now gone. Not much else offered a clue as to where one might hide a treasure. The only hint of riches in the portraits had been admirable lace and a few pieces of jewelry, all of which grouped together would not even be half a respectable fortune.

He had been shown the public rooms: The unused ballroom, its furnishings shrouded in covers. Mr. Harwood's study. A small sitting room that Miss Harwood kept for herself. A shooting room, its guns well-oiled and hung in racks. The dining room and library, both of which he had seen before, and a half dozen other rooms which now blended together into a maze.

Books had been scattered in most rooms, and he now carried two volumes tucked under his arm. Nothing of great value. But he had not read the *Iliad* in years, and the copy of Sterne's *Tristam Shandy* seemed a good thing to have by his bedside in case he could not sleep.

He wandered to a window that overlooked the back of the house and which gave light into the upstairs hall and looked out. The autumn day invited rambles outside, not in. The sun lay golden in the sky, and the clouds were far too white to threaten rain. They scudded past, and his thoughts began to drift with them.

Then a movement below caught his eye.

He glanced down from the upper story to see a cloaked figure leave the house. The hood of the gray cloak fell back, revealing golden-brown curls. Miss Cecila, then, though it would be difficult to imagine either her stern elder sister or her shy younger one stealing from the house in so dramatic a fashion.

She skirted the brick wall that bounded the kitchen garden and then turned toward the woods that stretched west of the house. Curious, Bryn watched. Was she out to visit some neighbor? But then why did she glance back as if guilty and expecting to be caught?

He frowned and shook his head. Most likely, she planned a tryst—with that Winslow fellow, no doubt. He really ought to mind his own business. Still, he stayed at the window, watching her disappear into the woods. She had grown up here, so she could not be in any danger of getting lost. Nor could he imagine any harm coming to her.

And still he did not like it. If that Winslow fellow was anything like his elder brother, then Miss Cecila ought not to be meeting him. Particularly not alone in the woods.

With another sigh, he gave up the battle and turned away, starting downstairs.

Had he not just been thinking it was a good day for a stroll out-of-doors?

He had, however, become rather lost, and instead of finding the main staircase, he came across the servants' stairs. Hoping he would not startle one of the few maids, he started down, his boots echoing on the uncarpeted wood.

The steps ended in a dark, narrow hallway, and he glanced both ways, uncertain. Then he chose left. That ought to lead to the back of the house.

After the hall turned and widened, he came across a door to the left, and he entered. This did not seem to be part of the house he had seen before. He found another door and opened it, stepping into a large room well-lit by sunlight and comfortably done in blue drapery and wall hangings.

An older woman looked up at once from a four-poster bed, which stood opposite the door. Before he could apologize and leave, she smiled and lowered the drawing pad that lay propped on her knees.

"Oh, hello. Are you Mr. Dawes, or Lord Nevin? How nice of you to visit. I am Mrs. Harwood, and I think you really must be Mr. Dawes, are you not?"

He hesitated, cursing himself for a block and realizing he had no choice but to enter. He would look the most uncivil brute in the world if he turned around and left. Besides, he found himself charmed by the smile offered and rather curious as to why Mrs. Harwood lived in such seclusion.

Lord, when would he ever learn to resist women in need?

Penelope had to do something—anything. She sought some task that could occupy her, but sewing did not have enough movement, the linens were few enough these days for counting to take more than a quarter hour, and Mrs. Merritt flatly refused her assistance in the still room to dry flowers or the last of the summer fruits since they had guests to entertain.

That drove Penelope to her room to fetch a shawl and bonnet so she might flee those very guests.

She went walking, and she kept walking. Down lanes, skirting meadows where the hay lay scythed and stacked, past fields harvested and now dug into brown, fallow rows to await winter's kiss, through woods where she startled pheasants from their coverts, climbing over stiles and jumping over streams.

At last her legs began to ache, and she stopped and looked about her.

Her rambles had taken her to the old Norman tower that overlooked Halsage. From the tower hill, she had a view of farmlands and the tidy, winding lanes of Halsage. Houses and treetops formed patterns that intersected green fields. She took a deep breath and let go the rein she had kept on her thoughts.

Why should Nevin's words so upset her? He had been speaking of a horse, and yet she had cringed as if he had been peeling back her own skin.

Distrust. Loneliness.

Oh, heavens, why did those words echo in her own soul like a voice down a stony chasm?

She sat down on the ground, not caring if the grass stained her skirts.

Was she becoming as dangerous as that stallion, both to herself and others? Did she, too, lash out too quickly?

But she had reason to be wary. She had had her heart torn open once, and she had no wish to repeat that agony. Oh, but how she also ached for something more in her life. And why could she not at least be kind to a gentleman?

She thought back to her encounter with Cecila. She had been pricked this morning by Cecila's speech, but she turned it over in her mind now without passion, trying to be honest with herself.

What she glimpsed, she did not care for.

She had been harsh with Cecila. And unkind. And Cecila had been right: she was becoming a disagreeable woman.

In truth, she doubted she could change. Too much had happened. But she could not allow her experiences to continually shadow Cecila and Sylvain's futures. She wanted them to find love, honest and lasting. But how she feared they might make the same mistake she had, in giving more than would ever be given back to them.

Her mind kept wandering in that circle. How did she allow her sisters the chance at love without also giving them its risk?

She had no idea how long she sat there, her thoughts

turning, but at last she glanced up at the sky and noted that the sun had begun its arc downward. She ought to go home. She had duties. She had those confounded guests.

Slowly, she rose, then started back to the house.

As she walked, she unknotted the ties to her bonnet and let it dangle from her fingers so the wind could tug at her hair and the autumn sun could warm her cheeks.

Lifting her face into the breeze, she half closed her eyes.

As a girl, she had run through the woods, pretending she could fly. How long had it been since she had allowed herself such play? Perhaps too long?

It took her another mile to work up the courage, and then she glanced around, feeling foolish, but she lifted her arms anyway and began to run.

A laugh startled from her, and she stopped and put her hand over her mouth. She glanced around the empty woods. What if someone heard? And then she decided she did not care. Besides, no one was there to see.

And she wanted some fun for a change. Just simple fun.

With a grin, she spread her arms again, holding her shawl out for her wings, and then she ran, pins popping loose so her hair streamed behind her, a smile pulling her mouth wide.

She jumped over roots and heard leaves crunch under her boots, and she pictured herself soaring. Heavens, what freedom that would be.

And then she came into a clearing, a shaded circle in a thicket of old maples, and came to an abrupt halt. Two figures sat on the log opposite her.

Cecila turned at once, her eyes wide. Theo Winslow sat next to her, far too close for propriety's sake. But Penelope could only think that they must have seen her acting silly as a child.

Her face flamed. Then she straightened. A sharp rebuke rose in her to chide Cecila for her misbehavior, but she bit it off. What a shrew she would sound—and a hypocritical one at that—to scold Cecila for folly when she had just been skipping through the woods like a demented nymph.

She could not do it. Even though everything inside her urged her to protect her sister, she saw too clearly that she had no right to speak.

Heavens, what a horrible sister she had turned into. Well, that she could mend.

Pulling in a deep breath, she gathered the tatters of her dignity and then wet her lips and said the first thing that came to mind. "Cecila, do not stay out so late as to catch a chill. Good day to you, Mr. Winslow."

Wincing at how inane she sounded, she turned and fled back into the woods, her shawl hugged tight to her body and her face still warm.

Heavens, would she ever learn to really grow up?

Cecila watched her sister turn and leave. Then she blinked and turned back to Theo, somewhat disturbed by her sister's abrupt appearance and uncharacteristic disappearance.

Theo had been staring after Penelope, his forehead wrinkled, but he glanced down at Cecila and asked, "Does your sister tipple?"

"Tipple?"

"Yes—drink a bit, you know. Not that I'm saying, mind, that there's anything wrong with her being a touch bosky, except that it seems rather early in the day for it."

"Bosky!"

"Well, yes. It's either that or she's looking a bit touched upstairs. I mean, I never thought much about m'father's claim, but if she's taking up running about like a—"

"What do you mean, your father's claim?" Cecila demanded, now thoroughly affronted on her sister's behalf.

He glared at her for the interruption, but then answered, sounding cross, "Oh, it's just that he swears an unmarried female over the age of five and twenty always goes a bit peculiar. You know, gets a bit unsettled."

Cecila rose and set her hands on her hips. "So now my sister is peculiar! Theo Winslow, I thought you had some regard for my family!"

He rose as well, glaring back at her. He had taken off his hat earlier, and now, with his free hand, he pushed back the black locks that fell nearly to his eyes. "Well, of course I do. But I've never seen your sister act like . . . well, as if she were a bit bosky. She was almost civil to me, and that's damned odd, if you ask me."

"Do not swear at me, Mr. Winslow."

"Oh, so it's oh-so-proper now, is it? First it's excuses why you won't be able to meet me tomorrow to slip off to the harvest dance at Spaxton. And now you—"

"I told you that we have guests. Besides, Mr. Dawes has promised to help me find the treasure, and tomorrow we are—"

"Help you! I thought I was to help you." His blue eyes had darkened, and now his mouth pulled into a sullen pout.

Cecila let out an exasperated sigh. "How are you to help when you cannot even come into the house without irritating Penelope?"

"She did not seem irritated a moment ago."

Cecila opened her mouth to argue this, and then pressed her lips together. Actually, Penelope had not seemed bothered to see Theo—though at least for a moment Cecila had glimpsed disapproval gathering in her sister's eyes, but it had vanished, and she could not account for the change.

What had come over Penelope?

And what, she wondered suddenly, would she do if Penelope withdrew her objections to Theo?

Head tilted, Cecila looked at Theo—really looked. He was, of course, quite the most handsome gentleman in the neighborhood . . . or he had been until Lord Nevin's arrival. Like Nevin, he had dark hair. But touches of red streaked Theo's straight black hair and his eyes were angelic blue, not black. Nor warm brown like Mr. Dawes's.

Theo also had the true pallor of a gentleman—due mostly, Cecila suspected, to not often being awake during daylight hours. However, even upset as she was with him, she not could help but admire the firm set to his jaw, and that oh-so-straight nose, and those lovely long, long lashes that framed his eyes.

Only just now those eyes glittered not with the play of amusement, but with anger, and Cecila's resentment deepened. How arrogant of him not to concern himself with her feelings.

Did he not think that at such a harvest dance as he had proposed, he would expose her to the riff-raff of the district? And why should he not be happy that she had Mr. Dawes's aide in finding the Harwood treasure? The sooner she found it, the sooner Theo could begin to court her properly, for she would have a dowry then.

Only perhaps he preferred her as she was—a lady whose financial circumstances left her quite ineligible as a prospective wife.

But that could not be the case. Of course not.

However, he had to learn she would not tolerate this lack of consideration. So she gave him a cold stare. "Well, if she has no objection to your presence, I do. For you are being quite rude and heartless, Mr. Winslow."

His dark eyebrows flattened. "I'll tell you what's heartless—it's a jade who babbles about love and when a fellow with a title comes along, she turns a cold shoulder."

Clenching her fingers around her shawl, she struggled to remember that a lady did not strike a gentleman—no matter how provoked. "Oh, so that is what you really think of me, is it now? That I would chase a title! Well, I thought being heartless was someone who pretended interest in one person while still sporting with a certain redheaded tavern wench who is employed at The Stag and Crown!"

The tips of Theo's ears reddened. "Now, Cecila, you know Tess means—"

"So it is true! Oh, you . . . you . . . oh, I never want to see you again, Theo Winslow! You may keep your tavern wench and your . . . your farmer dances, and your . . . your brother's careless ways. But I, for one, am done thinking you will ever care enough for me to reform yourself!"

Turning, she started for the house, ignoring Theo's calls for her to come back. If he came after her, she honestly would box his ears, and she braced herself for his hand to catch her arm. When it did, she would spin about and slap him. And she would not listen to his explanations—or at least she would not until after he had begged her forgiveness.

Oh, how she ought to have paid better heed to the gossip of the neighborhood, instead of finding excuses for him. His conduct could have no excuse. However, she would forgive him if he repented. But only if he did so truly.

She slowed her steps.

He certainly was taking his time in coming after her. No doubt he found it difficult to think up a suitable way to express his regrets. Oh, he really was the most wretched man! But if he cared for her, he would come after her. He would explain.

Would he not?

She half turned her head to glance back. Anger still churned in her stomach with a sickening agitation, but so did worry now.

Where was the sound of boots crunching on the fallen leaves? And he had stopped calling after her.

Well, she did not care.

Lifting her head again, she started back to the house.

Let him suffer! She hoped he felt horrible and quite sorry, and then he would send her a note, begging her to meet him. When they met, she might be gracious. And if he begged enough, she would forgive him.

Perhaps.

Then she glanced back to the clearing, now hidden by trees, her forehead tight and her heart twisting. Only what if Penelope was right? What if she had given her heart to a man whose only delight would be throwing it aside at every opportunity?

Cecila decided that if she did not speak to someone soon, she would burst. And she knew but one person in whom she could confide.

Her step quick, she started for her mother's room. She knocked lightly on the door and did not wait for an answer, but opened the door, the words already slipping out. "Mother, I must—"

She broke off her speech, for opposite her mother, a china cup balanced on one knee, sat Mr. Dawes, looking quite at home.

He rose at once, saying "'She danced along with vague, regardless eyes, Anxious her lips, her breathing quick and short . . .'—Keats for you, Miss Cecila. But where have you been walking that your breath is so quick, and your lips so anxious?"

Nine

Cecila hardly knew what to answer. She had expected to confide in her mother, not bandy words with Mr. Dawes, and she rather disliked that look in his eyes, as if he knew she had been with Theo, and did not approve.

Well, he had no say in her affairs. Only that look stirred a guilty reminder of how improper it was to go around meeting Theo in such a clandestine fashion. It had been easy to shrug off a sister's complaints, but the critical stare of a London gentleman left her twisting the ends of her shawl.

It also reminded her just how much her mother would worry, if she knew. So what could she say now? She had rushed here, thinking to pour her heart out, but might that fret her mother into another attack?

As if nothing were amiss, Cecila's mother smiled. She reclined on her daybed, next to a drum table that held a silver tea set. A chair had been drawn close for Mr. Dawes.

"What a pretty poem, to be sure. And how clever you are to recall it, Mr. Dawes. I can never summon more than stray bits of Shakespeare, as in 'rosemary for remembrance.' But then I used to be so very fond of gardening."

Sitting up, she patted the spot next to her on the daybed. "Darling, do come in and take tea with us. Mr. Dawes and I have been having a most lovely chat."

Cecila shot him a questioning glance. What in heavens had he been talking to her mother about?

He met her gaze, his expression maddeningly bland.

"And what did you discuss?" Cecila asked, coming into the room. She sat on the edge of the daybed, and took the thin china teacup her mother handed her.

"This and that. Did you know his mother was from Wales? From the Tregons of Wales. I went to school with an Agatha Tregon, and I think she must have been a cousin."

Her mother continued to talk of trivialities, of people she had known, of places from her younger days. Her voice, low and melodic, gradually soothed Cecila, until she realized that she must have burst into the room looking quite distraught. She drank her tea and glanced from under her lashes at Mr. Dawes.

He sat still, listening to her mother, his expression attentive, and she realized she had never seen anyone listen so well. Particularly not a gentleman. He leaned forward in his chair, and his eyes never left her mother's face. An occasional smile told of the parts that amused him.

How very odd that sitting here with him and her mother, sipping tea, should be so comforting. And the certainty swept through Cecila that while she had expected to pour out her worries, this had calmed the jangled agitation inside her far more.

It was so civilized. And while she loved Theo for being so exciting—well, there were times a lady needed something else.

Finally, Mr. Dawes finished his tea, put down his cup and rose. "Mrs. Harwood, this has been a delight, but I think we have worn you out."

Cecila rose as her mother stretched a hand out to Mr. Dawes. "I wish you would not go, but you are most likely in the right of it."

Bryn took Mrs. Harwood's hand, then bent and kissed it. Such a courageous lady deserved honors. He had learned much in his hour spent with her and had found much to admire in the way she faced her confining illness, and in the affection she so clearly held for her family.

"Your servant, Mrs. Harwood," he said. And then he turned to Cecila and offered his arm. "Shall we?"

Cecila leaned down to kiss her mother's cheek and stayed long enough to help arrange a shawl over her mother's legs. "I shall send Mrs. Merritt in later for the tea tray."

Mrs. Harwood frowned for a moment. "But, my dear, you came in looking as if you had something to tell me."

Cecila glanced at Mr. Dawes, who stared back at her, a caution in his eyes that perhaps they had overtired her mother. Then she turned back to her mother. "It was nothing important. Nothing that important at all."

She kissed her mother's cheek again, and then allowed Mr. Dawes to lead her to the door.

Once outside, she turned to him, unable to bottle her curiosity any longer. "Just how did you come to be visiting my mother?"

"If I tell you, will you tell me what happened between you and young Winslow that you came bursting into your mother's room, looking ready to enact quite the scene?"

She gave him a scathing look, one that seemed an imitation of her elder sister's prickly manner. "Mr. Dawes, I am quite able to handle my own affairs, thank you very much."

Then she turned and walked away, her head high.

Bryn watched her for a moment, certain that something had happened. A lover's spat? Or perhaps the start of a more serious break? In either case, he really ought to take the hint and leave matters alone.

But as he started down the hall, thinking about all that Mrs. Harwood had told him of her daughters, he wondered if, rather than discovering a treasure, he could be of more use in assisting Cecila to see that one of the wild Winslows was not at all in her best interest.

The rain settled in on the following day, bringing cold, gusting winds and a taste of winter. It then proceeded to rain for the next five days.

Sylvain took to spending her days in the stables with her owl, whom she was now exercising in the hopes of making his wing strong enough that he could fly again when the rain broke. Penelope did not approve, but as it did seem the only way Mr. Feathers might find his way back to a home in the woods, she said nothing to Sylvain about it.

For herself, Penelope found the rain irritating. She wanted to go out and ride or walk. But a lady was not supposed to soak herself to the skin. And so she stayed inside.

On the fifth day, restless and bored, Penelope had glanced out the drawing room window, longing for even a glimpse of sun. She was surprised to see a dark-clad figure in the paddock with the stallion.

Lord Nevin, it seemed, did not alter his plans for any reason, not even a slanting rain that pelted down, blown sideways by the wind so that it streaked the glass panes and flattened the grass into mud.

Curious, she watched Nevin. He simply stood in the paddock, unmoving, his arms at his side, a coiled rope dangling from one hand and the rain slicking off his bare head and dripping from the capes of his greatcoat. The stallion stood at the far end of the paddock, head up, ears twitching, his black coat equally drenched. Horse and man seemed to be watching each other, but neither made a move toward the other.

It looked a silent battle of wills, and Penelope wondered who would give in first, for they seemed equally matched in obstinacy. She could not quite decide if that attribute lay in Nevin's favor.

Finally, she grew bored of watching them, and so she went to see if Mr. Dawes needed amusing. She found him with Cecila, wandering the upstairs gallery. Cecila fussed with her dress, as if guilty to be caught in something. Her cheeks pinked and she muttered a hasty excuse that she was simply showing Mr. Dawes about. Penelope slanted a knowing look at her sister. Obviously, Mr. Dawes had been dragged into Cecila's futile game of treasure hunt.

She might not have thought anything about that, only her mother had asked just that morning if their guests were enjoying their stay. And Penelope began to think that perhaps she had allowed her distrust of the Daweses to overrule good manners.

That simply would not do.

So she went to her father to ask if he could not find something better for their guests than an ill-tempered horse and a wild goose chase about the house.

She found her father in his favorite wing chair in the library, a book open on his lap and his three hunting spaniels stretched out at his feet. Lazily, he scratched Freckle's ear as she spoke of her concerns.

"But, my dear, Nevin does not have to go out in the rain—and he swears he is making progress. And I thought you, of all people, would be pleased to have Cecila's thoughts taken off young Winslow."

"But, Father, that is a rather selfish view, is it not? I mean, we are thinking of our benefit, not theirs. And they must be a little bored. Heaven knows I am. Even Cecila has not seemed herself these past few days. And if we could come up with some amusement, it might even lure Sylvain from the stables."

Her father thought this over, his hand still stroking Freckle's ears. "Oh, I shall take them shooting when the sky clears, but that is not much fun for you girls." Then his face brightened. "But there is just the thing—the assembly."

"The assembly?"

"Well, yes. At Taunton. Your mother always enjoys the stories you bring home, and Sylvain ought to accompany you this year. She is not really out, but then, none of you have made your bow at court, and Taunton is not exactly the highest of circles. It would do you all a bit of good."

His smile widened, but Penelope continued staring at him. She had forgotten the upcoming assembly, and she had no wish to attend under the escort of Lord Nevin and Mr. Dawes. It would seem . . . well, it would simply seem uncomfortable, she thought, struggling for a reason not to go.

Besides, for two gentlemen accustomed to London's grand affairs, she could not see how this would seem a treat.

But then she stumbled over the thought of Sylvain.

Taunton was indeed just enough decent company without being overwhelming. Quite a few neighbors would attend. And going out into society would help Sylvain acquire more social ease and grace. So perhaps Cecila and Sylvain could go.

Only how could she send them with the Daweses and no other chaperon? She could just picture her father, much as he loved them all, becoming caught up in a conversation and forgetting that he had daughters to look after.

And, of course, Theo Winslow might be there. The rain had certainly kept him and Cecila from meeting, but what would keep him at a distance if she did not attend?

With a sigh, she decided the Taunton Assembly, with its country jigs, its weak punch, and its talk of crops and weather, would have to do. And if it made the Dawes gentlemen long to be elsewhere, so be it.

But it did seem rather odd that, when only a few days ago she had been wishing them gone, the thought of their departure now stirred an odd mix of feelings.

He would rather be back in the paddock at Harwood, even in the pouring rain, Nevin thought, glancing around the assembly room. But he set a smile in place, determined not to show an ounce of discomfort.

By London standards, the room was not crowded. Narrow and long, with white painted walls, austere gold chandeliers with few crystals, and a well-worn wooden floor, it had to be judged plain by London standards. But he liked the lack of pretension.

Few jewels sparkled on the ladies. The older gentlemen clung to the formal knee breeches and heavy, cuffed coats that had been the fashion of their youth. The younger gentlemen imitated the pantaloons, trousers, and nipped coats with padded shoulders of London fashion plates with more enthusiasm than success.

What came with them, however, left Nevin feeling almost as if he were stepping into society for the first time again.

Glances slid his direction, then turned away as his own stare traveled the room. One of the matrons looked him over, scorn tightening her face as she turned to whisper something to her neighbor, who glanced at Nevin, eyes wide, before hastily averting her gaze.

So it always began, he thought, his mood darkening.

He had no idea who had started the talk. That never did matter. Society, he had learned, loved only one thing more than to have someone to admire, and that was to have someone to despise. And what could be lower than a half Gypsy, for were they all nothing more than liars, thieves, and vagabonds?

At least he had learned to imitate his brother-in-law, the earl, in that he knew how to smile, instead of showing the simmering resentment such whispers stirred in him. He had never thought to be thankful to know St. Albans, but he had to admit the man had his uses.

Of course, the Earl of St. Albans actually did not care what others thought of him. Nevin could only wish he had also learned that trick.

He did care. And the ache of injustice burned in him that others so casually judged him—and found him lacking.

Turning, he glanced at Bryn, but his cousin, as always, seemed oblivious to the stir that drifted through the room like the breeze before a storm. Bryn's attention remained focused on the Harwood ladies, and Nevin decided he had the right of it to focus only on the beauty before him.

With that in mind, Nevin offered his arm to Miss Harwood and asked for the first dance. She hesitated, glancing at her sisters as if worried over their having partners, but of course she must accept. The eldest daughter of the house merited the courtesy of the first dance with him.

For him, duty combined with pleasure tonight. She looked . . . well, she looked remarkably lovely.

She wore her hair in loose curls, gathered up in the back with a gold chain that wound through the dark brown strands, offering intriguing glimmers in the candlelight. Her dress, also gold, fell in soft folds from just under her breasts, curving over her hips. He liked the simplicity of the gown and its elegance.

He led her out to the center of the room, and as they waited for the set to form, he knew he ought to make some sort of polite talk. He could only think to speak the truth, so he said, "I have been remiss in making my compliments to you."

She glanced at him, one skeptical eyebrow raised. Then her expression relaxed. "Oh, I see. You have remembered my request for the polite part of conversation, but, really, you should not sacrifice honesty simply to flatter me. I am beyond the age to need such a thing."

His mouth quirked. "Is any woman ever beyond compliments? And why must one given to you be dishonest?"

"Why? Well, because my mirror tells me so. It shows my freckles and my years. It shows that I am too tall and lack the least pretension to beauty. And, yes, I should hope it is possible to outgrow the need for the approval of others."

"It was not approval I offered. It was admiration." He stepped closer, his mouth curving as he looked down at her. "And you are not too tall for me, Miss Harwood."

The warmth from his breath brushed across her cheek, and an answering flush of heat stole across her face, flooding down her neck, spreading through her. Her skin tingled. Her mouth dried. And she wondered, how did he do this? How did he make her feel so . . . so . . . so however it was she did feel? He confused her so much she could not even think.

Fussing with her fan, she tried to meet that steady dark gaze with one that at least appeared as unshakable. "I am presentable, my lord. Handsome for my years, perhaps. If you wish for more, I would direct your glance toward my sisters, for they actually warrant such admiration."

Suiting action to words, Penelope looked toward her sisters, who stood conversing with Mr. Dawes.

Sylvain had her eyes down and her shoulders hunched as if to make herself smaller. Other than that, she did look lovely, with her red-gold curls piled high to emphasize her heart-shaped face. She looked a touch pale in white, but as a young miss just out of the schoolroom, she had to wear the color of innocence. If only she stood a touch straighter and smiled, the gentlemen would see her worth at once.

Cecila did smile—a little too much as she gave Mr. Dawes a coy glance, Penelope thought with a frown. But white looked far better on her, emphasizing the translucence of her skin. The blue-green ribbon that trimmed her gown, and which wound through her hair, brought out the color in her eyes. Now, if only she would take on some of Sylvain's reserve, she would appear the perfect miss.

The gentlemen began to gather around her, but Penelope noted with approval that it seemed Cecila did not intend to dance unless she also secured a partner for Sylvain.

She could, at times, be the best of sisters.

The music for the dance began, and Penelope turned back to Lord Nevin, ready to do her duty. *At least we will have the obligatory dance done with,* she thought, nervously wetting her lips.

Nevin's expression seemed critical, and Penelope decided he must not care to be contradicted—or perhaps he did not enjoy dancing. She gave him a curtsy, he bowed, and the dance began.

It was a country dance, a sedate one that required no more than that they stroll through the steps with grace and ease. They moved up and down the two facing lines of dancers—gentlemen on one side, ladies on the other—separating too often to allow more than the exchange of a word or two. Still, she found her glance sliding toward Nevin to admire that liquid grace of his. And she had to own to a pleasure in dancing with a gentleman taller than herself.

But, more than that, he drew the eye.

His black coat set off those admirably broad shoulders and nipped along the narrowing line of his back. Close-fitting black pantaloons outlined muscular legs, and other than a gold watch chain that hung across a white embroidered waistcoat, he wore no ornament. She liked the lack of ostentation in him. Of course, with his dark looks, he hardly needed anything else to attract admiration.

He also did not step on her heel. His hand always waited for hers to guide her though the next steps. And she found herself enjoying herself far more than she had in years.

With a shock, she realized it had been years.

For the past three years—since Cecila had been old enough to attend, in fact—she had brought her sister, but she had put on a matron's cap and positioned herself along the wall in the chairs with the other chaperons.

Tonight, however, Cecila had come into her room as Penelope was dressing. She had snatched up the lace cap, swearing that Penelope had no right to make them all look dowds. Sylvain had walked into the argument and sided with Cecila, insisting that if Penelope could bother so little about her appearance, she could as well. And so Penelope had given in, but only after achieving agreement that, in turn, Sylvain would also undergo the tortures of the curling iron.

As she had stepped into the rooms, she had felt self-conscious about not having her cap. And the low-cut gown that Cecila had dug out from the back of her wardrobe had seemed too revealing.

Oh, heavens, why did Nevin have to comment on her looks? Mutton dressed as lamb was the condemnation for women who clung to the folly of youthful fashions. And she did not want to be one of those desperate creatures who refused to admit that fine lines now creased the corner of her eyes, and she had not the bloom of six years ago.

She glanced at Nevin as they met in the dance to take hands and for a turn round.

Perhaps he flattered her because he still thought she might convince her father to invest in his scheme. Only he had said nothing more of it since that first evening. But why else would he offer such a compliment?

He smiled at her as their hands touched.

Too aware of him, she had to look away. Then, despising her lack of courage, she forced herself to look up again.

His gloved fingers tightened on hers before the dance required that he let go and move away, and the pulse fluttered treacherously in her throat.

Irritated with herself, she turned away.

Of course he meant nothing by it. London fashion no doubt demanded such insignificant flirtations. But as the dance ended, she began to think she had planned this evening badly. For she had not planned on her own weakness.

How delightful to have a handsome man dance with her. How wonderful to have a compliment. And how very much she had to keep in mind that she knew better than to think any of this meant anything.

With that in mind, she allowed him to lead her back to her sisters. She then made certain he would dance with them later and took her seat with the other matrons and spinsters.

Unfortunately, Mrs. Graves came over to her, looking quite full of gossip and bursting to share.

A stout woman with a florid complexion and blond

curls that had begun to silver, she shunned the high-waisted gowns for the stiff brocades of two decades ago. She had been a widow for twenty years, and Penelope tried to be charitable and think her gossiping stemmed from loneliness. That excuse, however, had worn thin as her own mother, bedridden for six years, still managed to find only good things to say about others.

Seating herself next to Penelope, Mrs. Graves snapped open her fan. "Dear Miss Harwood, you must be mortified at having to grant Lord Nevin a dance with you. But how is it that he came to stay with you? Surely your father must know of his background. Such a dreadful thing."

Shocked, Penelope stared at Mrs. Graves's profile, for she sat so she could watch the room as she spoke. Penelope certainly understood her own aversion to any Dawes, but why should Mrs. Graves think less of him?

The hairs on the back of Penelope's neck tingled as she remembered the gossip of last year. Was Mrs. Graves referring to how Nevin acquired his title?

For a moment, she tried to tell herself that she was not interested. But her fears returned in a rush. She had sensed that Nevin hid something from her. Now her pleasure in the evening evaporated.

Mrs. Graves turned to her, and her voice dropped to a low, excited whisper. "Oh, you do not know the story, do you? I can see you do not. Such a shame, and I know he does his best not to talk of it, but blood will out."

"Blood?"

"Why, yes—his mother is a Gypsy!"

Ten

Mrs. Graves's voice held a mix of pity and distaste as she confided, "Of course, Mr. Dawes is the one for whom I feel such sympathy. Imagine having a cousin appear from nowhere, claiming to be the rightful heir! That alone must have been shock enough to carry off Mr. Dawes's father, the late Lord Nevin, you know. And, if you ask me, I do not discount the stories that perhaps the current Lord Nevin did have something to do with his uncle's demise, for I heard tell of a dreadful confrontation between them. Still, the courts did find his claim valid enough, so *everything* went to him. And poor Mr. Dawes must now depend upon his cousin's good graces, for he has not so much as a penny, since Nevin's father was indeed the elder brother. But I still hold that no gentleman in his right mind would actually wed a Gypsy. Can you but imagine!"

Penelope had been frowning at this speech, and now she glanced at Nevin. He stood by himself, nursing a glass of punch. It all made sense now—those dark looks, his skill with animals, that odd language he had spoken to the stallion, and even how he seemed to prickle at the least suggestion of a slight. Yes, it made sense.

Half Gypsy. A man caught between two worlds. No wonder his character seemed to shift. Of course, she still saw no reason to trust such a man, but she understood better why he might adopt a rather fierce arrogance as a shield.

Mrs. Graves went on, as if Penelope's silence must express interest. "And then, of course, Lord Nevin's sister went and married the Earl of St. Albans." She raised her brows and nodded, as if to give that name an even greater meaning.

Penelope stared back, and the older woman added, her voice quickening with enthusiasm. "Oh, but you *must* have heard of him—the worst rake in all England. Why, some say that he ruined the sister of the Duchess of . . . oh, but I really must not say her name. Poor thing. You would recognize it in an instant."

"But I do not know any duchesses, ruined or otherwise. And if Lord Nevin's sister did marry an earl, what is there for me to remark? Has he gone on being a . . . a rake?"

"Well, no, but rumor holds she was his mistress beforehand—at least, that is what Mrs. Edgewell heard from Lady French, and she lives in London."

Penelope's patience began to slip. This seemed the worst sort of hearsay tattle, and it ought to be stopped.

Keeping her voice even, she said, "How very clever of her to know so many things that have nothing to do with her own family. Personally, since I have not met Lord St. Albans, nor Lord Nevin's sister, it is nothing to me how they conduct themselves."

Mrs. Graves stared at her, eyes wide. "Oh, but you cannot wish a man with such a background as Nevin's to have anything to do with your sisters!"

Penelope arched one eyebrow. "It is indeed unfortunate that Lord Nevin is a Dawes, but my mother encourages me not to hold that against him."

Mrs. Graves drew back a little, her brow tight, and then she forced a tittering laugh. "Oh, you and your jesting, Miss Harwood! For, of course, the Dawes have nothing to blush for in their pedigree."

Only a man who swindled his friends, Penelope thought. However, she would not utter those words. She would not tear apart another's character, no matter how deserving, and certainly not when that gentleman lay in his grave and beyond the ability to answer any charges.

However, such ridiculous prejudice against Nevin because of an accident of his birth seemed absurd.

And then those words sank in.

An accident of his birth.

Cold tingled across the back of her arms. She saw and judged Mrs. Graves's condemnation so clearly, but she had blinded herself to her own bias. And now shame washed through her in uncomfortable waves that left her shifting against the wooden-backed chair.

Half Gypsy or half Dawes—what matter did it make if she looked at him and saw only his breeding and not the man himself?

She struggled to think of one action he had taken which merited condemnation. The investment scheme he wanted to put before her father? That had come to nothing as of yet—and it had seemed a sound venture, one he had even offered to guarantee. He had certainly encouraged her father to keep Squire Winslow's horse, but he also risked his life to remake that horse into a useful breeding stallion.

And Nevin had said that he had come to Harwood intending only to make amends for his uncle's actions.

Penelope glanced at Mrs. Graves's bright eyes, but she saw reflected her own eagerness to find only flaws in Nevin. Just as others had once wanted to see only her faults.

The feelings of six years ago came back in a rush, as did the memories of the humiliating whispers that had circulated. *How shocking of her to break her engagement. Such a cold, jaded thing. How sad that she chose to break Treybourne's heart.*

She had kept the truth locked inside, for Jonathan had kept his word about one thing. He had not told anyone just how deep her father's losses went.

That had served—for a time. Only later, when loss began to pile upon loss, did their neighbors begin to realize that the Harwoods had fallen on bad times. By then, almost everyone had forgotten about her broken engagement, and she had not cared to bring up the subject again.

She had hated, however, being the center of such attention. And she would not participate in putting anyone else through such an ordeal. Not even a Dawes.

So she forced a smile and said, "I supposed if the Dawes name is so old and respectable, that must count for a good deal. And Lord Nevin is so very eligible."

Mrs. Graves frowned. "Well, if one could bring oneself to overlook the rest."

"But do we all not have those family alliances we would rather disown? In fact, did not your second cousin marry a Frenchwoman? An actress, even, I do believe?"

Pink flooded Mrs. Graves's plump cheeks. "Oh, we do not really speak to her, you know. And one must allow that the French are rather odd creatures. And she did give up the stage when she married."

"Yes, allowances do have to be made. For example, no gentleman with a title—and, I understand, a respectable fortune—ought to be shunned. Not entirely. It would be quite different if he lacked such qualities, of course. Or if he were in trade."

The frown tightened on Mrs. Graves's forehead, but then it cleared. "Oh, my dear—now I see just what you mean. And what a clever girl you are, to be sure. Given your circumstances, why, I might do the same. The neighborhood has been so lacking in young gentlemen since that horrid war with the French, which would go on and on so ridiculously. And I suppose if Nevin marries . . . well, let us say that a lady of breeding and unblemished reputation would certainly add to his credit."

Penelope had begun to frown at this. She had meant only to point out that Lord Nevin had some assets to his name and title, but it sounded as if Mrs. Graves had taken this as some sort of matchmaking hint.

Before she could correct that impression, Mrs. Graves noticed an old friend and excused herself, bustling away and leaving Penelope with an uneasy feeling that she had been misunderstood.

And had she actually done Nevin any good with her comments?

She glanced at him now and saw him with Sylvain. He looked to be asking her for a dance, and he had coaxed a smile from her. Offering his arm, he waited—as did Penelope, silently urging her sister to remember that a lady did not refuse such a request. It would be too like Sylvain to decline for no better reason than that she did not enjoy dancing. However, she put her gloved hand on his sleeve, and Penelope relaxed. Sylvain might actually realize the joy of dancing with so skilled a partner as Lord Nevin.

Only that thought also stirred an odd longing in Penelope. She told herself to ignore it. She could not dance with him a second time, for only a gentleman with the intent of courtship stood up twice with the same lady. And she could not imagine anyone wanting to court her, not when so many other younger, more attractive ladies offered flirtatious smiles and would no doubt be far more amusing partners.

The weight began to settle on her chest, though she tried to throw it off. She had a good life. Yes, she did. What matter if she now had to seat herself with the matrons and other spinsters? At least she had avoided the folly of an unhappy marriage.

Only why did that seem no consolation whatsoever?

Why did she still ache to be able to laugh and dance and flirt and act a girl? She ought to be old enough to know better.

Oh, but how she at least wanted to dance one more dance tonight.

As she thought that, a shadow fell across her and she glanced up at the dark form that loomed over her.

"You've not heard one word I've spoken," Theo Winslow said, a petulant edge to his tone.

Cecila glanced at him. He stood beside her, his black hair looking hastily combed into no particular style, the front locks already falling across his forehead. He had left off his customary riding boots, choosing dancing slippers and buff trousers. But he wore a black-spotted, knotted kerchief instead of a more formal white cravat, and his blue coat looked as if it had never seen an iron. Cecila really did, however, try to overlook these defects, for they could not detract entirely from his handsome features and those compelling blue eyes.

She reminded herself for the third time that evening just how handsome Theo looked.

But just now a frown creased his forehead. It pulled down the corners of his attractive mouth and darkened the blue eyes she admired. And she wished, with some irritation, that he would try to make himself at least a little agreeable.

She had forgiven him for his dallying with that tavern

wench, though he had not really offered an apology. He had not even mentioned the matter, and so she had not, either. But how long did he intend to go on being disagreeable?

Holding out her hand to command his arm, she said, her tone sharp, "Do not be ridiculous. Now dance with me."

In truth, she had not been minding. She had been watching Bryn Dawes as he asked Penelope to dance. Penelope, of all people! He had not asked her, now had he? That rankled. Of course, she did not really care about dancing with Mr. Dawes. It was simply a point of pride not to be left standing along the wall tonight.

Within a quarter hour of arriving, she had encountered that dreadfully vain Sarah Aldrich, who had become insufferable since going to London this past year. Sarah had proclaimed the evening void of any really suitable partners, and, with a deep sigh, had said to all within earshot that she supposed she would have to dance a few times anyway. And, of course, none of this could compare to how wonderful it had been to waltz at Almacks. She then went on to describe, yet again, her attendance at that bastion of exclusive, highly bred Society.

Cecila's temper had begun to simmer, and she had said, loud enough for Sarah's ears, how sad it was that some young ladies left their manners and the enjoyment of life behind them in London. For good measure, she added that she looked forward to having to choose partners from so many gentlemen.

With that, she formed the intent to dance every dance, even the dull, slow ones, and even if it meant by the end of the evening that she must stand up with the stout Mr. Langton or the spotty Mr. Gills or Squire Winslow himself. And she very much hoped Sarah ended up standing alone for most of the time. That would teach her to act so superior.

Glancing at Theo, Cecila began to tap her foot. He seemed oddly slow to obey her command. "Well?" she asked.

He scowled at her. "Time was, you waited for a fellow to ask you."

She angled her chin downward to offer up a teasing smile to coax him from his sullens. "Do you not wish to dance with me?"

Folding his arms, he gave back a cold stare. "Perhaps I do—or perhaps not. It depends on your answer to my last question."

Cecila scrambled for what he had been saying, but she had not heard one word. The first notes of the dance began, and desperation sparked the need for an immediate solution.

Turning away, she lifted a shoulder as if she did not care. "I will answer you after the dance. And if you wish to be churlish about it, then please do not stand up with me."

She heard a low growl of frustration, and she tried not to feel too smug with herself. Gentlemen, she had learned ages ago, really were such poor sports about losing any encounter.

"Oh, very well," he said, then thrust out his arm.

"Very well, what?" she asked, eyebrows arched and determined to punish him just a little.

"Very well, will you dance with me?" he asked, teeth clenched.

She smiled. "Why, Mr. Winslow, I should be delighted."

As she put her hand on his arm, he leaned closer, "And after, you had better have an answer for me that makes sense."

She glanced at him, resenting that dictatorial tone which had crept into his voice this evening. However, the grim set to his mouth left her hesitant to answer with a rebuke. He looked as if he really meant what he said.

Oh, heavens, what had he asked?

A faint alarm shivered across her skin, but she told herself not to be silly. What would he do if he learned she had not been attending? Go off in a huff for a few days again? Then he would miss her, and she would write him a charming note, and all would be mended.

They had had such disagreements and hurt feelings before.

But it seemed—well, it was becoming rather annoying that she must always mind him, while he could ignore her for days, going off with his brother and heavens knew what sort of low company. He had not said one word about their last encounter. He had not written her, even. In fact, he had never written her, now that she thought on it. Not a note of repentance, let alone of passion or a pledge of affection.

And she wanted such tokens.

However, as the dance began, he began to smile, and she found her feelings changing so that she searched for more excuses for him. Why, what gentleman would write a lady unless he planned marriage? But that set her frowning again.

Could it be that he intended nothing by her, as Penelope had said? But if so, why should he be hurt by her neglect? No, he must care for her. She had done nothing but look after his well-being and try to take care of him.

Only it would be rather nice if he thanked her once in a while with something other than sulks and demands.

And she started to compare him with how Mr. Dawes had treated her over the past few days.

Mr. Dawes had joked with her. He quoted absurd poetry to her. He had even said he might write a sonnet to her eyes.

Looking down the line toward Mr. Dawes and Penelope, Cecila frowned. They made a handsome couple, both with their dark brown hair and their height, which made them look elegant together. Unlike Theo, Mr. Dawes had taken some care with his dress, and he looked rather attractive in his black coat, pantaloons, and bronze brocade waistcoat.

The dance required her attention again, and then the steps took her down the set so that she actually had to partner with Mr. Dawes for a two-hands-around turn.

As she put her gloved hands in his, he leaned closer to whisper, " 'The smiles that win, the tints that glow . . .'"

She lifted her brows. "Whom do you quote now? Or is that your own?"

This lines around his eyes crinkled. "It's Byron, for I've decided no other will do for you. Do try to leave a few hearts unbroken tonight."

She gave him an innocent stare, as if she had no clue what he meant, and then moved back to dance with Theo, who glowered at her, his chin lowered.

Let him scowl, Cecila decided. And she hoped he recalled how it felt to be on the wrong side of such jealousy the next time his path crossed that of a too willing tavern maid.

Ignoring his bad mood, Cecila skipped through the rest of the dance. But then the music ended, and Theo stood before her, his frown even darker, and his eyes like chips of blue ice.

"Well—what about my answer?" he demanded.

She played with the fringe on her shawl. He must have asked her about meeting him again soon. That seemed to be his continual complaint. And since she did love him, she decided to relent.

Tipping her head to the side, she smiled and said, "Yes. Your answer is yes."

His jaw tightened and anger flared so hot in his eyes that she almost stepped back. Then he gave a curt bow. "In that case, spend your time with your bookish London gentleman, and see if I care! I can always find more congenial company!"

Turning, he strode away, leaving her to stare at him, a numb weight on her chest. What had he asked? Something about a London gentleman? She tried to sort out what the question had been, and to invent a quick excuse, but her thoughts tangled in desperate panic. Oh, what had she done?

Her own anger began to simmer. What right did he have to walk off in so rude a fashion? Snapping open her fan, she waved it in fast strokes to cool her face. Well, he could just storm off for a few days, if that's what he preferred! Yes, and she, too, could find better company.

Only, oddly, the back of her eyes now stung, and her breath caught on the hiccup of what almost sounded like a sniffle.

Oh, blast him for having ruined her evening—and for having robbed her of any more interest in dancing with anyone else.

It seemed more than one Harwood lady required rescue tonight, Bryn decided as he watched young Winslow stride away from Miss Cecila, leaving her stranded. He had just seen Miss Penelope Harwood handed to another partner, and he hoped she might not insert herself again among the wallflowers, but he had not thought Cecila would be abandoned so abruptly.

Someone certainly ought to give Winslow a few sharp words on how to treat a lady. Only Bryn had no interest in the fellow's education. He did, however, have a regard for Miss Cecila, and so he started across the room toward her.

His cousin reached her first, securing a hesitant smile for something said, and then her hand for the next dance. Bryn checked his stride, then altered his path to make for the refreshments, laid out on a walnut table at the opposite end of the room from the platform that held the string quartet.

He told himself to be pleased that his cousin had stepped forward. Nevin normally did not care overmuch for these affairs. He told himself that he had known a lady as lively and lovely as Cecila would never lack for partners. And finally he told himself that a man such as himself, without property or prospects, had no business paying any lady too much attention. Particularly not when that lady's circumstances dictated a need for a husband with a plump pocket.

And that, he thought, staring into the glass of burgundy punch he had poured himself, *is why I am not much of a poet. I ought to put feeling first and damn the rest.*

Only he never had been able to bring himself to starve for his art, and he certainly would not ask that of anyone else, certainly not a lady for whom he felt anything.

An elderly lady, plump, with silver-blond hair and wearing a gray brocade gown with the low waist of bygone years, drifted closer to the refreshment table, deep in conversation with an older gentleman with bushy gray hair and black eyebrows. Bryn tried not to listen, but the woman's words caught his attention.

". . . he intends to marry one of them. Mind, I would not want such an alliance in my family, what with Gypsy blood. But I do see how the Harwoods must think first

of the money, and there is a title. In fact Penelope as
good as told me she hoped for an offer for her sisters—
and, well, just look at him now."

Bryn did just that—and then he realized the obvious.
Of course. Why had he not seen it before? A match between Nevin and one of the Harwood girls would make
restitution for past ills, and bring a respectable alliance
that would help his cousin.

And, damn all, but the youngest was too young, and
the eldest too tart, so of course Nevin must choose Cecila.

Letting out a breath, Bryn moved away from the gossiping old lady, unwilling to hear more. He might, after
all, be the next topic. Lord Nevin's indigent cousin. Poor
Mr. Dawes. The gentleman whose title and inheritance
had been taken from him by a half Gypsy upstart—oh,
yes, he had heard it all.

Only he had never really wanted that title—had
dreaded the day he would inherit, in fact. He knew himself well enough, after all, to know he would have done
right by it. He would have taken his seat in Parliament,
and would have spent his life running estates he did not
understand or care for. And he would have left his books
and his writing. It had been a relief to have a pair of
cousins he had not known existed appear—the answer
to a prayer. He had even discovered he liked them.

He had become their friend when they were but Glynis and Christopher Chatwin Dawes, with hot tempers,
few social skills, and a desire for more. Then Christo became Lord Nevin in fact as well as by right, and Glynis
had become Lady St. Albans. Still, he stayed with them.
Not, as word had it, to hang on his cousin's sleeve, an indigent relative. No, he had helped smooth Nevin's
rough edges—and there were more than a few from too

many years spent in a rough life. And he had provided a buffer between his cousins and the world.

Of course, it had been a delicate thing to offer advice, as well as support, without too much interference. But he had managed to redirect a good deal of the gossip that came his way—and, Lord, had it ever come. He had even heard rumors, early on, that Nevin must have committed murder to gain the title.

Nonsense, of course. But also a little too close to the truth. Only it was his own father who had had family blood on his hands. Brotherly hate—Cain and Abel replayed—had been that tale. But Bryn had known that it would do the family no good to allow such stories to spread. So he had used himself, and his presence at his cousin's side, to prove such a tale ridiculous. Gradually the rumors had faded.

However, the time drew near when he would no longer be of such use. No, Christo had become more than Lord Nevin in name. He had gained assurance and polish, and if he took a wife, she would do far more to smooth his future path in Society.

By then Bryn knew he had better have some sort of employment or something, or he would start to become that despised creature—a useless relative. He would grow to resent such a situation. So would Nevin.

He liked his cousin far too much to allow that.

With an inward sigh, he watched Cecila Harwood flirt with his cousin. She had her smile back in place, and her fairness seemed a lovely contrast to Nevin's dark looks. Bryn could imagine a worse match for his cousin, and Cecila would enjoy being a titled lady. She certainly would cut a dash in London.

All in all, a depressing thought, them married.

Bryn drank back his punch. Then he put down his cup and made himself a promise.

If Cecila and Nevin made a match, he would do all he could to be their friend. But before that happened, and if Nevin really did intend to marry, he would try to direct his cousin's interest elsewhere. For Cecila, he had learned over the past few days, was not really the right lady for Nevin. No, she needed someone more gentle. Someone who understood her dreams and could encourage them.

And Bryn carefully kept his thoughts away from the temptation of casting himself in such a role, for he simply could not afford to think of a wife.

Penelope heard the story circulating at the first interval. The musicians had barely put down their instruments when Sarah Aldrich approached to remark that Penelope must wish to hear such laughable tattle so she could refute it.

Miss Aldrich's smug tone had set Penelope's teeth on edge, but she merely asked, "What must I wish to refute?"

"Why, the story that Lord Nevin is courting your sisters. So preposterous!"

"And just what is preposterous—to think that a Harwood might marry a baron? Or to think a Harwood might marry at all?"

Miss Aldrich forced a laugh, as if Penelope must be joking, but Penelope stared back, her expression blank, and then she said, "Do share, Miss Aldrich, why you find either myself or my sisters so ridiculous."

At that, Miss Aldrich's face tightened. She blinked at Penelope, tried to recover her poise, and then excused herself, claiming she had seen someone she must speak to.

With her hand clenched around her fan, Penelope's mouth tightened into a line.

Mrs. Graves, of course. Too late she saw that those

matchmaking hints had been suppositions. It almost could be laughable, only Penelope had no wish for her sisters to be objects of such gossip.

She glanced around the room, looking for them and wondering if they, too, had been informed of this story by some obliging soul. She hoped not. It would leave Sylvain mortified, and Cecila might feel goaded into outrageous flirtation with Nevin just to provide a genuine scandal.

But neither sister looked concerned. They both sat close to the entrance, Sylvain looking bored as she smothered a yawn behind her glove, and Cecila—well, Cecila looked tired, actually. It seemed unlike her to be sitting so quiet, staring at the floor, a frown pulling her brow tight.

Perhaps she had heard. Or perhaps she was not feeling well.

And that, Penelope decided, gave her an excellent reason for them to take their leave. The talk would die away when nothing more came of it.

She glanced around for her father, who had come with them, so that she might ask him to take them home. The gentlemen had come in their own coach, and so could stay, which would also help settle wagging tongues.

But as she turned, she realized that a gentleman was striding toward her—and her heart stopped. For a moment, she could not breathe, could not move. She could only think—*Jonathan.*

And then she realized she must be staring like a fool when the last thing she wanted was to show any trace of emotion to the man who had already been so reckless with her feelings. The man she had almost married.

Eleven

Jonathan stopped before her and offered a hesitant bow, looking so achingly the same—and distinctly uncertain, as if he did not know what she might do.

His hair still lay golden and straight, a touch long so that it curled at the collar of his green coat. His narrow face and figure still looked boyish and slim. His smile still tilted in a crooked, off-center slant, his mouth too wide for his face, which made his jaw seem a touch slight. Under his dark brown brows, his green-gray eyes filled with the same kindness they had always held, even when he had told her their love could not possibly survive financial hardships.

He looked so much like the gentleman who had once kissed her—the only one to ever do so—that the pain lanced through her chest, as fresh and sharp as six years ago. Too many memories began to crowd her—all of lost dreams which lay forever beyond her grasp.

Then he smiled, and his voice, that clear tenor which had once sung country ballads of tragic love, washed over her. "Hello, Pen."

She gave a silent prayer of thanks and let out a breath.

She had always hated that particular pet name. Hearing it on his lips brought back another set of memories. Not the moonlit walks, nor the other dances they had attended, nor the spring wildflowers he had once picked for her, nor the rides they had gone on that summer he had been in the district, visiting his uncle.

She focused instead on how she had confided about her father's change in fortune, had cried on his shoulder, even. He had offered sympathy. Then his visits became less frequent—and shorter.

He always had reasons. Always reasons. His uncle needed him. His aunt had an errand for him in Bath. She had not thought anything of it. Until, after an absence of nearly a month, he had come to her and stood before her, not even putting down his hat or taking off his gloves, and had told her he must return to his home in Sussex. Without her. He had offered nothing but excellent reasons why they could no longer think of marriage, but they all came down to her family's lack.

As a younger son, he had little income. He hoped for an inheritance from his uncle, but it might not come for years. And his father would disapprove of an alliance with a lady who brought nothing with her—might even cut him off.

"I am only thinking of you," he had said, his eyes ever so kind, and his voice so gentle.

She had almost hated him, for she could think of ways they could manage. If he wished it. And she knew then that more than money had been found lacking.

He simply did not love her enough to make the effort. She could see that in his expression. She knew then that she had failed to inspire a deep enough love. That failure had torn apart her confidence in an instant.

Trembling inside, she had walked to the door, her hands so icy she could not feel the tips of her fingers. Somehow she had gotten the door open. Then she had managed to say, her own voice held steady by force, "I trust you will say nothing to anyone of my family's . . . circumstances."

He hesitated, turning his hat in his hands, and she understood then that he worried what others would think. A gentleman, after all, did not break a promise, particularly not one so sacred as an offer of marriage.

That splinter in her chest twisted deeper, but she managed to get the words out, thinking only that perhaps somehow this might change things. "You may say I cried off."

There. Now he must know how deeply she loved him—so much that she was willing to take the blame upon herself.

He will get to the doorway, and then he will realize that I would make any sacrifice for him, and he will not be able to leave. Please, God. Please let it be so.

Only he did leave. He walked out without a glance at her.

Numb, she had stood there until the room grew dark. Stood there almost as if she still hoped his heart would change and he would return. And she tried to convince herself how well off she was without him—imagine wanting to marry such a man!

Only it still hurt that he had not cared enough.

She had begun then to train herself to hope never to see him again. He would not be back to visit his uncle in the nearby village of Durston. If he had not the courage to marry the lady he loved, no matter what, then how could he ever have the courage to face her again?

Only now he stood before her, and the spice of his cologne stirred too many feelings.

She fought them, staring at him with her eyebrows lifted and her mouth set, wanting only to get this over with.

"Mr. Treybourne," she said, stressing his family name and offering only the slightest incline of her head as an acknowledgment.

His eyes clouded. "Ah, Pen, we never used to be so formal."

"*Mr.* Treybourne, there are many things we once were which no longer lay between us."

His mouth tightened, and she hated herself for being so cold. They had once been so much more. Half turning away, she allowed herself to weaken, and dared to ask, "I trust your uncle is well?"

"Actually, I am here because he is dying."

She glanced at him, the long-hidden wish blossoming with treacherous hope. For months after he had gone, she had dreamed that his uncle might die. She hated herself for wishing ill on someone she had never met. But she prayed Jonathan would get his independence. He might come back then, full of regret and missing her so much that she would forgive him.

Gradually, that fantasy faded. She had thought it dead, but it seemed that it needed only the breath from his voice to fan those ancient embers. And she did not want that.

No, I am done with wishing for things I cannot have, she told herself. And then she wished she could forever throw away those desires for someone who might desire her.

As penance, she forced the words out, making herself mean every word, "I am sorry to hear such news."

He gave a small, sad smile. "He lived a good, full life. My own wish is that he may pass easily now. Ah, but it is good to see you again, Pen."

Pressing her lips tight, she wished he would not use that name. She could feel her control slipping.

And then his smile widened. "But, come, I want you to meet my wife."

* * *

Nevin had been talking to his cousin when a gentleman he did not recognize approached Miss Harwood. Something in the man's posture spoke of intimacy—he leaned too close to Miss Harwood, and that annoyed Nevin. But Miss Harwood must know most of those here. And the protection of his escort, and Bryn's, could only be considered a mere formality, what with their father in attendance tonight.

Still, knowing this did nothing to mitigate Nevin's mood, and it bothered him all the more that he could not give a reason as to why this fellow's attitude should dig under his skin.

Then Miss Harwood's face turned as white as her gloves, and Nevin realized that her discomfort mirrored his own.

What had that fellow said to draw such a reaction from her?

He watched as Miss Harwood went with the fellow, crossing the room to be introduced to a small, dark-haired lady. He watched the tension gather in the line of Miss Harwood's back—an elegant back, but now taut as a blade. Her face remained pale. She stayed only a moment, then turned and walked away, her eyes unfocused and her steps hesitant, as if she did not even notice the room around her.

Nevin leaned towards his cousin. "Who is that fellow Miss Harwood just left?"

Bryn glanced around the room. "What fellow?"

Gesturing with his glass, Nevin indicated the fair-headed, narrow-faced gentleman in a green coat. To judge by how he hovered next to the small, dark lady, Nevin decided she must be a wife, for the swell of her gown showed she would soon have to forgo such events as these. She looked to be increasing.

Bryn studied the couple, and then shook his head. "Have no idea. Does it matter?"

Nevin put his cup on the long plank table that held the refreshments. Miss Harwood had found a seat in a corner of the room and seemed to be doing her best to imitate an ice sculpture. With a word to his cousin, Nevin excused himself.

The gossip drifted to him as he crossed the room.

"Did you see how white she went? How she must regret her folly. . . "

". . . she threw him over . . . so heartless . . ."

". . . his wife—so sweet. He must be relieved now that he did not win such a cold woman as . . ."

". . . beyond attracting a husband now. And she must know it, for did you not see that look on her face?"

Nevin needed no names to guess their topic, and his stride lengthened.

Miss Harwood did not even glance up as he approached, so he leaned down, took her hand and pulled her to her feet, ignoring every rule of etiquette that his cousin had drilled into him about a gentleman waiting for a lady to allow any such contact.

At his touch, she recovered enough to look at him, but instead of the sharp stare he expected for his forward action, she gazed at him, her eyes glassy. The pallor on her cheeks left him wishing he could have just five minutes with that idiot she had not married. What thoughtless stupidity to introduce her to his wife, as if nothing more than casual acquaintance had ever been between them.

Well, at least he could act the gentleman, and so he said, "Miss Harwood, will you take a turn with me about the room?"

Since he had already tucked her hand into the crook of his arm, he did not wait for an answer but began to walk with her.

With a weak effort, she tried to pull away. "Please, I do not feel well."

He clamped his arm tighter to his side and then leaned closer to say, his voice soft, "You will feel worse if you encourage what is being said of you."

A spark flared in the depths of her eyes, and he found a smile lifting the corner of his mouth. She needed that fire just now. He knew well how such a flicker of anger could keep the world from seeming unbearably cold.

"What is being said?" she asked, and then she lifted her chin. "Actually, I ought to have said that I do not care."

His smile twisted and he kept walking, compelling her to stroll with him. "Then you had best smile at me and show your lack of concern."

She tried to do just that, but the expression quivered on her lips so tenuously that Nevin's heart twisted. He covered her hand with his. "Forget the smile. Flirt with me instead. That will give these gawkers something else for speculation."

She stopped, forcing him to stop as well. "Flirt? Oh, I could not."

She looked so shocked that he had to smile, and then he coaxed her to move again. If they kept walking, others would not interrupt. "You make it sound such a sin."

"Well, it—it is just not something I do. Or ever have, really."

He thought of how tempting she had been in the stables that one dawn. Oh, she could flirt all right. But only when that mind of hers stopped turning, it seemed. So how did he lure her into forgetting herself? He had no helpful Cinder to provide beguiling tricks.

Leaning closer, he said, "Then I shall flirt with you to show you how it is done."

She stiffened again, and that unhappy haunted look

returned to her eyes. "Please, you do not have to do this. I . . . I—"

Her voice broke, and Nevin knew he had to get her someplace private. She sounded on the verge of falling to pieces, and he could not imagine anything more distressing to a proud woman such as her—or to him.

The assembly rooms occupied the upper story of a brick building. It took only a moment of maneuvering to lead her to the doorway, and then down the stairs. A quick word with the porter at the entrance, a coin slipped into a white-gloved hand, and they were shown into the cloak room and left alone with assorted hats, greatcoats, and cloaks, which all smelled faintly of damp fur and wool.

It said much about her state of mind that she went with him, her eyes downcast, not saying anything, as if she could find neither the voice nor the will to make any protest. Or perhaps she did not trust her own control.

In the cloak room, he glanced around, found a stool, pulled it forward for her, and told her to be seated.

She sat, so docile that he wished he had brandy for her. She had obviously had a shock—a bad one. *Devla,* but someone ought to throttle that fool of a *gadjo* for doing this to her.

"Breathe," he ordered.

She glanced up at him. Her hands had begun to tremble, so he knelt before her and rubbed them between his. "Go on—deep breaths. They will steady you."

Pulling in a breath, she held it a moment, then let it go and grimaced. "You must think me ridiculous."

"I think you have had much to endure tonight."

She winced. "I thought it all done with."

"And so it is. But who of us ever expects our past to walk up and say hello again? However, I also think you are quite extraordinary to have faced him and still acted a lady. My sister would not have managed so well."

Her shoulders slumped. Then she said, her voice scornful, "Lady—oh, yes a fine lady. And I know what the world thinks me. Did you also hear that I am a jilt, a woman without a heart to have rejected so fine a gentleman?" Tears glimmered in her eyes. "Why did he have to come back?"

Nevin could see no other choice. Rising, he pulled her to her feet and into his arms, and then he held her as the storm broke. It was not much of a flood—a few sniffles, a good deal of shivering. His sister would have exhausted herself with streams of curses and sobs, and would have made such a scene upstairs as to leave the county talking for a month. He could only wish Miss Harwood could lose just a touch of her too tight control. The woman must be strangling her heart.

Pulling away from him, she dug into the small, gold-embroidered bag that hung from her elbow and dragged out a square of lace and linen that she dabbed to her eyes. "I do beg your pardon."

"For what? You have been harsh in judging me, I know, but you seem to hold yourself to even higher standards. As for that gossip . . . well, I have too much experience on the wrong end of such talk to give it credence."

She glanced up at him, her eyes still watery and her brow furrowed.

He touched a finger to her cheek. "You forget that I have seen you with your sisters. I know you would not send away someone you loved."

Penelope stared at him, mortification creeping into her that her deepest thoughts could be so obvious—particularly to him. Must she lose every scrap of dignity this evening?

Stepping back, she dabbed her eyes again, then put

her handkerchief away. She had herself in hand at last. Oh, but why had she had to fall apart before him? He certainly ought not to have held her, she decided, trying to summon a sense of outrage. That had only encouraged her weakness. But all she could find inside was a warm gratitude. Oh, it had been lovely to have someone's shoulder to lean on. Particularly such a broad shoulder. Even if only for a moment.

Now, however, she really should act a mature, sensible lady. She had indulged herself enough—only she still felt fragile as glass.

She had to leave—soon.

"Thank you, my lord. Would you take me back now?"

For a moment he frowned at her, and she worried that he might dispute the matter. She had no fight left, but guilt consumed her that he had done so much for her. She did not want any more speculation to spring up around him because of their absence. She owed him that consideration.

Then he offered his arm.

Relaxing, she managed a weak smile. "Thank you. You have been wonderfully kind." The words came out stiff and halting, and she wondered if she sounded ungrateful.

He seemed not to think so, for he slanted a glance at her, a teasing light in his black eyes. "Kind—for a Dawes?"

The teasing softened her own mood and put her onto known ground with him so that she was able to answer, her voice almost even, "No, simply kind."

As they climbed the stairs, she had to remember his advice to breathe. It stopped that dreadful quivering in her stomach. Oh, heavens, she hoped Jonathan had taken himself—and his wife—away already.

How amazing that one simple sentence could smash every last hope within an instant, and could leave one so utterly shattered.

At least now she could finally get on with gracefully stepping into a spinster's life. She could bury that last secret in her heart that love would ever change anything in her life. It might do so for some, but there were, after all, many ladies who never married. It did not mean she could not have a happy and satisfying life.

They stepped back into the room, and it seemed as if every pair of eyes slid her direction. She knew that could not be true, but the avid stares and the whispers scratched across her nerves like the scrabbling of rat's claws across a dark floor.

The warmth began to drain from her again, and her respect for Nevin rose. Heavens, if he had to endure this every time he went anywhere, no wonder he had developed such brusque manners.

"My offer of a flirtation stands," he said, his voice a low rumble in her ear. "It would at least give *you* a distraction."

She glanced at him, not understanding why he was making such an effort on her behalf. She had done nothing to earn such regard. Indeed, her earlier treatment of him had now thoroughly been revealed as less than desirable, leaving her pride in tatters.

Only, perhaps she did understand. He must know about the discomfort of being the center of speculation. And it said a good deal for his character that he could extend himself to feel for another suffering the same plight.

She had misjudged him in everything, it seemed. Just as she had once misjudged Jonathan. No wonder she had ended a spinster. She seemed to have only flaws, and the biggest of these seemed to be an inability to really understand any gentleman. Heavens, did she even understand herself?

This time her smile, small as it was, actually stayed in place as she turned toward Nevin. "You will have to ex-

cuse me. I am sadly out of practice, and I actually was
never much of a hand at it to begin with."

"And do you also plan to give up riding because of the
rain and wet, and being so out of practice with that?"

"Now you are being absurd."

"Why? Both are skills. Or is it that you enjoy one, and
not the other?"

Penelope stared at him, the look in her eyes uncertain, the color still gone from her cheeks. And Nevin
decided she was reconsidering his offer. In truth, her
lack of seductive skills did not matter. She needed only
something else to think about. But he also knew a little
of the disinclination to attempt something that might
prove embarrassingly rusty.

He had once struck fires with only his knife and a flint,
had walked in the forest silent enough to surprise even a
fox, and had tracked deer by moonlight. Now servants lit
his fires, his stride made almost as much noise as his *gadjo*
brother-in-law's, and he would probably lose his way if he
tried to follow a deer's track anywhere.

Regret for that loss hovered at the edge of his mind,
but he put it aside. He had a lady's pride to restore just
now with compliments that would put a glow back on
her cheek. He had no time for foolish memories which
had been softened by the cushion of time and too much
comfort.

Oh, he might recall how bright the summer sky
looked at night, or the sweet sharpness of a spring
breeze, or the raw joy of the wind before a storm. But he
would do better to remember the bite of an early snow,
how hard the ground could be in February, and the
choking dust of a road in late summer.

He focused again on Miss Harwood. Her chin had
lifted only a fraction, and no spark lit her eyes. She had
not yet put back into place all her usual layers of armor.

Oddly enough, he rather missed that abrasive side of her. His mouth twisted. His sister, he knew, would tell him he loved danger too much.

"Come now," he said, his tone dropping lower. "All you must do is gaze at me as if my every word fascinates and offer inviting smiles."

Scorn flashed in her eyes. "I thought you preferred honesty."

"Could you not honestly find me fascinating?" The faintest blush tinted her cheeks. "Ah, so you could."

Penelope opened her mouth to deny it, only he kept staring at her, those dark eyes far too knowing. He had leaned closer to her—closer than he really ought to. Not so near that they touched, but near enough that she could see the faintest circle of golden brown at the center of his eyes.

The excuses dried on her tongue. And then she straightened. "You are flirting, and without my permission!"

He gave a low chuckle, then took her gloved hand in his. Through the thin kidskin, the warmth from him soaked into her cold fingers as welcome as heat from a fire. "No. Try again. You tell me I should prefer honesty. I ask you if you cannot honestly find me . . ."

"No. I cannot." With a shake of her head, she pulled her hand away.

His mouth now set, he took her hand again. "Come now, you can think of something amusing to say. If not, then offer a coy glance and rap my knuckles with your fan."

Penelope's frown tightened. She had never been able to toss her curls as did Cecila, or utter fatuous banter. Even as a girl, she had been serious and quiet. Far too like Sylvain, in fact. Now she let out a long breath. "It is just no use. I never was such a simpering miss as that!"

He laughed then, a low throated chuckle that left her puzzled and uncertain if she ought to take offense, or be intrigued. Was he amused by her failings? But he did not seem to be. He seemed, well, he seemed to actually be enjoying this rather odd flirting.

And then he said, "I think you will survive, Miss Harwood."

Sudden awareness swept through her that she had indeed managed to forget her circumstances for a few moments. She almost smiled. If she could forget for a little while, then she could forget for even longer. The earlier pain had receded into a distant ache, and would soon be no more than what it ought to be—a memory. She would indeed survive.

What a blessing to have someone so irritating at hand. She had not known what a tonic that could be.

"Now if you will gather your sisters, I shall take you home," he added, his voice still low, so that it set her chest to vibrating at that deep tone. "But do take your time. I cannot think you wish to look as if you are fleeing."

He touched a finger to her chin as he spoke. She did not know what to say. Or do. Did one thank a gentleman for being an annoyance?

Then her searching stare met his, and she knew she had no need of words. He understood her feelings exactly.

An unusual gentleman, to be certain.

Turing, Penelope strode away to fetch her sisters and to say their good nights.

Nevin watched her, his attention caught by that elegant back. Her stride had purpose again.

And then Bryn stepped up to his elbow, and said, his tone dry, "Best have a care, cousin, how long you spend with any Miss Harwood, for the gossips have you married already."

Twelve

"Married?" Nevin turned, his mouth crooked, certain Bryn must be mocking this evening's rumors with such an absurd one. His amusement faded as he took in his cousin's lack of a smile and the flat disapproval in Bryn's eyes.

Folding his arms, Nevin hunched a shoulder. "And what do I care what others are saying?"

Bryn's eyes darkened. "Don't be an ass. The Harwoods live here. They will care."

Nevin's mouth tightened. Then he said, "Do you have a point to make?"

"I should think it obvious. Miss Harwood found it so, for the account is that she now has hopes you will court one of her sisters."

Nevin glanced across the room, but he could no longer see Miss Harwood's tall figure. "Impossible. She hardly tolerates me."

"Oh, yes, she certainly looked so just now. And do you not think her capable of having an interest in getting one of her sisters a title, not to mention a comfortable income?"

Nevin muttered a rude comment in his Romany tongue.

"Go ahead, then. Ignore me. But that won't stop the

rumors. If this were London, bets would no doubt be laid whether you'll come up to scratch or run shy!"

Nevin's collar seemed to tighten as he turned to glare at his cousin. "So I am thought to have already raised the ladies' expectations?"

His face grim, Bryn's voice dropped lower. "I don't know about anyone's expectations, other than my own. And what *I* expect is that now such tattle has started, the longer we stay, the more it appears that you do have a particular interest in the Harwoods. And if we leave in a few weeks', the gossips will have a lovely time inventing reasons for our departure—all of which will center on expectations having been raised and not met. That will not be pleasant for the Harwoods."

Nevin eyed his cousin, his brow tight and his thoughts dark. He did not like this conversation. Even more, he disliked that his cousin spoke only the truth.

"So you think I should take my leave now and run from these rumors?" he asked, scorn icing his tone.

"You could, or . . ." Bryn paused and pulled in a breath, then said, his voice strained, ". . . you are not going to care for this."

Nevin continued to stare at his cousin, and Bryn shifted on his feet. He had known this would be difficult, but someone had to remind Nevin that they had come here to make the Harwoods' situation better, not worse.

As Nevin continued staring, Bryn decided he might as well get it out. "You might actually consider marriage, you know. As practically a son, you could aid them far better and more easily."

Nevin's frown deepened to so dark a scowl that Bryn stiffened. Would he turn and stalk away, or would he un-leash that smoldering temper? He had a wicked right, and there would be the devil of a fuss if Nevin chose this moment to revert to the rough ways of his youth. But seconds passed and Nevin did not move. Bryn let out a breath. Nevin had, it seemed, learned some control over the past year. But the effort to hold himself in check appeared in lines that tightened around his mouth.

What was he thinking? Bryn wondered. That his cousin had lost his mind, perhaps? Bryn had not cared for his own conclusion, but a gentleman had a certain responsibility to protect a lady's reputation. One simply did not go about doing things that started gossip such as this—and if one did, one then stepped up and did the right thing.

Only Nevin might not choose to see it that way.

And it grated on Bryn that he could offer no help in the matter. An offer from an indigent gentleman such as himself would be worse than an insult, and could do nothing to remedy the situation.

Finally, Nevin moved. One black eyebrow lifted. Then he asked, his voice thick with mockery, "And have you also picked which sister I ought to now court?"

Bryn's jaw tightened at the sarcasm. Did Nevin think he enjoyed this? That he liked having to step into a situation in which he knew his counsel would be unwelcome? He allowed an answering bitterness to shade his voice as he replied, "Sorry. I forgot that as Lord Nevin you are now head of the family, and you must be tired of all this advice."

He started to turn away, but Nevin's hand caught his arm. Fists clenched, Bryn spun around, but then he saw the crook to Nevin's mouth and a glimmer of humor in his cousin's black eyes.

"You are no end of irritating—because you are right about every blasted thing, damn you."

Letting out a breath, Bryn gave back a hesitant smile and accepted the peace offer. "I can only imagine how galling that must be, but it hardly alters the situation."

"Yes, yes, I know. You have more than made that clear, and I have not spent all this time as Harwood's guest only to do him mischief, even unintentionally."

"Then we are leaving?"

"No. My business is hardly over, but I will make certain this speculation ends."

"And just how—"

"Leave it, cousin. I said I would manage. And the Harwoods are ready to depart, so go and ask for the carriages, if you please, and I will meet you downstairs."

Bryn hesitated, a tight furrow between his eyebrows, but then he shook his head and started for the doorway.

Nevin glanced around the room. He disliked discussing his affairs with anyone, but had to admit that Bryn was right, both in his warnings and in forcing the issue. The gossips would invent more tales until something else was given them. Only what could he offer? Not the full truth. It held too much shame for his family, as well as for Harwood. However, there was one reason that might serve.

Noticing an older gentleman who had been introduced to him earlier, Nevin went to exchange a word, making certain to drop a mention that he had become interested in buying Harwood's stallion, and how difficult the task was proving. He spoke loud enough for others to hear, and then left the tattlemongers to add what embellishments they would.

That excuse, however, would seem reasonable only for a time. After all, what man chased after a horse for weeks on end? And the thought teased that perhaps his cousin was right about all of it.

But marriage?

It seemed an extreme step to take, and yet . . .

He had never really considered tying himself to any woman. The Rom regarded him with the same disdain for his half-blood as did the *Gadje,* and so an alliance with any of the traveling folk had not really seemed an option. But that, he knew, was only part of the truth. His mother had defied her own family to marry a *gadjo,* and had been banished for it. In truth, he had never met a woman willing to make such a choice for him.

In fact, the women he had known before he had become a lord were not the sort that a man brought home as a wife. He had chosen them just because they offered such easy smiles and such fleeting passion.

But if he wanted a son to inherit, he would have to marry, so why not wed a Harwood? It would put him in a far better position to make up for the harm caused by his uncle, and a wife would give him a hostess who could better establish his position in the world.

All of that seemed quite reasonable. So why did the notion still seem so . . . so awkward?

Because he had expected to find love?

He searched his memories now, but could find no trace of desire for such a thing.

He had grown up with an adoring mother, a doting older sister, and an intense dislike for the hard life that came with living on the road with no possessions, no home, no place to belong. But he had never had a clear idea of what else he wanted. And then, when he turned twenty-one, his mother had told him the truth of his inheritance—that his father had been a nobleman.

Everything changed. He had been angry at first that she had kept silent so long. He could remember that well enough. And then it became clear that his mother had been wise to protect him until he came of age. He learned that quickly enough. His uncle had hated him and would have been happy to remove him, and his sister, from this earth by any means possible. But his uncle had been the one to depart this life, and there were times Nevin liked to think the man's hate had eaten away at his heart until it must fail for nothing had been left.

A poetic thought, but nothing to do with his present— or his future.

Marriage.

Could he better mend the past with such an alliance? Arranged marriages among the Rom were as common as anywhere, and this would be little different. But while Harwood might accept him as a guest, would he really welcome a son with Gypsy blood?

Uneasy, he rubbed at his temples. He did not care to think himself a coward, but he also had no taste to court any more scorn. So what should he do?

And how had such a simple plan to give Harwood back some of his fortune become such a personal tangle?

Over the next few days, Penelope did her best to change her manner toward Lord Nevin. After all he had done for her at the assembly, she wanted to offer him a greater courtesy and ease. If only she could stop that urge to fidget and fuss every time he came near.

She could at least start over with him. And she would stop being so aware of him. She would not speculate when his mouth crooked in that curious half smile what thought had amused him. She would not watch him when he entered or left a room, admiring that lovely grace. And she would not avoid him just because she could not control her reactions. She would, in fact, treat him with a better deference due his title.

So she said yes when he offered to ride with her in the mornings, even going so far as to accept his invitation to borrow his cousin's horse. It proved no hardship to accept such a proposal, for Mr. Dawes had a handsome bay hunter with a long stride and sloping pasterns that made for a comfortable, springy ride. And after a morning gallop, with the wind in her face and a fine horse to ride, it seemed the most natural thing in the world to walk back to the stables with Lord Nevin, talking about everything and nothing in particular.

She still watched over her sisters. However, Cecila had seemed oddly distracted since the assembly, sitting for hours in the evening, staring at nothing. Penelope could guess that it had something to do with Theo Winslow, but the attempts she had made to talk about it met with a sharp change of subject, so she allowed the matter to drop. And Sylvain seemed only to seek out Nevin for his advice on Mr. Feathers, drawn out of her shyness by some mystery that Nevin worked.

He practiced the same magic on the stallion, although Penelope decided he must be going about the process entirely wrong. Each time the horse made hesitant steps toward Nevin, he chased the stallion away. That seemed to her the opposite of the goal of catching the horse and training it.

Finally, she asked him about this, but his only answer was to smile and offer back a cryptic comment, saying, "Ah, but every creature is tempted most by that which it cannot have."

She did not see how such logic applied to a horse.

However, four days after the assembly, she walked into the stable yard and then stopped dead, her eyes widening and her mouth falling open in shock.

Nevin stood on the cobbles, the stallion next to him, a monstrous, dark form.

Nostrils flaring, the horse lifted his head, his ears flicking back, then forward, as if the least thing might send him into one of his fits. Sunlight filtered through the clouds, sometimes offering bright moments, and then moving the day into chill shadows, so that the horse's coat gleamed one moment, and then dulled to a brown so dark as to appear black.

In shirt sleeves, breeches, and boots, his coat abandoned across one of the stable doors, Nevin kept his attention on the stallion. Muttering soft words—Gypsy words, no doubt—he reached into his breeches pocket and pulled out a sliver of apple that he offered on the flat of his palm.

The horse tossed his head and stamped a hoof, and Penelope noted that no ring of iron against stone echoed through the yard. The horse had not been shod. If he struck out, that might be a life-saving factor. On the other hand, she would rather not find out just how much damage he could cause even without iron shoes on his hooves.

With another toss of his head, the horse blew through his nose and then slowly lowered his head to take the apple, eating greedily and quickly.

Penelope eyed the horse, hardly daring to believe he could now be so tame. He no longer wore his headcollar. Nothing whatsoever, not so much as a rope, hung on him to enforce control.

Deciding on caution, Penelope gathered the skirts of her green riding habit in case she needed to sprint to safety.

Then it occurred to her just how Nevin might have worked this miracle, and she asked, "Did you feed him an opiate?"

At her words, the stallion tensed, his head lifting again, but Nevin laid a hand on the sleek dark neck, and then glanced at Penelope, his eyes alight with amusement. The wind tugged at his black hair, tossing it, just as it did the stallion's mane, and she wondered if these two had made peace with each other just because a common wildness ran through them—an edge of something untamed.

Dangerous unpredictability, you mean, she told herself. Not exactly the most comfortable of traits. And all of it errant nonsense, of course. Nevin might be part Gypsy, but he was a lord and gentleman, after all.

Oh, why must the man be so confusing about just who he was?

Nevin offered a smile. "Come and make friends. But move slow, and keep your hands low. He is still shy."

"Thank you, but I think I shall remain where I am."

"What—are you afraid? I can assure you, he is far more frightened of you. He will not lash out if you do not threaten him."

As Nevin spoke, he begun to scratch just in front of the stallion's withers. The horse lifted its head and turned, his head tilting and his eyes narrowing with obvious pleasure.

Penelope almost refused, but Nevin's words stung. She was not afraid. No, she simply had a sensible amount of caution.

So she edged one step closer. Then another step.

The stallion glanced at her, flattening his ears, and she stopped at such a warning, but Nevin had already muttered something to the horse, distracting him again.

"Just what are you telling him?" she asked, frowning as the horse began to nose Nevin's pockets.

"Nothing. Just words. A horse listens more to your tone, to your body. And just now you are telling him he can dominate you, so he is thinking about doing just that."

Penelope straightened. "I am not."

"You are. You challenge him with how you stand and stare at him. Turn sideways and stop looking him in the eye. Invite him to come to you. But you have to do so in a way he understands. You have to learn his language."

It seemed silly, but she decided she ought to at least try his odd ideas. So she turned to present her shoulder to the stallion, and then said, "Where do I look if not at him?"

"Watch his body instead of his face. And his tail. Just do not lock stares with him, for that makes him think you want to fight. He thinks of you as just an odd, two-legged horse, so you must be that. Ah, there, see him relax. See how his head dips and he nibbles like a foal with his first grass."

"How do you know all these things? Is it some . . . some . . ."

"Some Gypsy skill?" he asked, his tone dry.

She glanced at him. He sounded faintly amused, and his mouth lifted with a smile, but she heard a tainted echo of the prejudice from the other night.

Without waiting for her reply, he answered his own question. "Actually, it is just that I know how to think like a horse. I spent too many hours as a boy watching them, trying to learn their language. See, he is talking to you now. He is nibbling again, and shifting his weight. Come closer."

Intrigued, she moved a step forward.

"Stop there. Let him take the last step," Nevin said, coming to her side. "He must be the one who comes to you in the end."

"Should you leave him alone like that?" she asked, frowning.

Amusement slipped into his voice. "Worried he might run away? If he does, he would only come back, looking for me. And for this." He slipped a slice of red apple into her hand.

"Do I just hold it out?" she asked. And then she realized how ridiculous she must sound. She had been around horses all her life, and she certainly knew how to feed one an apple.

Forcing her shoulders down, she took a deep breath and let it out, willing her muscles to loosen.

Nevin stood next to her, muttering words to the stallion that meant nothing. The horse's ears swiveled. He stretched his neck forward, and his nostrils flared. He pulled back and away, then leaned closer again, and finally took a hesitant step forward.

Penelope almost stepped backward, but she came up against Nevin's chest and she stopped herself.

Nevin leaned over her shoulder, whispering to her now, his hands on her arms, "No, do not ever move away from this one. He gets all his bad habits because too many have backed down from him. That makes him think he can be a bully. Stand your ground. He must respect you."

Easy enough to say, she thought. Far harder to do when staring up at so much power. Yet, with Nevin behind her, she had to trust he would not put her in danger. So she stood still, her heart pounding rapidly in her throat.

The stallion edged a step closer.

Heavens, she had not realized he was so large—a good six inches taller at the withers than any horse in their stables, with a deep chest and that massive, arched neck. If he could sire offspring with his size, they could not help but outrun anything on four legs.

Again the stallion flattened his ears, as if threatening an attack. Skin cold, Penelope held still and waited. Would he choose now to revert to his old habits? Or had Nevin really managed to convince him to behave?

And then the horse pricked his ears forward, as if wondering why his usual horrible face had not made her cower.

"You imposter! You honestly do try to intimidate everyone," she muttered to the horse.

The horse's ears flickered again. He stretched his nose toward her, and velvet lips nibbled on the apple she held.

Her fear left in a stirring of delight.

Taking the apple, the stallion stepped away. Then, as if to let her know he had not entirely changed his conduct, he flattened his ears and bared his teeth.

She almost pulled back, but Nevin was there. He stepped forward at once, muttering a rebuke to the horse and driving it away. Then he turned aside from the horse, and slowly the animal edged closer, almost like a puppy seeking forgiveness for his relapse. A very large, very dangerous sort of puppy, Penelope decided.

When the horse stood quiet again, she glanced at Nevin, a frown tight on her forehead. He had, she supposed, done as he had promised. And she would have to abandon her plan to ask her father to return the stallion.

But would this change last?

Her thoughts tumbled out as she turned to him, saying, "And what are we to do with him after you leave?"

Pressing her lips together, she wished she could take back her words. She ought not to be putting her problems onto his shoulders. Heavens, no.

"I beg your pardon—you must excuse me," she muttered. Then she turned and fled for the house, keeping her eyes on the ground, embarrassment churning inside her.

Of course he must go. Had she not been wishing him on his way? Why should it matter to him if he left them with a stallion now only half a rogue? Oh, why had she said anything, as if this predicament somehow meant anything to him? Why could she not compliment him on his skills and leave it at that?

She must be losing her wits.

Or perhaps she still was off balance from seeing Jonathan again. However, that seemed a less than honest explanation. Of course it had been a shock, but she had been amazed to find how quickly that tightness around her heart had faded. Relief had bloomed that she had not married such a man, but regret for lost dreams still shadowed her. And now here she was, looking to Lord Nevin as if he were . . .

Her mind blanked.

As if he were what?

He was nothing to her, other than a guest of her father's. She really had to keep that firmly in mind. And she was nothing to him, other than perhaps an annoyance.

Stepping into the hall, she stopped at once. Cecila stood by the side table where the morning post lay on an ebony tray, her face pale and a note held in trembling hands.

With a start, Cecila glanced up and then thrust the note behind her. "Oh . . . good morning."

"Is it now?" Penelope said. "Or is it Theo Winslow again?"

Cecila's cheeks pinked, betraying the truth.

Shaking her head, Penelope folded her arms. "So he thinks nothing of writing you without Father's permission, as if you were already promised to each other? That should show you how little true regard he has for you!"

Cecila's chin came up. "Well, we are not promised, are we? And not like to be if you have your way—and I . . . I just wish you would allow me to live my own life!"

She swung away, the hem of her gown spinning out, and then stalked up the stairs, her back stiff.

"Cecila!" Penelope called out. She took a step forward

and then hesitated, feeling worse than she had a moment ago.

Ignoring her call, Cecila disappeared upstairs. A moment later, the slam of a door echoed down to the hall.

Penelope let out a sigh. Would nothing go well today? And just what exactly had she said to put her sister into such a temper? She had only offered her help. Perhaps it was not so much what she had said. Was it more what Winslow had written? Yes, that had to be the case.

Her hands fisted.

She could throttle Theo Winslow for tearing apart her sister's peace. It would be a different matter if he showed signs of stability, or less inclination to follow his older brother's wild ways. Instead, he was a thoughtless boy, and very like to ruin her sister's happiness with his careless ways.

Well, this could not go on.

Hugging her arms, she glared at the other notes upon the tray, one addressed to her father.

Father would have to do something. He would simply have to be made to see that he had to call upon the squire and put a stop to this. The squire might even send young Winslow away for a time, for Penelope could not believe he wished either of his sons to marry one of the poor Harwood daughters.

With her determination fixed and the hurt from Cecila's dismissal hardening into a justified anger with Theo Winslow, Penelope set out to find her father.

In the kitchen, she learned from Mrs. Merritt that Mr. Harwood had gone out with his gun and with Mrs. Merritt's son to act as his beater for grouse. After thanking the housekeeper, Penelope put on a shawl and bonnet, then let herself out the back of the house. He would not have gone far, and the sound of his gun would be quite easy to follow.

Glad to have the task before her, she strode toward the woods. Cecila would certainly shed a few tears when Theo Winslow was sent away, but it would not be as bad as having Winslow break her heart over and over again.

By the time she reached the bounding stream that lay between Harwood and Winslow Park, her irritation began to lessen and her steps slowed. The squire had purchased the unentailed land from her father, but he had extended the courtesy of allowing her father to continue hunting the area. Now she started to wonder if she really ought to say something to her father after all.

Perhaps she ought not to interfere. Cecila had thrown out the comment that she wished she could live her own life. Only how could she stand by and watch Cecila be hurt?

At the echoing boom of a shotgun, Penelope halted. The startling of doves into the air gave her better direction as to the origin of the shot. Starting forward again, she picked her way along the narrowing path between maples and beech and oak trees. The clouds had thickened overhead, and the cold bite of the wind stung her cheeks.

As the underbrush thickened, she stopped to listen again. Oh, heavens, perhaps she ought to just go home and leave this until she had a better frame of mind. She might even try again to speak with Cecila, or at least lay the matter before her mother for advice.

The path narrowed and tangled with nettles, brambles, and wild berries, slowing her steps. Then it opened into a small clearing. Penelope paused to catch her breath, and then the crack of a branch and the crunch of leaves from someone else's heavy step made her turn.

Her skirt caught on a thorn, pulling at her and forcing her to turn back to unsnarl it. As she did, a deep

voice made her drop her hem and spin about. "Hullo—
here's better sport."

With a hand to her bonnet, Penelope glanced up at
the grinning face of Terrance Winslow.

Thirteen

A tall black beaver-skin hat sat at a rakish angle, and a shotgun lay tucked under his arm. Oddly, he wore not shooting clothes, but evening attire—black coat and pantaloons, white shirt, waistcoat, and cravat. From the wrinkles, he had either slept or traveled a good distance in them, or perhaps both. The shadow of a beard darkened his square jaw, emphasizing the pallor of a face that had seen too little daylight, and Penelope did not care for the glitter in his tawny, bloodshot eyes.

The sharp aroma of brandy washed over her as he moved closer.

Stepping back on the narrow path, she stretched her skirt to tearing point. Still tugging on it with one hand, she gave him the briefest of nods. "Good day, Mr. Winslow."

Grinning now, he came even closer. "Ever the correct lady, eh, Pen? Wishing me good day, but you ought to school your eyes not to reveal so much. You're really wishing me to hades."

"It is Miss Harwood to you, and you look well on your way without my wishes. Now, if you will excuse me." She tugged again on her skirt, hearing fabric tear.

"Hold still," he ordered.

"Really, Mr. Winslow, I—"

"You are caught fast. Now for once listen to someone

else and stand there." He slurred his words only slightly, but enough that Penelope decided he must be well drunk. She paused in her efforts to untangle herself and glanced at him.

He had propped his shotgun against an oak, and now he stepped toward her. The aroma of brandy and the smell of tobacco strengthened, then he went down on one knee beside her.

She edged away and he glanced up at her, his expression tightened with irritation. "Gad, you are the most obstinate female."

Reaching up, his hand came around her waist and he dragged her closer even as she stiffened and glared at him. "Now, stand there. I need some slack if I'm to get these thorns out of your hem." He grinned again suddenly. "Unless you'd rather stay here?"

Mouth pressed tight, she folded her arms and looked away. Heat crept up her chest and into her throat and face as she remembered a dozen other encounters between them, most of them ending with him laughing as his taunts drew her anger. Well, she was no longer a girl to be tormented into undignified behavior. As soon as she was free, she would take her leave.

Shrubbery rustled as he struggled. He swore once, and she hoped he had pricked himself on the thorns from the brambles. Then he rose to his feet in front of her. Automatically, she tried to step away, and found her back against the rough bark of a tree.

She stared up at him. He was taller than his brother, his face more lined by dissipation, and far too muscular, she thought. He looked, she decided, as if he ought to be brawling somewhere in London.

"Thank you. Good day now," she said.

He leaned a wide hand on the tree beside her head. Thick underbrush hemmed her in on either side, and if she tried to duck away, she would only end up tangled and caught again.

"Come now, I deserve a sweeter thank you than that."

"What you deserve is cold water over your head and a few lessons in polite behavior. I should like to leave now."

His grin widened. "You think I'm flawd to be out dressed like this and with a shotgun?"

"You certainly are flawed."

"No, Pen. Flawd—drunk. As in four sheets to the wind. Aren't you even curious what I'm doing here? Ah—you are. I can see that in your eyes, too."

"What you see is irritation with boorish behavior. Now pray excuse me. My father is out shooting also, and I expect he shall happen along at any moment."

He grinned, showing a flash of white and the almost wolfish points of his two incisor teeth. "Shall he? Well, I hope he has a brace of grouse on him. I've staked a hundred pounds that Winslow Park boasts the fattest birds in the south of England, only I can't find a damn one of them to take back with me."

His grin faded, but the glint remained in his eyes, and Penelope pressed herself even tighter against the tree. "'Course, there's another bet I've not yet made good on. I've not yet kissed every woman in the district, now have I?"

Her irritation with him flared. "Of all the vulgar—Mr. Winslow, I have told you for two years now that you may as well forfeit that . . . Mr. Winslow!"

Her rebuke came as his hand darted out to catch her bonnet, pulling it off her head so that it dangled from its ribbons, digging into her neck and half crushed against the tree. She pushed against his chest with both her hands, and he stumbled back, unsteady on his feet.

"Touch me again, and I shall box your ears so hard that they ring for the rest of the day!"

His grin flashed again, and he rubbed his chin. Then he stepped up and stuck out his jaw. "Well, come on, then. Let's see how handy you are. Go ahead, have at me."

She hesitated. "Why? Because you wish to goad me into such unladylike behavior, or so you can grab my arm when I attempt it?"

"Well, perhaps you'll be quicker than I. Care to make a bet on it?"

She clenched her teeth and decided that even brambles and a ruined dress were to be preferred over this.

Gathering her skirt, she turned. As she did, his hand caught her arm. He spun her around and pushed her against the tree. She let go her skirt and struck him, a sharp echoing whack that left the red imprint of her hand on his face.

Eyes narrowing, he had hold of her wrist in the next instant. Then he grinned at her. "Do you bite as well?"

She glared at him, mouth pressed tight before she turned away, refusing to even look at him.

"Damn, if you are not the most disobliging female! Now, hold still. It is only a kiss."

He began to lean toward her, and Penelope squeezed her eyes tight and pressed her lips even tighter, scrunching her face with distaste as she braced herself for the worst.

After pacing her room for a quarter hour, Cecila decided that wearing a hole in the carpet did no good for anyone. She could almost wish she had spoken with Penelope about Theo's note, but she did not want more lectures.

How she had wished he might write her.

Well, she had her wish—he had written to say that after thinking the matter over, he had decided he would accept an apology from her, but only if she begged his pardon very nicely for her behavior at the assembly.

She had read the note, irritated at first, and that had flamed into a hotter anger. What—she must apologize for enjoying herself? And for doing something with her time other than forever waiting on Mr. Theodore Winslow's pleasure?

He had not used so much as a single endearment. Just made his demands, then scrawled his name to the letter. As if he could not be bothered to do more!

For a moment, she thought of simply tearing the note apart, as if that would tear Theo from her life. Only how could she? Theo was supposed to be her life. Or he would be if he could only be brought to his senses so he could see it.

But did she really wish to marry a man who could write such a note as this? One that demanded and offered nothing.

With a frustrated sigh, she pushed the note under her pillow and left her room in search of paper and a sharp quill. At the least, she could write a note back to Theo. Something that would make him twist with shame. Something that would make him see just how far in the wrong he stood. Something that would set him straight about who ought to be admitting faults.

After all, he had started all this by paying more court to a tavern wench than he did to her.

Her step quickening, she made for her father's study, where she might find pen and paper.

Mr. Dawes already occupied the room.

He rose at once, juggling a book, sheets of paper, and his quill. More papers and books, as well as an inkwell, sat on the side table beside his chair.

She almost dropped a curtsy and backed out with an apology for having disturbed him. Then she realized, who better to help her write a reply to Theo? With all that poetry in his head, Mr. Dawes must know something of love.

So she came into the room, closing the door behind her and giving him a good day. Then she asked, putting on a bright tone, "Are you working on a poem?"

He frowned and shifted on his feet, and the papers slipped from his fingers to flutter to the carpet. Muttering what sounded like a curse, he bent to retrieve them. She came to his side, kneeling on the carpet with him to pick up one of the scattered sheets.

He plucked it from her fingers before she could even scan the page. "Don't bother. It's nothing of significance."

"You might allow me to decide that," she said, then picked up another sheet, which had four lines inked and a number of crossed out words.

Again he pulled it from her grasp. "And what would you know of poetry?"

Stung, she shot back, "I know that it ought to rhyme, and that that does not." He frowned at her, so she rose and shook out her skirts. "You need not be so rude about it."

Bending down, he gathered the last sheet and then stood. "I am not being rude."

"You are. Is it because I said you have no rhyme? Well, I am certain you must have better ones. Or is that why you quote everyone else's poetry, and never your own— because you do not like it yourself?"

He frowned at her. "Quoting myself would be arrogant."

"And quoting others is not? I will have you know all that quoting can make you sound quite as if you are setting yourself above others."

His frown darkened. "What it shows is that someone other than I had better words for the situation."

"And what is wrong with your own words for a situation?" she asked.

Bryn opened his mouth to tell her just how an apt quote more clearly conveyed his feelings, but then her remark sank in. What was wrong with his own words? He had spent the morning, in fact, struggling with finding those words, and not succeeding.

Could it be he had no words to uncover? Was his mind nothing more than a container for the wisdom of others, with nothing original to add?

He glanced at the sheets in his hands, the desolate urge building to toss them all into the fire.

And then he glanced at Cecila. Just how had they gotten on this topic, anyway?

"Did you come looking for me?" he asked, fighting gloom by directing his irritation toward her.

"No, actually. But I interrupted, did I not? Would you rather I leave?"

She glanced at him, her eyes troubled.

"No, no, please stay," he said, his annoyance already fading. He gestured to a chair with his papers, and when she had spread her skirts and seated herself, he sat down again in the chair opposite.

The sun slanted in from the window behind her, giving her golden-brown hair a halo. He had to smile at that. Perhaps what he had lacked this morning was inspiration. A lovely face and smile to conjure dreams.

She began pleating the end of the blue satin ribbon that trimmed her gown—a very fetching gown with bits of blue strewn across a white background. "I am sorry about your poems."

"What's that?" he asked, pulling himself back to the moment.

"Your poems—the not-so-rhyming ones. You know, the world also needs those who appreciate poems as well as those who write them. And you have a very great appreciation."

Bryn straightened. "Look here, you barely glimpsed them."

"Well, yes, but I must tell you that even Penelope can at least manage a rhyme. Very pretty ones, too. I should think you would want to do that if you aspire to being a poet."

"I'm certain your sister writes charming nonsense, but I am trying to do something a bit more."

Looking offended, she straightened. "Her poems are very good—better than yours, I dare say."

He resisted the urge to roll his eyes. He had lost track of the efforts shown him over the years by ladies seeking to impress him with their literary skills. Amateur seemed too kind a word for such efforts.

Something of his thoughts must have shown in his expression, for Cecila rose, scowling now, as if he had insulted her personally.

"I will show you—just you wait."

She flounced from the room, and Bryn let out a sigh. He should not have said anything. He ought to have asked about those troubled eyes of hers and not allowed the conversation to slip out of control. Now he would have to dutifully admire the efforts shown him and do his best not to offer any more insult.

He glanced at the sheets in his own hands. Well, they might at least make him feel better about his own struggling efforts.

By the time Cecila returned with a hatbox in her hands, Bryn had decided to be charitable to himself, as well as to her. He had folded his own papers and set them aside, and he would see what he could manage with them later.

Cecila sat down on a low sofa, the round hatbox beside her, and pulled off the lid. Taking out a dozen sheets, she riffled through them, then selected one and gave it to Bryn.

"That is my favorite, but she does not think it her best."

Putting on a polite face, Bryn began to read.

And then he really began to read.

I traveled in my dreams last night, to places of bright starry flights.

He scanned the lines, a brief work and no challenge to Byron, but the sweetness charmed him. Looking up, he glanced at Cecila. "What else does she have?"

Half an hour later, dazed, his mind spinning, he put down the last sheet. A good deal of these showed youthful efforts—and less than success. But some of them—some of them dazzled.

And they had changed his view of Miss Harwood.

He had thought her hard—a woman of reason and severe judgment. Now he knew her for a creature of sentiment and passion and deep feelings, all masked by that shell she wore. Her poems ranged from expressing exuberant delight, to the terror of facing a beloved parent's death, to despair of love's trust being shattered.

"Some of these ought to be published," he said, handing the last of them back to Cecila.

"Yes, well I should not tell Penelope that. She is as touchy as you about showing her poems to anyone. Not that she writes very much anymore."

He frowned. "Then I should not have read these."

"Oh, but I knew you would appreciate them. Probably better than I. Actually, I like the ones that are a bit tragic, such as the one about the two who cannot seem to meet, as if the dance of life always must separate them."

She let out a small sigh, then went back to settling the sheets into the hatbox.

Bryn glanced at his own pages. Rising, he picked them up. Then he tossed them into the embers in the fireplace.

Cecila scrambled to the grate, her fingers darting in to snag the papers and pull them to safety. "What are you doing?"

He took her hands and lifted her to her feet. "Leave them. They are no loss."

"But you must have spent such time on them. You should not just toss them aside."

He shook his head, feeling tired and far older than his years. "Do you know how long I have struggled to be a poet?"

Staring up at him, she shook her head.

"I was ten when my mother began to read Shakespeare to me. And then we moved on to Donne and Pope and Milton. My mother loved words, and she had the loveliest voice. Just the faintest hint of Welsh lifted her words. Because of her, I started to write my own. I so wanted to impress her."

"And did you ever read them to her?" she asked, her voice soft.

He shook his head. "She died that winter. Cholera. I read . . . I read one to her. I don't think she could hear much by then. The fever had her."

Cecila's hand tightened around his. She could not bear the empty look that had come into his eyes. "Oh, she heard. I am certain of it. A mother always hears things such as that, you know. Why, I learned that my mother heard us all when we asked her not to leave us when she was . . . was so very ill."

The distant look retreated from his eyes and he glanced down at her. "Thank you. It is nice to think so. My father, of course, wanted me to give up such nonsense. He had little use for the written word, unless it was a contract or a letter of business. But I thought . . . you know, I rather think you are right. I think I do quote others because I know my own words are not enough."

"You make it sound so awful, but I think it is terribly clever of you. I cannot quote anyone."

He let go her hand and ran his own through his hair. "Yes, but that leaves me a rather useless sort of person. I'm not much fitted for the army, but I suppose I could always see about taking orders." He gave her a lopsided smile. "Perhaps that meddling streak in me has always marked me for the church, and I could quote scripture in sermons."

Cecila stared at him, a hollow ache in her chest. What had she done? She had only meant to show him that she knew something of poetry, for she had not liked how he discounted her comments. Only she had done far more.

Somehow she seemed to have shaken his faith in himself.

Oh, but it seemed melodramatic to think that. Then she glanced to the sheets in the fireplace, now charred into black curls by the heat.

He would still write, she told herself. This must be but a passing mood. She knew enough about those. Only she could not leave him in this gloomy state, not when she had been the cause of helping him into it.

Fixing a smile in place, she pushed her own troubles to the back of her mind. They—and Theo—could just wait a bit. Mr. Dawes—Bryn—needed her just now. And the pleasure shivered through her that he did need her. She so very liked to feel she could be of use. With such a daunting sister as Penelope, there were times she could not help but feel a bit like a superfluous ornament.

"I am certain you would be an excellent vicar," she said. "But, really, I think you already have a far better calling. Have you ever thought to ask your cousin about investing in a publishing venture?"

"You are not very attractive when you do that," Terrance Winslow said.

Penelope pried open her eyes. He had leaned away from her and now stared at her, his eyes still glittering, but with a bemused twist to his mouth.

"Neither are you," she offered back, scowling and hoping he might find that even more unappealing.

Instead, he smiled. "You've grown into a shrew's tongue. Let's see if a kiss won't sweeten it."

He leaned closer again as he spoke, and Penelope struggled to pull away from the brandy fumes, her stomach churning.

A sharp thwack above her head made her—and Winslow—startle and glance up. Winslow's hat now stuck against the bark of the tree, held by some invisible force, a dent in its side.

She blinked up at it for a moment, as did Winslow. Then his grip on her loosened as he muttered, "What in . . ."

Penelope jumped for her chance, slipping from his hold and darting under his arm before he could gather his brandy-soaked wits. Head down, grasping her bonnet with one hand, she ran across the clearing—and straight into an arm which snagged her around the shoulders.

Breaths coming in ragged gasps, she whirled, one hand coming up to grasp the black-clad arm that held her. Then the fight drained from her, leaving her sagging against that strong, hard arm.

Nevin.

He must have followed her for some reason, and she had never thought to be so happy for such a thing.

Only then the embarrassment began to seep into her at being found in such a situation. Hands trembling and with a knot tightening in her chest, she stiffened. His hold on her did not slacken, and his attention remained fixed on Winslow, who was still cursing but who had swung around, bracing himself with one hand against the tree as if to steady himself.

From the murderous look on each man's face, she could only think that this fiasco now seemed likely to degenerate into a complete brawl.

And she had the most ghastly, weak-willed urge to simply break into tears and fling herself into Nevin's arms.

Fourteen

Glancing from Winslow to Nevin and back again, Penelope struggled to push aside such an unseemly wish. The breeze stirred, ruffling the few leaves overhead. Penelope shivered, and then pushed a loose strand of hair from her eyes.

Nevin's coat and waistcoat hung open, and they held the pleasant aroma of horse and apples. Nothing about him, however, looked pleasant. With his feet braced apart and his eyes narrowed, he looked far more dangerous than the squire's stallion.

Square jaw jutting forward, Winslow glared at Nevin. "Who the bloody hell are you?"

Penelope took the only refuge she knew—in good manners that might let them get through this without further unpleasantness. "Lord Nevin, may I present our neighbor, Mr. Terrance Winslow. Mr. Winslow, this is our guest, Lord Nevin."

Strain squeaked in her voice, but the gentlemen ignored her, and she found a flicker of vexation to hang onto. Bad enough to be forced to endure Winslow's inebriated attentions, but she simply would not endure further indignities.

Nevin's arm still held her shoulders, so she stepped away, shrugging off his touch. At that, he glanced at her, and the look of concern in his eyes nearly undid the meager control she had gained over herself.

Looking away, she pulled in a ragged breath. He must see her as an object of pity. Poor Miss Harwood, the frigid, shrewish spinster. Well, she would correct that. She would pull herself—and the situation—together.

"Thank you, my lord, for coming to escort me home. I was just taking my leave of Mr. Winslow." She struggled to keep her tone casual, as if nothing had happened, when in fact her stomach still quivered, and the disgraceful desire to turn and run away from this all was beginning to grow stronger. That would not do, however.

Instead, she forced herself to give Winslow a cool stare, and then said, "Good day, sir."

He did not even glance at her, but continued to stare at Nevin, realization glimmering in his eyes. "You must be that half Gypsy Theo was talking about. Only a damn Gypsy would throw a knife at a fellow's back."

The corner of Nevin's mouth crooked, but Penelope could not see any humor in the hard edges, nor in those black eyes, as he answered. "Oh, that was but a reminder to remove your hat in a lady's presence."

Nevin glanced once more at Penelope, and then started toward Winslow, his long stride taking him away so quickly that she had not time enough to reach for his sleeve to stop him.

Of all the fool-haste notions!

Biting down on one knuckle, she prepared to close her eyes at the impending carnage. Winslow not only stood several inches taller, but his heavy shoulders and frame gave him a decided physical advantage, and she could only be sorry that Nevin must now suffer for having intervened on her behalf.

Well, it was his own fault. He could have gone away

with her, if he had but taken up the broad hints she had dropped.

As Nevin approached, Winslow pushed away from the tree, those tawny eyes glittering with unholy delight, as if he relished finding trouble. He swung, his right hand bunched into a fist, and Penelope flinched.

Ducking the blow, Nevin came up, moving so fast Penelope only knew that one moment she waited for the worst, and the next, Winslow lay on the ground, his hands clutching his stomach as he rolled on the fallen leaves and crushed vines, gasping.

Nevin stood over him. "And that is but a reminder to treat a lady with proper respect."

For a moment, Nevin remained tensed and alert, waiting to see if the fellow would rise. His own knuckles ached, and he resisted the urge to shake the pain from his hand.

The man lifted his head and fell back with another struggling gasp for air. Nevin knew he had caught him just under the rib cage, forcing the air from him. Winslow would roll there, gaping like a fish, for at least a quarter hour. About what he deserved for being idiot enough to pick a fight with his wits slowed by drink. And fool enough to think he could best a half Gypsy who had grown up learning every fighting trick known to Gypsy or *gaujo*.

Stepping around the prone form, Nevin reached up and pulled his knife from where it pinned the man's hat. He flung the damaged beaver onto Winslow's chest. Then he turned and strode back to Miss Harwood.

Back rigid, her mouth thinned into that disapproving line, she looked the opposite of fawning feminine gratitude. Had his interference annoyed her? Perhaps. But then he thought of the white-faced panic that had strained her features when she had blindly run into him, and he knew he had behaved with admirable restraint. His knife, after all, had not found its way into Winslow's back.

And he had been tempted.

However, a gentleman and a lord was not supposed to go about murdering ruffians, not even such deserving ones.

After tucking his knife back into the thin leather sheath that lay under his left coat sleeve, he offered his right arm to Miss Harwood. "Shall we?"

She glanced back at Winslow, her forehead bunching with worry. Then she seemed to decide he had no need of her concern or assistance, for she gave a brief nod and gathered her skirts with both hands. "Thank you, but I can manage."

He had to smile. He heard the faintest tremor under that frost, but better to have her this way, with her armor in place, than to have her as shaken as she had been the other night at the assembly.

Turning away, she started down the path. He followed a step behind.

At the edge of the woods, where the land opened into pasture and field, she stopped and turned to him. "I suppose I ought to be grateful that you came along," she said, sounding reluctant to admit such a thing, as if somehow it equated with conceding some defect in herself.

Devla, but this one seemed to think she ought to be able to handle anything and everything on her own. Did she always have to fight to be so independent of everyone?

Striving for a truce, he offered a smile. "I thought we were friends enough that there is no need for gratitude or thanks."

A smile softened her expression for an instant, but

then her gaze shifted to his arm—to where his knife lay hidden. Her smile faded. He sensed her withdrawing, moving behind those barricades of hers, and he could do nothing to stop it.

He had followed her after she had left the stables, and after he had coaxed the stallion back to his paddock. He had been irritated by her comment. Did she think he would abandon his task half done? And the more he thought about it, the more he wanted to make it clear to her that given enough kindness, the horse would lose the worst of his temper, even if he never became one to grow careless around.

Well, perhaps Miss Harwood was much the same. She, too, had been hurt enough so trust did not come easy. That lack showed in her face now, and he decided she must be wondering what else he kept concealed.

Almost he could wish he had abandoned the habit of carrying his *tshuri*. But, like Miss Harwood, it seemed he, too, could not do without his defenses.

Perhaps because he was not quite the gentleman he wanted to think himself.

He scowled at that, uneasy with implications he did not want to face. No, he was Lord Nevin now. And he would act accordingly, meaning he would not continue to make Miss Harwood uncomfortable with his presence.

Stepping back, he offered a brief bow. "Of course, if really you wish to thank me, you may do so by having a greater care for where you walk. Good day."

And with that, he turned and strode toward Harwood, almost wishing his fight with Winslow had not been over so quickly, for at least that might have given this gnawing restlessness inside him an outlet.

* * *

A publishing investment.

Cecila had posed the idea, then argued its merits, and then had somehow gotten him off on the topic of writing love letters and how to go about it.

She had praised him and flattered, and almost made him think it possible. And she would not relent. Each day she had some new embellishment to the plan.

For three days, it spun in his head, teasing him with possibilities. And terrifying him. She kept arguing how it might be done, insisting it did not really carry the stigma of trade, which would sully any gentleman's reputation. After all, it was not like opening a shop or a manufactory.

Of course, the matter of making money could be a vulgar thing, but if a gentleman could make a fortune from owning land or from the invention of others or from putting money into the Exchange, why not from selling books? It was, in fact, a sort of patronage, like sponsoring a painter or a sculptor.

Only a patron did not make money from his artist's creations, Bryn thought. And no gentleman-patron ever participated in such a vulgar thing as hard work and effort.

Thinking of how his father would have reacted to such a notion, Bryn grimaced. His father had come from the old school where gentlemen had soft white hands and hired others to do for them. Gentlemen simply owned things that made money without the least application.

He could, in fact, recall his father doing everything possible to discourage every interest, making it clear that idleness for a gentleman was a requirement, not a sin. But only look where that had taken him. Not the best example.

So why should he care now what his father would have thought? His father had been a man whose notion of honor had allowed him, at the least, to intentionally steal a title from his brother's child. At the worst, he actually might have helped his brother into his grave.

Bryn preferred to think that could not have happened. But the cold, hard man he had known had been capable of it.

Frowning, Bryn glanced now at the books that lay before him on the library table, and which he had been attempting to catalog today for Harwood.

'And men forgot their passions in their dread, Of this their desolation.'

Byron again, with his thoughts on darkness. Yes, that seemed an apt analogy for his father, Bryn thought. A man with too much darkness in him. He did not want to be such a man.

So could he go into a publishing venture?

He picked up a book, smoothing his palm over the tooled leather, allowing his fingers to trace the embossed gold lettering on the spine. The pages had that smell of knowledge, that musty scent peculiar to old books and which Bryn associated with the fonder memories of his life, spending hours in the library at Dawes Manor.

Books. Now there was a passion.

He had assembled the best he could scavenge from Harwood's shelves where they had stood, no order to their arrangement. Neglected, in fact. Tucked behind and between quite ordinary works in German and Latin, he had even found a copy of *Roman de la Rose* that looked as if it could be an original edition of the French romance, which would make it quite valuable.

That should please Harwood.

But could he really make a profession from publishing such works? Or was he setting himself up to fail, as he pitted himself against the men in London who knew this as their trade?

There was that word again. *Trade.* Such an innocent word. Such a tainted word to Society.

What would it do to Nevin's standing to have a cousin in trade? Bryn rubbed at his forehead. He could imagine the talk. Half Gypsy, with a cousin who sold books. It would make Nevin an even worse pariah.

He could not do that.

No, despite Cecila's urging, he would have to set this aside. His father had already done too much harm to Nevin and his sister, and Bryn could not add to the weight that already lay on his conscience for their having suffered as outcasts during their youth. Far better to stay an idle, indigent relative than to become such a social liability to them.

With a last glance at the books on the table, he stood. Tomorrow he would finish his catalog for Harwood. In all, if his estimates on the few works of value were correct, they might fetch as much as a hundred guineas at auction in London. He suspected Harwood would welcome those funds.

He would be happy to have as much in his pockets. At least then he might try the gaming tables to see if he could turn that small sum into a larger one, though he had never been particularly adept with cards. Still, luck might come to sit on his shoulder.

And then he thought of Cecila.

Lord, her confidence in him almost made him think that with such a lady nearby, no man needed any more luck than that.

But he told himself he had no right to entertain such dreams. What, after all, did he, a gentleman without prospects or fortune, have to offer any lady—particularly a lady who needed to make a good match for herself and her family?

Besides, Miss Cecila had her Theo already. Not, of

course, that that seemed likely to be more than an infatuation. Still, if she had made her choice, he had no right to intercede.

And I am going to have to remind myself ten times a day that we came here to do right by the Harwoods—not to turn their lives into everything that is wrong.

She had been awful again, Penelope decided.

Sitting before her dressing mirror, staring at her reflection and frowning, she noted the line between her eyebrows. She relaxed her face, but the line remained visible. Which showed just how frequently she did scowl.

With one forefinger, she rubbed at the crease.

The line remained.

She had promised herself to start over with Lord Nevin, but after that day in the woods, she had actually done her best to avoid him. She had to admit it now.

Quite intentionally, she had started rising too late to ride with him. And she had either taken her sketch pad outside to the Norman tower to sit and draw nothing much of anything or she had found meaningless household tasks to occupy her hands, if not her thoughts.

She ought to have thanked him nicely for what he had done. Instead, she had been unable even to admit that she had needed or welcomed his aid with Terrance Winslow. A shrew's tongue indeed. Terrance, it seemed, had the last word on that.

Propping her chin on her hand, she decided it was time for brutal honesty with herself.

Nevin had acted with nothing but chivalry. But she— well, she had hated that, not an hour after she had embarrassed herself by starting to make demands of him, he had found her in such an improper situation. Her own wretched pride had gotten in the way.

She wanted to be perceived as a paragon, a lady beyond reproach. She did not want to appear lacking in the least, and she knew now that she held onto that perfect pose as if it might keep everyone from looking into her heart and seeing the inadequacy she felt.

She let out a sigh. Perhaps the only person she really deluded was herself. Perhaps, as Terrance Winslow had said, her thoughts showed too clearly in her eyes.

She searched her image and decided that, indeed, what was wrong with her must be there for all to see.

In her quest to make herself a strong, independent woman, she had somehow also made herself hard. She had wanted only to be capable, to be a good example for her sisters. She could even recall her mother saying she must do so when she had stepped into the bedchamber to be first introduced to Cecila, her face still wrinkled from her birthing, her hair invisibly fair, and her tiny body wrapped up in a white shawl. At six it had seemed an enormous responsibility. It still did.

Then, after Jonathan, she had wanted only to somehow deaden that wrenching pain that wrapped around her heart. And when Mother nearly died, she had decided she must be even stronger.

But along the way, she had given up her softness. Just look at how Cecila did care not to confide in her, and how Sylvain kept to her own world in the stables and the woods. And could she blame them? Would she want her own brand of assistance?

Almost she could wish for some cream to restore herself—something she could rub on herself which would soak deep.

A faint smile lifted the corners of her mouth. Like her grandmother's recipe of chamomile and rose water for the skin, she would certainly forget to use it, or, worse, all that softness might bring back all that desperate heartache, as well.

Heavens, what a ninny I am, wishing for the impossible.

Straightening, she pinched color into her cheeks.

She was what she was. But she could stop moping about it. Besides, part of this dismal frame of mind came from that monthly time when even her own skin irritated her.

However, she would have to start yet again with Nevin. This time, she would be kind, even if she had to do so with gritted teeth. For he would not stay much longer. Autumn was fading, and with winter coming, he would not want to be caught with muddy roads between here and London.

Only now the thought of long winter nights with no gentlemen to make noise and interrupt the routine and be there to be entertained seemed utterly depressing.

Oh, heavens, it had to be this mood of hers.

Rising, she took up a Spanish shawl, a present from better years, and went to meet the others in the drawing room before dinner.

Since their guests had come to stay, Mrs. Merritt and Bridges had put the drawing room to rights, lighting candles in the wall sconces and a fire every evening. The candles smoked a bit, for they were tallow, not costly beeswax, and everyone tended to gather close to the fire, for the nights had grown cold. But the pools of yellow light, the smell of lemon oil to polish the tables, the carpets taken up from other rooms and laid down, had brought the room back into elegance.

As Penelope entered and started toward the fireplace, Cecila broke off some heated words she appeared to be having with Mr. Dawes. The treasure hunting must not be going according to Cecila's plans, Penelope decided. She would have to talk to her sister about that, for Cecila really must not hold Mr. Dawes at fault for not finding what was not there in the first place.

Reaching Cecila's side, she asked Mr. Dawes how he did. He looked a touch pale, as if he did not feel well—or perhaps that was Cecila's badgering—and then Lord Nevin came into the room, Sylvain on his arm.

In a plain yellow round dress, her hair actually combed and pulled up, and without a twig or leaf in it, Sylvain had her full attention focused on Nevin. Her expression serious, she spoke softly to Nevin, and Penelope caught only enough phrases to know she was talking about the upcoming release of Mr. Feathers into the woods.

At the sight of such easy rapport between them, a jolt skittered down Penelope's back and then settled in the pit of her stomach. She started to frown, then caught herself. It must be the old worry for Sylvain come back, of course.

Then, with a shock, she realized that Nevin and Sylvain might indeed be forming a close connection.

Was that not wonderful?

She tried to summon a smile.

Of course, it had been different when she had been uncertain as to his character, but she could no longer see any reasons why such an attachment might not be welcome.

It would be marvelous to see Sylvain happily married to a gentleman with money and a title, and so obviously kind.

Yes, it would, she told herself, trying to unknot the depression gathering inside. And she would be the worst sort of sister not to encourage this.

Glancing at her, Nevin offered a tentative smile. She smiled back and nodded, and after he brought Sylvain to the fireside, he left her and came to Penelope.

She had not expected that, and his presence reacted on her as always, making her too aware of that innate grace of his, of those wide shoulders, of his scent, which held a touch of the exotic.

Smoothing the fringe on her shawl, she tried to relax. Oh, why could she not be as comfortable with him as Sylvain? Why did just his standing next to her make her want to fuss with her hair and straighten her gown and say something cross to him so he would go away?

He must also be aware that she had been avoiding him, so she began inventing an excuse.

Heavens, she was at it again. Trying to make herself the too proper lady, with no flaws and a good reason for every behavior, even the inexcusable ones.

His voice, low and beguiling, brushed over her skin, as warm as the fire behind her, pulling her from her thoughts. "Good evening, Miss Harwood."

She gripped the ends of her shawl tighter, and forced out the truth before it could hide again. "I've been avoiding you."

Black eyebrows tightened above those unreadable black eyes, and he began to move away. "In that case, I shall—"

"No, please." She put a hand on his arm, and he glanced at her touch. She did as well, then snatched her fingers away, her face warm. "I mean, it is not anything you have done. It is just that I . . . well, I . . . I haven't felt well."

Her conscience winced at such an evasion, so she took herself in hand. "Actually, what I have felt is embarrassed, and quite dreadful that I never did properly thank you the other day. I am very sorry. And thank you."

There, that had come out pretty enough—except for the forced tone she could hear in her voice.

He stared at her for a moment longer, still frowning. Had he taken her into such dislike that there could be no hope of ever mending things between them?

Thankfully, her father entered, and called for everyone's attention, saying, "I have a surprise for you tonight."

He then stepped back, pulling open both tall, gilt doors to the drawing room, and Bridges and Peter—Mrs. Merritt's son—entered, their arms linked to carry Penelope's mother into the room.

Fifteen

Penelope heard Cecila's startled gasp, and then everyone seemed to be moving and talking.

The gentlemen came forward to offer assistance as Bridges and Peter hurried to settle Mrs. Harwood in a wing chair near the fire. Sylvain plucked pillows from the couches to prop under her mother's feet, Cecila kept asking if the fire was too warm or the room too chill, and Penelope took the opportunity offered by the disorder to move closer to her father.

"Is this wise?" she asked, laying a hand on his sleeve to draw his attention and speaking low enough that no one else would hear.

He glanced at her, his smile dimming, and Penelope glimpsed her own concern mirrored in his pale, blue eyes. "Your mother swears she feels well enough, or I should never have allowed this. And she does fret about being a poor hostess, you know. But, mind you, we shall both watch her close to see that she does not overdo."

He gave her hand a squeeze, and then Mrs. Harwood called for him, looking delighted to be the center of attention, and asking him to perform a formal introduction to Lord Nevin.

Stepping aside, Penelope tried not to worry. Her mother did seem to be enjoying herself, holding court with her daughters at her sides and the gentlemen so attentive. And she could detect no strain in her face. The doctor had been strict in his warnings against such excitement, but perhaps if they kept the evening singularly uneventful, it would do no harm.

And so she stepped forward again, determined to offer only the blandest of topics, such as comments on the weather.

A quarter hour later, Bridges announced dinner, and Penelope moved to her mother's side. "Are you certain you do not care to retire now?"

Though her mother's face had lost some of its color, she still smiled and said, "No, my dear, I would much rather stay. And sitting in a chair is not too taxing, after all."

Penelope started to urge her mother to reconsider, but before she could utter a word, Lord Nevin stepped closer. "I could not help overhearing. I should not wish you to overexert yourself, Mrs. Harwood, but I think there may be a way to give you both your desire and your comfort."

"And how is that, my lord?" Mrs. Harwood asked.

"Allow me to see what can be done," he said. He stepped away to speak to Mr. Harwood, and a moment later they left the room, taking Mr. Dawes and Bridges with them.

Mrs. Harwood turned toward Penelope. "What a curious gentleman he is, to be certain. But he seems quite amiable, my dear. You must have gotten off on the wrong foot with him."

Penelope's smile stiffened. She thought back to her awkward exchange with Nevin tonight, and decided she still seemed to be on the wrong foot with him.

She said nothing, however, and Cecila's speculations on what the gentlemen might be doing soon took over the conversation.

"Do you think I should go see?" Cecila asked finally, already on her feet and turned toward the doorway as if she could not wait for her curiosity to be satisfied.

Penelope frowned at such impatience, but Mrs. Harwood merely said it would not do to spoil the gentlemen's surprise, if one was intended.

A half hour later, her empty stomach rumbling, Penelope began to wonder if perhaps she ought to go and see if anything at all was planned, or if the gentlemen were simply standing about, arguing ideas.

Just as she thought that, the door opened and the gentlemen returned, her father looking pleased, Mr. Dawes still looking a touch haggard, and Lord Nevin's expression as unreadable as ever. Bridges and Peter followed them into the room.

As they took up Mrs. Harwood, Mr. Harwood offered his arm to Penelope. "Shall we go in to dinner?"

Bridges and Peter went before everyone, carrying Mrs. Harwood. Penelope took her father's arm, while Lord Nevin offered Cecila his escort, and Mr. Dawes gave his arm to Sylvain. Instead of leading the way to the dining room, they started toward the back of the house, to Mrs. Harwood's rooms.

Penelope glanced at her father, her lips parted to ask him what she ought to expect, but he winked at her and laid a finger to his lips. So she waited.

She had not long to hold back her questions.

The door to her mother's rooms stood open, allowing Bridges and Peter to carry her mother to her bed. Then Penelope stepped into the room, and stopped in surprise.

The dining room—or at least the crystal, china, silverware, and serving platters of food—had been transported to this room. Dining chairs now stood about her mother's bed, and a pair of round tables with pedestal bases had been pulled close to make a rather crowded but adequate surface for the meal.

"How wonderful," Cecila exclaimed, smiling for what seemed to Penelope like the first time in days.

"Does this mean I do not have to be so careful with my table manners?" Sylvain asked, eyes bright, and Penelope shot her a censuring glance, which left Sylvain muttering about how much easier owls had their meals than did ladies.

It took a few minutes to settle Mrs. Harwood in her bed, and then Bridges remained by her side to serve her. A few of the dishes had gone cold, but Penelope noted that no one offered any complaints.

Both courses for the meal had already been laid out, but this made for a good deal of conversation in having to ask for dishes to be passed, and in having to find space to return them to the table. For a change, at the meal's end, the gentlemen, not the ladies, rose to take their leave, with Mr. Harwood saying, "We will take our port in my study, my dear."

Bridges, aided by Peter and Mrs. Merritt and Mary, their one maid, began to clear away the dishes as Mrs. Harwood stretched a hand to her husband. "Thank you, Stephen. This was most thoughtful of you."

"You must thank Nevin on that score. He invented the scheme," Mr. Harwood said.

He dropped a kiss on his wife's hand, then stepped away, gesturing for Nevin to take his place. Penelope watched as he bowed over her mother's hand, looking the proper gentleman—and she could not help but wonder if, even now, he carried that knife under his coat sleeve.

She decided he probably did, and that she would also probably never really understand him. He would always surprise her, just as he had with his thoughtfulness tonight. And a twist caught around her heart as she looked to his going. But what a foolish thing that was.

For now the gentlemen were merely leaving for their port.

Penelope did not allow her sisters to remain long with their mother, for she had noted her mother's eyelids starting to drift closed and her head nodding, as if she might fall asleep at any moment.

By the time Bridges cleared away the last cover and dish, Penelope rose to kiss her mother good night. Tomorrow would be soon enough to put the furniture right. Or perhaps they would leave it and dine again in this fashion, though not so soon as to strain her mother's strength.

"Do thank Lord Nevin for me again, my dear," her mother said as Penelope shepherded Cecila and Sylvain from the room. Penelope promised she would, but she found herself a little daunted at having to fulfill such an obligation, for she would no doubt make a botch of it, as she seemed to with everything to do with Nevin.

By the morning, Penelope had worked out a new approach for dealing with Lord Nevin. She needed more safe topics. She had decided that last night as she lay awake, staring at the tester over her bed and thinking of him. Looking back on the evening, she could not count one instance in which she had said anything unkind, or taken Nevin to fault. She had stayed to neutral conversation, and that had worked quite well.

She had a limited supply of nothings, however. So what else could she speak about? Herself? That thought left her twisting uncomfortably in her sheets. Nevin? No, even worse, for that hinted he interested her a good deal, and she could not admit to such a fascination. Besides, she did not want him to think her one of those avid gossips who dug for hints of scandal.

And then it occurred to her that perhaps she had the ideal subject—her sisters. Why, if she kept her talk focused on them, she might even encourage a possible match.

The frown tightened between her brows again.

She ought to encourage Nevin to court her sisters. It was an excellent opportunity for them. And it was not as if she might push Nevin into anything. Heavens, no. One had only to look at the stubborn perseverance he used with the squire's stallion—her father's stallion now, actually—to see the man was even less biddable than the horse he sought to gentle.

So why not praise her sisters to him, and then leave him to fix his interest as he would?

Yes, she would do just that. But still, as she dressed in her riding habit that morning, she found her limbs oddly sluggish and the desire to crawl back into her bed and bury herself there almost overwhelmed her resolution.

Straightening her shoulders, she made a point of going down to the stables with a firm step, her back straight, and her decision set.

However, she did not meet Lord Nevin, and that left a hollow disappointment inside, which she tried to pass off as being nothing more than a cold morning and depressing low clouds.

But she would ride, and she would enjoy herself.

She had Peter saddle her mare, for she did not wish to take Mr. Dawes's horse without the consent implied by Nevin's presence.

Ambling along country lanes with the elderly Juno soon had her heartily bored, so she turned the mare for home and found her patience rewarded in the sight of

Nevin leading his black gelding from the stables. She realized a smile had stolen into place, and she tried to school it into decorum.

As she slid from her side saddle, he gave her a good morning and then asked, "Giving up your gallops?"

She gave Juno a pat. "I thought she might need a stretch of her legs today."

"And did she stretch anything other than your patience?"

Penelope tried not to smile, for that was exactly the case. Instead, she insisted, "It was most pleasant."

"But not exhausting, I should think, so why do you not come out again with me on my cousin's horse?"

She hesitated only long enough not to seem too eager. A few moments later, her saddle lay on Mr. Dawes's raking hunter, and she and Nevin rode down the drive, gravel crunching under hooves.

The stallion lifted his head from grazing in the paddock, his ears alert, as if curious. He even took a tentative step toward them before bellowing out a call that sounded half a challenge and half sulking displeasure.

Nevin's mouth crooked. "He hates it now when his visits do not come first. I think, soon enough, he'll start demanding to be ridden out."

She started to ask him just how soon that soon would be for that wretched horse, but she caught the words.

Nothing critical, she reminded herself.

So instead, she asked about Mr. Feathers's progress, then praised Sylvain's skill with animals, noting it must certainly indicate that Sylvain would be as attentive to her own children someday. "Though I would like for her to have a London season," she added. "She still needs more polish in company."

Then she realized this did not put Sylvain in the most

favorable light, so she switched to speaking of Cecila, noting quite honestly that it pleased her no end that Cecila's beauty had never gone to her head. And she spoke freely of her sister's generosity in always being the one to remember baskets for those most in need at Christmas.

It did seem to her that Nevin grew increasingly quiet as the ride progressed, almost withdrawing a little. But perhaps that came from her talking so much. Or from the gallops he urged, which prevented any conversation.

Overall, however, it went well, she decided as she dismounted again in the stable yard. She had not once been sharp. But still, as she stood next to him, that urge to fidget with her riding crop or touch her hair to ensure it remained tucked into her hat or fuss with the buttons on the front of her riding habit crept into her.

Oh, heavens, why did the man leave her so awkward and uncertain? Was there nothing she could do to put herself on a more comfortable footing with him?

"I . . . I must thank you on my mother's behalf. What you did for her last night, well . . . I cannot express my gratitude enough."

The corner of his mouth quirked. "I thought we were friends enough not to need thanks or gratitude."

She heard the echo of the words he had given her that day he had rescued her from Winslow, but this time she found she could smile back. "It sounds a rather awful sort of friend to have one who never says thank you."

Then she bit the inside of her cheek. Here she was, offering yet another sharp comment. Heavens, could she not stay away from them?

However, his smiled widened, and he offered to take her horse into the stables. "But only, mind, if you do not bury me with more thanks."

She would not allow that, insisting only a poor horsewoman did not look to the comfort of her mount.

With Peter's help, the horses were soon rubbed down and back in their stalls, with Peter carrying a wooden bucket to the kitchen for boiling water to make a hot bran mash.

Deciding she ought to quit while still ahead, Penelope excused herself to change from her riding habit.

Nevin offered a bow, gave his escort into the house, and then remained in the hall, staring up at the empty stairs long after she had gone, his thoughts tangled.

He was still standing in the hall when his cousin came down the stairs. "Why so glum?" Bryn asked, his own voice sounding less than cheerful. "Not had your coffee yet?"

Roused, Nevin offered a brief smile. "Oh, I have had that and more, including a ride with Miss Harwood in which she did nothing but praise her sisters. Endlessly."

Bryn frowned. "So she does indeed have hopes of you as a prospective brother-in-law. Gossip, it seems, can have the right of it at times."

Irritably, Nevin had to agree. He disliked having his hand forced, of course. Need had driven him for too many years. But there was more behind this reckless urge to do something to show Miss Harwood that he had no interest in her sisters.

Only he *had* been considering courting one of the Harwood girls. However, the more Miss Harwood spoke of them, the more he saw just how impossible it was.

He could admire Miss Cecila, but with the same feeling he might have for a painting—one he had no interest in possessing. As for Sylvain, well, he could not shake his initial perception of her as more child than woman. And he strongly suspected she thought of him more as a brother. She certainly treated him with such casual ease.

And as to Miss Harwood herself—well, he could not

deny the tug of attraction. Something had stirred between them, once in the stables and again at the assembly. But from her words today—and how utterly boring she had made herself—he could only believe she intended to make it clear that she had no interest in him other than for her sisters.

Irritation rippled under his skin again, like needles prickling from the inside out. He itched with the desire to show Miss Harwood just what did interest him, and to show her in such a way as left no doubt in her mind that he was a man who could make his own choices. He was not some timid rabbit of a fellow who decided to marry, then changed his mind about it.

But while a Rom might act so, a gentleman could not.

No, a gentleman had to restrain and defer and watch always for those unspoken signals that a lady used to encourage or discourage. And he did not want to do that just now.

Which left him unable to stay in this house. Not at the moment. So he clapped a hand on his cousin's shoulder. "Come on, let us go and see if we cannot hunt up something stronger than coffee in whatever passes for an inn nearby."

"Now that is the best idea you've had in ages," Bryn agreed.

By midday, the rain had begun to fall. Nevin and Bryn waited out the worst of it, snug in the Four Feathers with a comely tavern maid, decent ale, a fire, and a chessboard. Bryn had taught Nevin the game, but he could now best his cousin, and today he trounced the man soundly. Bryn shrugged off his lack of focus, but for once he did not credit it to the lines of a poem forming, nor did he quit the game and pull out a pencil and paper.

That puzzled Nevin, and he began to tease his cousin

about his muse having deserted him, but that put such deep lines around his cousin's mouth that Nevin left off his jesting. However, he did not pry. A man ought to be entitled to keep his thoughts to himself, if he wished.

When the storm broke and the clouds parted, they called for their horses, but the wind soon drove the sky into dark gray again, and the rain caught them halfway back to Harwood, soaking them.

By dinner, Bryn had begun to sneeze. The following morning, Nevin had word from his cousin's valet that Bryn planned to keep to his bed.

Nevin stopped to look in on his cousin and found him bleary eyed and pale, his hair dampened to his forehead with sweat. However, Bryn only glared at him when he suggested a visit from the nearest doctor.

"I only need rest," he said, his voice raspy, as if what he needed was a new throat.

Nevin left him to his misery.

The rain had departed, leaving behind sodden ground but a glorious day, with billowing white clouds that chased across a sky so brilliant it almost hurt the eyes.

Instead of making for the stables or the stallion's paddock, the lure of sunshine and the lazy warmth in the air drew Nevin to the gardens at the back of the house.

He did not want to think about difficult stallions—or women, for that matter. Or about any of the Harwoods. A remembrance of summer drifted in the air, a last touch before the days darkened and the land slumbered. Such a day ought to be savored. His mother had always said that. He could remember, in fact, that such days on the road were days when she insisted they stay in whatever camp they had made. Those were days for stealing apples and lying under trees with them. Days for idle chatter. Days for doing nothing—a rare enough treat when every moment went into thinking of the next meal.

He had different worries now.

And he wanted to escape into just a moment of indolent freedom again. Why had he ever thought a lord had an easy life?

His boots crunched on the gravel drive as he strode around the front of the house, and then the path changed to a stone walkway. He skirted the back terrace of the house, with its shallow, gray stone steps, and strode through the roses, cut back to thorny stumps. Then he spotted a stone bench, set so it offered a view of the alley of oaks that framed the distant silver ribbon of river.

Birds chattered and sang, as if the day had to be celebrated. From one of the oaks, Nevin heard a pair of squirrels arguing territory. A few sheep grazed on the grass between the trees—an excellent way, without a dozen gardeners and scythes, to keep the lawn shorn.

He stopped at the bench and the peace of the spot began to seep into him, mellowing his restlessness, just as had the ale yesterday.

Then a soft voice interrupted. "Good morning, my lord."

Sixteen

Nevin turned, startled, then moved at once to Mrs. Harwood's side. She looked fragile in the sunlight, her skin translucent, her frame thin. "Good morning, but should you be out on your own?"

She gave him a smile that reminded him of her eldest daughter—a stubborn look, which said she pleased herself. "Actually, I come out most fine mornings, but do not tell Penelope. She would worry."

Offering his arm, he helped her to the stone bench. "And your husband and other daughters would not?"

Seated now, she glanced up at him, her eyes narrowed against the sun, the white lace cap on her head doing little to shade her face. "They would, but not as much. Ella takes it as her duty to look after us, and she is too good at it."

"You make that sound a bad thing."

"Oh, it is wonderful to be skilled at something. However, too much of anything is always a disaster. And I would that my Ella had more amusement. More gaiety. But I cannot see to it, for this is now the extent of my abilities."

She gave a sigh, and he wished he had comforting words to offer. He could only imagine how much she must chafe at the restrictions imposed by her illness.

As if she sensed his concern, she smiled. "However, I

do not mean to darken the day. And since I am advised to do little, I shall ask you to entertain me, for I hear your mother is a Gypsy, and I wish to hear all about her."

Nevin stiffened. He disliked such patronizing curiosity, as if his mother's Romany heritage made her an exotic thing to be pulled apart, not a person of flesh and feeling.

Leaning back, Mrs. Harwood's eyes drifted closed. "Do you know, I cannot imagine a more glamorous life. To go wherever one wishes, be always out-of-doors—it seems a bit of heaven."

He understood then, and his hostility faded. He had thought her like the others, expecting stories of fortune-telling and superstition. But to a woman held prisoner by infirmity, he could see that what interested her was the illusion that nothing restricted a Gypsy. Of course, everything did—laws, poverty, and the threat of illness with no coins for a doctor.

But he did not want to give her harsh truths. Sometimes, he knew, the hope from dreams could be what kept one going from one dawn to the next.

So he began to talk of his mother, dredging up what few good stories he could recall. A summer day when his sister had taught him to swim by throwing him into a lake, and his mother had taken a switch to her for nearly drowning her brother. His mother's lack of sight, and how, when he was a boy, she still seemed to know exactly what he had been doing.

It surprised him to find more than a few tales, good memories he had not thought existed. He even recalled a few humorous ones. At least Mrs. Harwood chuckled, though she ought to have frowned with censure at how, when he had first learned to take years off a horse's age by filing down the teeth, he overdid his efforts. The gelding's teeth looked six, but the animal's swayback, sunken eyes, and hoary coat told everyone the truth far better.

She only shook her head, then admitted, "I have never cared overmuch for gentlemen without a little rogue in them. But now you may help me back, for I am in need of my morning rest."

Rising, he took her hand. She leaned on him as he walked her to the house, moving slowly, and he could feel the frailty in her thin fingers. No wonder Penelope worried over her.

He kept his step short and slow, until she could sit again on the edge of her bed.

She glanced up at him then, her smile reminding him again of her eldest daughter as she asked, "You will come and see me again, I hope, before you go?"

He agreed, thinking it no hardship. In truth, he had never met a more tranquil woman—and she showed him so well his own restlessness.

She had shown him something else about himself, a past worth remembering. But as he bowed himself from her room, he wondered how could any man be a gentleman and a lord if he did not also shut away the Gypsy in him.

Theo's boots squelched in the mud as he paced the clearing. Stopping, he glanced over the surrounding trees, with their scattering of leaves that clung to skeletal branches. He could just glimpse the smoke drifting up from Harwood's chimneys.

Where in blazes was she?

Cecila had sent him a note, a very frilly sort of thing, asking him to meet her at the fallen log. Did she now mean to keep him waiting in a cold breeze?

"Women!" he muttered, and resumed pacing.

Of late, he had begun to think perhaps it would be a good thing for him to find a reason to take himself elsewhere for a bit. The fun had gone out of Cecila. She seemed to be entertaining expectations of late. And that led to trouble—to weddings, in fact.

Of course, someday he might see his way to having a bit more than fun with Cecila. She was temptingly pretty, after all. But why rush matters? Besides, they had gotten on very well as they were. Or at least they had used to.

Damn, but why must she now kick up all this fuss? Must be those London gents putting notions in her head, he decided, his jaw tensed.

Can't ever let a female get the bit in her teeth with their notions, or you're done for. That's what Terrance would have said. And he could imagine his brother telling him, his voice harsh, that he'd given Cecila too much rein.

"Ought to hold fast," Theo muttered to himself.

Fond as he was of Cecila, she had to learn to check her stride. And not go about allowing other gentlemen to make sheep eyes at her, as she had at the assembly! Nor to keep him kicking his heels. Particularly in a chill wind.

Folding his hands behind his back, he kept pacing.

A quarter hour later he heard her steps crunching on fallen leaves and he swung around. She came into the clearing, the color in her cheeks, her golden-brown curls wind tossed, and her cloak and dress lifted to show a trim pair of ankles.

Theo forced a frown. He would not allow those sweet looks of hers to turn his head. Not this time, damn it.

"You're late," he growled.

She had been walking toward him, her skirts dropped and hands outstretched. Now she stopped, her smile fading. "Well, are we not in a terse mood?"

"Terse, is it? That another of those fancy words you've

had from that Dawes fellow? And don't think I couldn't see a dozen of 'em in that letter of yours!"

Cecila stiffened. "What, do you think so little of my intelligence that I could not write you? Well, I wrote you entirely on my own. But I did not come here to argue."

Theo folded his arms. "No, you'd better have come to apologize."

Frowning now, Cecila caught the tip of her tongue between her teeth to keep from saying anything regrettable. Did he wish to start a quarrel? Perhaps he was just out of sorts that she had kept him waiting—and she had a little, but only because she had wanted to look her best.

She struggled into a smile, then said, her voice only a little clipped, "Very well, if I have done or said anything to cause you offense, I beg your pardon."

"And you'll not do it again?"

She blinked at him. "Not keep you waiting?"

"No, I know you females can't help that. I'm talking about your behavior at the assembly, and you flirting like a . . . a . . ."

"A what, Theo?" she asked, voice dropping and temper flaring. "Like a tavern wench—such as the ones you entertain? Well, you must be spending too much time in such low company if you can mistake me for anything but a lady!"

"Lady? And what sort of lady allows some London gent to dally with her?" Unfolding his arms, he stepped forward. "Don't tell me he did not—or has not been! I saw him staring at you in Taunton as if you were a present he could not wait to open."

A surprised pleasure feathered through her. "Did he really?"

"Yes, he did! And don't give me that wide-eyed look, as if you did not know it. His influence was even stamped all over that note you sent me! And I won't have any more of it! I am not going to have you making a fool of me!"

Tilting her head, she studied him, her mouth pulling down. Then she said, "So that is all that concerns you— how you look to others! And I once thought that you . . ."

She broke off the words, unable to trust herself not to betray her hurt. She had wanted only to see him, to mend things between them. But now she saw that what she had been trying to mend perhaps did not even exist. Well, it was time to find out if it did or not.

Plunging ahead, she said, "If you wish the right to dictate my behavior, why do you not apply to Father for permission to take such a responsibility from him?"

Shock widened his eyes for a moment, and then he scowled at her, his shoulders hunched. "Permission? You mean . . . that is . . . I . . . well, dash it, Cecila, a fellow's got to have some fun before he settles, you know."

She stared at him, the hurt welling stronger, but an odd sense of relief mixed with it to have the truth in the open. "You mean you do not really want me. You only want to have me waiting."

Dragging a hand through his hair, he stared at the ground, then at her. "That's hardly fair. And I'd hope you'd at least thank me that I'm not making you any false promises."

"Thank you, but I have just discovered I want promises. I want them very much."

Watching him, her forehead tight, she waited. *Oh, why can't you change—just enough to give us a chance?*

She realized then that, just like Theo, she had also been guilty of wanting not him, but someone to be there for her. Just so she would not end a spinster like Penelope. Shame rushed into her.

With a shake of her head, she knew that a chasm had widened between them. Or, more like, it had been there for ages, and she had not seen it until she had taken a step away from him. Loss already lay heavy on her chest, but she could see no other choice.

She did want promises—and she wanted them kept.

Turning away, she looked up at the clouds drifting on a fast wind. "This is not at all what I intended."

He came a step closer, the mud sucking at his boots. "Why fret so? And over what? Some bounder from London?"

She glanced at him. "You may leave Mr. Dawes out of this. What I am fretting over is the promises you will not make me!"

His forehead wrinkled as his eyebrows lifted. Helpless regret shadowed his eyes.

Oh, heavens, am I making the worst mistake? she wondered.

Well, if she was, she could not undo it. She would not. And for once she tried to see Theo as he was—impetuous, quicksilver charming, a light flirtation, and not at all the steadfast lover she had had in her mind. Or in her heart.

At last he slanted her a roguish smile, softened with the merest hint of boyish charm. "Least I got my apology."

Reaching out, he touched one finger to her cheek. She put her hand up to touch his before he pulled away. For a moment he seemed to struggle with unspoken words, and hope flickered.

Then he turned and strode away.

She watched for a moment. Then she turned to walk back to Harwood, her stare focused on the ground, on her muddy hem, on the tips of her boots. She had to focus on something.

Oh, heavens, what did she do for a future now?

* * *

The thumping woke Bryn. Pulling open eyelids still weighted by sleep, he realized that the worst of his illness had receded. His head no longer throbbed and he no longer ached in every joint. He swallowed and found that his throat also no longer felt as if a dozen cats had clawed their way down it.

Sitting up, he glanced at the pale sunlight drifting in from behind the drapery. Late afternoon, he judged. He had not slept the entire day away.

Another set of thumps pounded, paused, then started again, farther away this time.

Throwing back his bedcovers, he took up a purple satin dressing gown and dragged it on. Padding to the door, he opened it to glance into the hallway. Cecila Harwood paused, her hand upraised as if about to knock on the wall again.

He leaned against the doorjamb, puzzled annoyance shifting into amusement. "I thought the dead of night to be the mandatory treasure hunting hour."

She lowered the hand that had been about to start knocking the walls. And then Bryn straightened as he noted her pallor and the hollow look in her eyes.

"I do not care if you want to make sport of me. I am going to find it!" she said.

The hot insistence in her voice caught at him. Something was not right. "And why such urgency now?"

Her glance fell, and she began tugging on one bare finger. He half thought she would not tell him, and he wondered how he could coax the truth from her.

Then she glanced at him, obviously struggling to contain her feelings, and looking all the more miserable for it. "Because if I am not to marry Theo now that we've broken, what am I to do?"

Bryn stared at her, his jaw slack and an odd lightness

in him. Must be the fever still. Only that did not account for why a dizzy delight now danced in his chest.

Then he heard her small, sharp intake of breath. She had her head down, as if searching the hall floor for something she had lost. Hiccups of muffled whimpers lifted her shoulders in spasms as she struggled with her tears.

In the next moment, he had her in his arms, her head tucked under his chin and her body held tight. "Oh, my dear. I am sorry."

He knew just how much it must hurt. His own first love had been a pointless affair with a married lady, which had thankfully never gone anywhere, but that had not taken the sting out of the rejection he had felt when it ended.

Burrowing against him, she let loose her tears. With his free hand, he brushed the wetness from her cheek, stroking away each crystal drop, allowing his fingers to trace the line of her face, the edge of her jaw, the curve of her mouth. And then she pulled back to stare up at him, her eyes wide and full, like lakes after a spring rain.

Such lovely eyes—so yearning, so wounded. It seemed the most natural thing in the world when his mouth found hers without effort or thought.

It simply happened.

He bent closer. Lips touched to lips. She tasted of salt. Of a sweetness that left him aching. His mouth traced the line from her mouth to her eyes and back again, and when his lips found hers again, that lick of desire inside him flared into something far hotter.

The touch of her fingers on his skin, grazing the hairs on his chest, startled him from the growing haze of pleasure.

Penelope Harwood's shocked voice jolted him into a final, mortified awareness. "Cecila! Mr. Dawes!"

Cecila jumped as if a hot poker had been touched to her. Then she pulled away. Cold replaced the warmth that had been in Bryn's arms, and for an instant he could not tell which he regretted most—the kiss, or its conclusion.

Dragging a hand through his hair, he tried to think of some excuse—only there could be none. Not really. He glanced at Cecila, wondering if she, too, now regretted their madness. She stared at her sister, her chin high, her lower lip quivering as if it would not take much to restart the tears. He must be careful, and he could only think that perhaps the fever still lay upon him and had taken his sense.

Miss Harwood glanced from her sister to Bryn, and then she said, ice in her voice, "Cecila, you had best go to your room. Mr. Dawes, I think my father will have something to say to you!"

Nevin stood by the window in his cousin's room, watching him turn the carefully styled curls his valet had created into true disorder with a swipe of his hand. The story had already spread through the house as it must, like fire through August grass. Sylvain had brought the tale to the stables and to Nevin. So now he had come to find Bryn and the truth.

What he had found was his cousin, grim faced, getting dressed to see Harwood. And not a sign of the Harwood ladies.

Nevin frowned. His cousin must feel something for Miss Cecila to have kissed her, but he had also seen the girl flirting and tempting that Winslow youth. He did not know who to blame most for this lapse in proper conduct, so he asked, "Just how did this happen?"

Dragging his hand through his hair again, Bryn

clutched a handful of dark strands, then released them.
"Blazes if I know." He glanced up. "I . . . she was . . . oh,
blazes, I only wanted to comfort her. And after—she
looked utterly confused after. Then her sister marched
her away before I could say a word."

"To offer her marriage?" Nevin asked, frowning.

Bryn slumped into a chair. "Oh, yes, that would be
kind, when I've no income to support a wife. No property. Not even prospects to lay before her. Hell, if I offer
and then go away to seek a fortune in India, I might even
hope she will marry someone else while I'm gone!"

He spoke with such bitter harshness that it surprised
Nevin. Eyes narrowing, he studied his cousin. Bryn had
never seemed anything but eager to see the title and
lands given over to Nevin as his due inheritance. And
Nevin had simply assumed he would someday make
some provisions for his cousin. He had not seen any rush
to resolve Bryn's future until his own past had been settled. Now he saw his mistake.

"I could—" he began, and cut off his words as Bryn
shot him a hard, resentful stare.

Voice soft, Bryn asked, "You could what? Buy me for
them? Give me enough money to marry so you will not
have to?"

Nevin's hands clenched, and he had to consciously
relax his fingers. He had been about to suggest that, only
not in such crude terms. He could think of at least two
livings he could give his cousin—the care of some small
village churches, in which Bryn could be vicar in name
while leaving the real spiritual tasks to some lowly curate
who resided there. It happened often enough.

But it would not do. Not for Bryn. Such charity would
eat at his pride, becoming a canker that must fester into
a deeper wound. Not the best way to start a marriage.

And not something he could do to Bryn. Not when he owed his cousin everything. If only Bryn could see that.

Changing his mind, Nevin gave a small smile. He would find another solution. "I meant to say I could come downstairs with you to face Harwood, if you wish it."

Color stained Bryn's cheeks, and he shifted in his chair, then stood. "I beg your pardon. And it's cowardly of me, but I shall take you up on that. Blazes, but I wish I had not gotten out of bed."

Nevin came over to Bryn's side and clapped a hand on his shoulder. It felt like grasping stone. "So do I. Well, at least Harwood is not like to shoot you."

Bryn offered an empty smile. "I wish he would. I deserve it."

Harwood, however, when they entered his study, looked unlikely to shoot anyone.

With his blue eyes even more vague than usual and his wispy ginger hair disordered, he seemed baffled, Nevin thought, as if he did not know whether to act the gracious host or become an outraged parent. He begged them to sit and offered glasses of burgundy. Then he stood before his desk, fidgeting with the gold watch chain that lay across his waistcoat.

Finally, he put his hands behind his back and cleared his throat. "Penelope says that I ought to . . . well, that is . . . Mr. Dawes, I ought to ask you your intentions. However, I must tell you I am loath to promote a match when I am uncertain if your affections—or my daughter's— are truly engaged. Yesterday, she sighed over Theodore Winslow and today she kisses you. That seems reason enough to perhaps forget all that occurred."

Bryn's face had paled. He sat in a high-backed wing chair near the fire, his hands tightly clasped before him, and Nevin could not tell if the color draining from his face came from a return of his illness or the effect of Harwood's words.

Nodding, Bryn said, his voice tight, as if a hand clenched his throat, "I quite understand your reluctance."

Harwood unfolded his hands and began fussing with his watch chain again. "On the other hand, I dread this story will get about. Everyone in the house seems to know, and tongues do wag. I should not worry, only . . . well, I am aware what is said of Penelope, and if Cecila were to be thought too bold for propriety—well, you must see that I am obliged to look to my daughters' futures."

Nevin did see, as must Bryn. Gossip had labeled one Harwood daughter a jilt, and if word spread that another was fast and loose, then what hope had they to ever gain a decent match? It would take a strong passion—or a rich dowry—for most gentlemen to overlook such faults in a possible lady-wife.

With a shake of his head, Harwood leaned against his desk, one hand resting on the smooth cherry wood surface. "I have no solution to this."

Nevin glanced from Harwood to Bryn, who sat with his head down, so Nevin could not glimpse his expression. *Devla,* but he could not allow his cousin to go on sacrificing himself for others. Not in this case. What had he said? He had only meant to comfort the girl. Nevin could kick him for his methods, but he could not leave him to deal with this on his own.

He glanced again at Harwood, still reluctant to do what he knew he must. He did not want this. But if Bryn could sacrifice for him, he must find character enough in himself to do the same.

He hesitated once more, then forced the words out. "Sir, I wish your permission to wed your daughter."

Harwood stared at him. Bryn said nothing. And Nevin did not look at him. It had started to rain, and Nevin could hear the patter of drops against the window. He also could feel his heart beating sluggish in his veins.

Would Harwood refuse him?

Straightening, Harwood frowned, glanced at Nevin, then at Bryn, and then to Nevin again. "This is something beyond my abilities, so I think you had best apply to Cecila. And if she consents, well then, I shall wish you happy."

He moved to the bellpull, and Nevin heard the distant clatter of the bell in the servant's quarters. When Bridges arrived, Harwood requested that Miss Cecila join them. Nevin glanced at his cousin then, but Bryn still sat with his head down. His knuckles had gone white.

A moment later, Cecila stepped into the room, her face pale, but otherwise looking composed. Nevin frowned. Already he began to regret his action. Then he glanced again at Bryn. His cousin had stood when Cecila entered, and he now stared at her, his face empty of any emotion.

Nevin put away his regrets. If he had seen any sign that his action troubled Bryn, he would have withdrawn his offer at once, but now he straightened and fixed his stare on Miss Cecila. He would leave this to her. If she cared for Bryn, she would reject him. And if she accepted—well, he had wanted to help the Harwoods, had he not?

But why, then, did he keep thinking of another Miss Harwood? Ah, he must learn to set that aside, to school himself to stick to the duty he had just taken on by declaring himself to Harwood.

Harwood had already stepped forward to take his daughter's hand, and now he said to her, his voice soft, "My dear, you have a decision to make. Lord Nevin has asked to marry you."

Seventeen

For a moment, Cecila held still. She could not even breathe. Nevin had asked for her? She glanced from one Dawes to the other. She had rehearsed half a dozen scenarios in her mind while pacing her room, and not one of them had been this.

Turning to Bryn, she willed him to say something. His gaze, however, had dropped so that he stared at the medallion pattern on the carpet. He said nothing.

Hurt welled into a fierce anger that warmed her face. *Please say something!* she wanted to shout. And then her shoulders slumped. How very tired she was of gentlemen who would not make promises.

She glanced at Nevin, so daunting with those dark good looks and that unreadable face. Wetting her lips, she said, her voice as steady as she could make it, "I would like to hear it from him myself, Father."

And let us see if he can, she thought.

Nevin lifted one shoulder, as if it mattered little, then said, his expression rather grim, "Miss Cecila, I would be honored if you would consent to become Lady Nevin."

Her throat tightened. There it was. An honest proposal. A promise to cherish her and endow her with his worldly goods. For a moment, the future dazzled. Society. Balls. She could take Sylvain and Penelope to London, even.

But at what cost?

He had not mentioned a word of love or feeling. She glanced at Bryn, who still did not look at her. Then she thought of Theo.

Oh, what did she know about love, anyway? She had thought . . .

Oh, you silly goose, stop thinking and act, or do you want to end like Penelope—unhappy and alone?

Straightening, her heart beating so fast it was starting to make her ill, she looked directly at Nevin. "Thank you. You do me the honor, and I . . . I accept."

There. She had said it. But even as Nevin came to take her hand, her glance slid to his cousin. He still did not look at her, just stood there, his head bowed as if with shame, his right hand clenched as if he could not bear this.

She turned away, unable to bear it herself. Oh heavens, what had she done? But she made her lips curve upward and tried not to think about that kiss, which had changed everything inside her.

It had changed nothing in the world around her, after all, except that she would now marry Nevin. And she hoped with all her heart that Mr. Dawes now regretted his cold silence.

She certainly did.

Penelope heard the news just before dinner, when her father, who stood before the fire in the drawing room, called for everyone's attention and said he had an announcement.

She glanced at Cecila, worried. Her sister had seemed far too quiet all evening. Perhaps she ought to have allowed Cecila and Mr. Dawes to sort out things between them, only all the old resentments against the Daweses had surged out in a flare of anger. She had hated seeing him take advantage of her sister in such a fashion.

But had the result been to force Cecila into an unhappy alliance? She had not intended that.

Then her father put Cecila's hand in Lord Nevin's and announced that they would wed.

A numbing weight settled over Penelope. Her fingers loosened and she almost dropped her wine glass, but then she caught herself, merely spilling her wine so that she had to occupy herself in brushing the red droplets from her gown.

Nevin? But, no . . . he could not.

She glanced at Mr. Dawes. He stood back from the others, his stare fixed on Cecila. Then he came forward, shook his cousin's hand, kissed Cecila's cheek, and excused himself, saying he still did not feel quite well.

Neither did Penelope.

From next to her, she heard Sylvain muttering, and one phrase drifted to her: ". . . utter disaster."

Blinking, fighting off that numbing shock, Penelope glanced at her sister. "Really, you must not say such things."

Sylvain frowned. "Why not? They won't make each other happy, and we all know it."

Penelope glanced at Nevin and Cecila—one so dark, the other fair. A striking couple. Cecila had begun to smile. Nevin held her hand.

Hot tears burned the back of Penelope's eyes, and an ugly jealousy clawed loose in her chest. Appalled by such emotions, she turned away, afraid her feelings would be noticed. Oh heavens, she ought to be happy at Cecila making such a grand match. Had she not even thought to encourage it?

She glanced at them again. And the truth struck her—she envied her sister not the match, but the man.

He leaned closer to Cecila to say something to her, and Penelope had to look away, the twist so sharp in her that she wished she could drag out her heart to stop the agony.

When had this happened? She had tried so hard to keep herself safe, but she had ended by only hiding her feelings from herself. She had not stopped them.

Squeezing shut her eyes, the loss began to widen inside her until it must swallow her.

A light touch on her elbow pulled open her eyes. Sylvain stared at her, her eyes quite serious and her expression intent. "You have to mend this."

She pulled in a breath. What did she answer? She glanced at Sylvain, then said, "There is nothing to mend."

Crossing the room, she congratulated her sister and Nevin, saying to him as Cecila moved away to speak with their father, "You have made a good choice."

He stared at her, black eyes impossibly inky. "I made no choice. I did what I must to repay my cousin's sacrifice for me."

She glanced at him, puzzled. Heavens, he had done this for others, not for himself? Oh, that would not do. She parted her lips to say something, but what? She could hardly demand he retract his offer.

His hand lifted as if he would touch her. Then he let it drop to his side again. "I leave for London tomorrow to make arrangements. And I hope . . . I hope you will visit us."

She shook her head, unable to say anything. Then she turned away, her mind spinning.

Somehow she got through the rest of the evening, dragging herself as if the air had become a cloying liquid that made every moment an effort.

By the time she reached her bed, exhausted, her emotions ragged, she had begun to think Sylvain had the right of it. Something had to be done. Cecila had put on a brave face, but looked unhappy underneath, and Nevin had the grim set to his mouth of a gentleman who knew his duty.

Only what could be done now?

Well, something must before the engagement became public and it became impossible to set aside without scandal.

However, when she lay down on her bed, instead of planning the future, her thoughts turned to the past, for she could not stop wondering just when she had fallen in love with Nevin.

Nevin left at dawn. He chose to ride, leaving behind his valet, taking with him only a clean shirt and an extra cravat tucked into the small satchel that attached to the D-rings on the front of his saddle. Light travel meant fast travel, and before he made for London, he had his mother to find.

She needed to know he planned to marry, and he needed to see her. She had always given him the best counsel, even if at the time he had often not cared for her wisdom.

It took a few hours to find the signs, cut into trees and left at crossroads in small piles of rock, that the Rom used to tell each other of good camping grounds and what direction different families traveled. By mid afternoon, he had found a Gypsy camp with a cart and a sturdy pony, white canvas tents, two men, a woman with a babe, and three ragged, rangy boys.

Dark, uneasy eyes watched as he dismounted, but when he gave them a greeting in Romany, their faces lightened into surprise. Soon enough he had a hot drink in his hand, questions to answers, and a story to give.

Word, he knew, would travel of his search, and would reach his mother soon enough.

That was the way of the Rom. One spread the word, and then one left the outcome in God's hands.

It unsettled him how easily he slipped back into the old ways—as if he had never taken on a title and the clothes of a gentleman. And when they offered to share their dinner with him, he almost stayed. But the restlessness drove him, and so he took his leave, a few coins tucked into grubby hands before he rode north.

That night, he bedded down under the stars. He had thought of hiring a room, only his stop that day—or perhaps the wedding that faced him—had left him with an odd desire for open space and the half-remembered freedom that his talk with Mrs. Harwood had stirred.

The ground was as damp as he remembered, the night as cold, but it did not rain, and the sharp glints of stars beyond count in a clear sky began to clear his thoughts. Nearby, Cinder cropped grass, a comforting, rhythmic sound that lulled the discontent from him.

He had forgotten the beauty of a cold night and the satisfaction of muscles well used. What else had he forgotten of himself in his rush to make himself into a lord? He frowned at that.

And what would Penelope think of a man who slept under the stars? What a mouthful of a name that was. What had her mother called her? Ah, yes, Ella. A softer name. She no doubt hated it. And she would probably think him uncouth to be sleeping outside. But then she would also probably set to piling leaves for a softer bed, and insisting on enough wood gathered for a fire all the night. Yes, she would manage.

Devla, what was he doing marrying one sister when his thoughts turned so easily to the other?

I am helping my cousin, he told himself. *As I must, for that is what a gentleman does.*

With that, he shut his eyes and his thoughts, but the dreams came anyway.

By the morning, Bryn knew he must speak with Cecila. The urge to explain himself had filled him to bursting, and he knew he could not remain silent. He ought to. He ought to allow her to marry Nevin. She would have a comfortable life then.

But he had to at least explain why he could not afford to wed her. And perhaps she might understand. Perhaps she might wait for him to make the fortune he needed.

And perhaps she might laugh in his face as he deserved.

He had to find out.

He sent Bridges off with a note for her. An answer came back five minutes later that she planned to remain in her room.

It seemed too early to start on brandy, so he settled himself in the library, busying himself in cataloging titles that no longer interested.

When a knock sounded and the door opened, he jumped to his feet, hoping for the impossible. But only the eldest Miss Harwood entered.

Shoulders slumping, he managed a good morning, then gestured to the books on the table. "I've almost done here—there actually are a few things of value—but I suppose that hardly matters. Nevin will see to your family's needs now."

Coming into the room, she glanced at the books, then folded her hands before her. "Mr. Dawes, why did you kiss my sister?"

And I ought to be horrified at how blunt I am being, Penelope thought. A sleepless night had left her beyond that.

She had started this by going to Father, and even now she interfered. But Sylvain had been right. She had to mend matters, for she had been part of the making of this tangle.

He blinked at her and shifted on his feet. "I . . . well, it started with my comforting her, and then . . . just happened."

"Yes, but you must have some feeling for her—or are you a heartless rogue who would kiss any female?"

He dragged a hand through his hair. "I am a miserable wretch—'like a fiend in a cloud, with howling woe.' And if I still had Nevin's fortune in my hands as my own, I would lay it at your sister's feet. Only I have not, so I did not."

His shoulders had slumped as he spoke, and Penelope's temper shortened. "Mr. Dawes, it is not my place to give you advice, but I shall do so anyway, for my sister is involved. A gentleman once told me he had not enough money to marry, but I still hold that had he enough true feeling, we would have managed. Cecila is as accustomed as I—or Sylvain, for that matter—to doing without luxuries. It might be different if she knew only wealth. But I can only suppose you are either being too noble for anyone's good, or you have a romantic's notion that love must always end tragic!"

He had stiffened at this, and she did not blame him. She had just abused his character, but then she was a rather desperate woman just now.

Eyes narrowing, he glared at her. "I may be a romantic, but I am not a fool. Cecila made her choice."

"And did you offer her any other?"

He stared at her, doubt lighting his eyes to the color of weak tea. Exasperated, Penelope shook her head and tried to soften her aggravation with him. She certainly had not been much better in expressing herself.

"It's no use, anyway. She won't even see me," he said, dejection in his voice.

Penelope drew herself up. "I will make you a bargain, Mr. Dawes. You leave that to me, and I shall leave it to you how you sort this out with her. But I do insist that you sort it out. I had the strongest feeling last night that your cousin is doing this for your sake, not his own."

Bryn's head jerked up. "The devil he is!"

"The devil, Mr. Dawes, is not the assistance you should be seeking just now." With a nod to him, she turned and left.

It took the better part of an hour to coerce her sister into going downstairs. Penelope finally succeeded by pointing out that since Cecila was about to become Mr. Dawes's cousin, if she did not reconcile with him, she could create a rift between him and Nevin that might not heal.

That drew a guilty look from Cecila, and Penelope took shameless advantage, urging her sister into a gown, pulling her hair up into curls, and insisting that Cecila at least attempt to entertain Mr. Dawes while Nevin was away.

"And since Mr. Dawes has almost finished cataloging the library, you should show him those books in the storage room. Something ought to be done with them," she told Cecila, as she invented a task that might at least throw them together.

Grumbling, Cecila agreed and left, and Penelope sent up a prayer that for once her meddling might do some good.

Bryn glanced around the musty room. Chairs, legs broken or upholstery tattered, stood in one corner.

Under shuttered windows, a couch tipped drunkenly to one side. Two heavy trunks, their curved lids closed, stood against the opposite wall, and he could only imagine they held more castoffs. To the right, in a wall of dusty, empty bookcases, stood the most hideous trio of porcelain figurines: a dog of some sort, with its broken head next to its body, a teapot made to look like a cabbage, and what looked a tipsy shepherdess, missing one leg.

"And what am I to do here?" he asked again. He ought, he supposed, to be glad Cecila had at least come down and had offered her hand to him, saying coldly that since they were to be cousins, they ought to cry friends. She had not allowed him to say anything on the matter that now lay between them like a double-edged sword.

She gave him another of those withering glances, and he almost wished she had not come downstairs at all. She obviously hated him. How in blazes did he explain anything to a woman who looked as if she would rather have him a thousand miles away?

"Penelope said I should show you the last of the books," she said, stressing her sister's name, as if to make clear this was not her idea.

He glanced around, seeking something that would at least lead to their talking again. "You never showed me this room before."

She gave him a scathing glance.

"For treasure hunting, I mean," he added, feeling foolish.

Folding her arms, she lifted her eyebrows. "I never showed you the still room, the laundry room, nor the waterclosets, either. Besides, they have all been searched before a dozen times, and there is no treasure. That was only childish nonsense, anyway."

Unfolding her arms, she swept past him to drag open one of the trunks. Its hinges screeched with lack of use. "These are all we ever found, in fact. Years ago. They were tucked into a niche behind the bookcase, but they are all German or Latin. Father did not find them terribly interesting, but then, he does not read German. Nor does anyone else in the house, actually."

"What niche?" Bryn asked, that damnable curiosity of his stirring. If he had not wondered what it would be like to kiss Cecila, he might not be in his present predicament.

He shut away that thought.

Cecila lifted her eyes as if impatient with him, but then she walked to the bookcase on the end of one wall. With a little effort, she dragged one end out so that it swung into the room, revealing a shallow opening, hardly more than a niche with more shelving.

Sounding disappointed, she said, "It had just those books in it and was not even large enough for games."

"Such as hide and seek?" he asked, offering a smile.

She stared back at him, her expression empty.

With a shiver, he glanced into the hidden cupboard, and then turned to the trunk of books. They sank his mood even lower. Plain leather bindings, not even a trace of gold lettering. Probably dusty grammars or boring travel accounts by some nameless soul.

Lifting out a book, he tried to shut out the awareness of Cecila—her perfume and that cold displeasure that emanated from her, as bitter as an east wind.

He opened the book, and then forgot everything else.

Eighteen

Hand lettering. German. He began to translate, struggling with his rusty skills, but a tingle spread across his skin as he read. Then his knees began to wobble, so he simply sank down next to the trunk. Closing the first book, he set it aside and took out the next, his fingers touching the hole that he suspected had once held the book chained to a shelf in a monastic library. His touch reverent now, he opened the book. Lovely, careful script, the ink still black on the thick vellum page.

"What is it?" Cecila asked.

He put down that volume and took up the next. And then the next. "You showed these to your Father?" he asked, still bent over the text, this one a Latin dictionary, a hand copy of the *Summa Hugucionis,* over six hundred years old.

"I already said we did. But the two we showed him were in German, which Father does not read. He said we ought to put them away, so we put them here, for they are too large and unwieldy for the shelves upstairs."

And they were. Books created in a time when their weight displayed the wealth of those who owned such luxuries. Reaching into the trunk, Bryn hefted out the next book. This time as he opened the page Cecila gasped.

Gold glittered. Even in the dim room, vibrant blues

and red flashed from the page, letters wrought with artistry and text scripted with intricate beauty. Illuminated. Yes, these pages brought their own light with them.

Bryn's hands trembled. "I'll wager you never showed him this."

He glanced up at her. Dumbly, she shook her head, then said, "The others seemed so dull."

Closing the book, Bryn sat back and let out a laugh. Then he put down the book with the others and stood. "Dull? You've a very dull copy of St. Augustine's *De Civitate Dei*, from the sixth century, if I do not mistake. And that last is an illuminated bible, though it will take a better scholar than I to place its date. This, my dear, is what poor Cecil Harwood hid from the Puritan Roundheads. He knew they would see it as Popish writings—scripts from Catholic monks, with idolatry in every golden image—and they'd have burned them. Wiped them away along with the monarchy they sought to destroy. So he sent his gold to his king, but he took the real treasures from his library and hid books behind books. And you found them!"

She stared at the books, then at Bryn, her eyes glazed.

He took her arms. "Don't you understand. There's at least two dozen books here, or more. I've no idea what they might fetch, but I can think of at least one collector who'd give your father whatever price he names for them."

"Whatever?" she repeated. With a squeal of delight, she threw herself into his arms. "Then we are rich!"

Bryn gave up the struggle before it had started. "Oh, hell," he muttered. And then he had his arms around her and his mouth covering hers, and this time he kept kissing her until his head spun and she leaned into him.

Pulling back, he glared at her. "You cannot kiss me in that fashion and then expect to marry my cousin!"

She began twisting the top button of his waistcoat. "Well, at least he asked me. You never did! And I was so angry with you for not saying so much as a single word!"

"Thank you, but your older sister has already as good as told me I am an idiot and that if I cared enough for you, I should not allow thoughts of genteel poverty to weigh on me."

She dimpled. "You ought to listen to Penelope, for she is invariably right about everything. Besides, now I have money."

"Well then, I suppose I shall have to marry you for it. Will you have me? Will you 'come live with me and be my love—and we shall some new pleasure prove'?"

"Are you quoting at me again?"

"Yes, I am. And I plan to go on doing so, only you may have to wait a bit while I make something of myself so that the pleasure part might actually be pleasurable."

She wound her arms around his neck. "But if Father has money now, why can he not invest in a publishing firm with you? And besides, you cannot expect me to sit by and—"

His kiss silenced her. After a moment of resistance, she softened in his arms.

Pulling back, he took her hand. One fence down, but others remained. "Come on. We must talk to your father about this."

Penelope heard raised voices coming from her father's study and could not resist their pull. A ride had been the only way to keep herself from hovering a step behind Cecila and Mr. Dawes to see what might happen.

But something seemed to have occurred, and she had to know what.

Glancing into her father's study, she found Cecila, Mr. Dawes, and her father gathered around his desk, a stack of dusty books piled high.

Her father gestured at once for her to come in, saying, "My dear, we have the most amazing news."

She listened as he explained the value of the books, and she could only stare at them, taken aback, a frustrated regret stirring. They had been here all along, a fortune to be claimed. All of it—Jonathan, the years of hardship, perhaps even her mother's illness—might have been avoided, if only . . .

Ruthlessly, she cut off such laments. If they had known of this years ago, the books might well have been sold to pay for some failed business scheme. Perhaps they came at a time when her father would now see the wisdom in holding on to what they had.

She started to say something to that effect, but Cecila interrupted, turning to her, eyes bright, "And Father is going to invest in Bryn's starting a publishing company!"

Panic skittered into Penelope. Oh, heavens it began again. To make it worse, Mr. Dawes, looking utterly besotted, took hold of Cecila's hand and kissed it.

Penelope scowled at him.

Smiling, Cecila took back her hand and tucked it into the crook of Mr. Dawes's arm, and then she beamed at her sister. "And Bryn and I are to marry."

Eyebrow arched with shock, Penelope glanced to her sister. "Do you not think you should at least settle matters with Lord Nevin beforehand?"

Mr. Dawes smiled and waved a hand. "Oh, he won't mind."

Clenching her back teeth, Penelope fought to keep from uttering something caustic. Lord Nevin might well be relieved—at least she hoped he would—but such callous disregard for his feelings seemed inexcusable. She knew if she did not leave, she was going to say something harsh about harebrain publishing ventures and inconsiderate relatives.

No one seemed to notice when she excused herself and left.

News of the books and their value spread rapidly through the household. Mrs. Merritt promised a celebratory dinner that would outshine even the best Christmas feast from any year past. Bridges dug in the cellar to scavenge something festive for a toast, managing to find a neglected port that had not turned to vinegar. And the family dined in Mrs. Harwood's rooms so she might hear the story and toast the bride and groom.

Penelope, however, found that the sight of her sister and Mr. Dawes gazing at each other, their hearts in their eyes, stealing small touches of hands, dug under her skin in an oddly irritating fashion. Oh, she did so hope Nevin would not mind—but what if he did?

Unable to enjoy the celebration, she excused herself early, but after she had changed into her nightclothes a soft knock sounded on her door. Opening it, she blinked at the sight of her father, burdened by five of the leather-bound books.

"Do you mind if I put these down? They are rather heavy," he said with a smile, and then he came into the room. He put the books on her dressing table, then turned to her.

"Whatever do you want me to do with them?" she asked.

Coming to her, he took her hands. "Why, keep them, my dear. From what Mr. Dawes says, they are the most valuable—and they are now your dowry. Your independence, if you like."

"My—" her throat tightened on the word. She glanced at the books, and then at her father.

His blue eyes softened. "My dear, I know things have not always gone well between us. But you must know I never wanted anything more than to give you girls what you most desired. Sylvain is so easy with that. And now Cecila seems quite happy. But . . . well, I have not managed well with you. So please allow me to give you this." His smile twisted. "I am certain you will invest far more wisely than ever I have, and it will gratify me and your mother no end to know you need never worry for your future."

His hands tightened, and Penelope found her vision blurring and her nose tingling. "Oh, Father . . ."

He gathered her into his arms to hold her close a moment, then stepped back, placing her at arm's length. "Just be happy, my dear. That is the best your mother and I could ask for you."

With a smile, he pinched her chin and left. Penelope stared at the door a moment, then walked to the books. She opened the top one and stared at the page, its colors joyous, as if in celebration of life.

Closing the book, she wiped at the wetness on her face.

He had only ever wanted to make her happy. And what had she wanted?

She had wanted him perfect. She had wanted him to do what she thought best. She had wanted so much, and all of it seemed so empty now. All along his love for her had been in her reach, just as had the books. A treasure overlooked.

Oh, how stupid she had been. She could do as she

pleased now. Could live as she wished. But she found what she most wanted was those years to do over again.

Curling up on her bed, the candle flickering, she stared at the books for a long time, and then she did something she had not done in years. Reaching under her bed, she pulled out the hatbox of her poetry. A scrap of leaded pencil lay at the bottom, and she dug it out. Then she sat reading her own words, and starting to write new ones. Better ones, she hoped.

When Penelope woke, her thoughts began where they had left last night, turning over yesterday's events. As she dressed, her gaze slipped to the books. It still did not seem real. So many new choices now. So what did she do with them?

In the upstairs hall, she met Sylvain, dressed in her oldest gray gown, clutching a half-grown fox in her arms, its pointed face poking out from a tattered blanket, one white-bandaged paw visible and its eyes wide with fear.

"Sylvain, you should no—" Penelope began, but then she stopped her words. She had to give up this habit of thinking she knew best for everyone. So she started again, her voice softer, "Dear, if you are going to keep a fox, you had best tuck him under your bed. He might at least think it a burrow."

Sylvain's expression changed from sullen resentment to suspicion. "You are not to say I must take him to the stables?"

Itching to do just that, Penelope managed a smile. "Just try not to let him get loose and frighten Mrs. Merritt."

Sylvain shrugged off such a notion. "Oh, I shan't. She would terrify him."

With a shake of her head, Penelope started toward Cecila's room to see what amends she might make there, but Sylvain's words stopped her. "Oh, don't bother with Cece—she and Bryn left already."

Penelope turned. "Left? For where?"

Sylvain snuggled her fox. "London. Something about a special license to wed."

"Well, of all the . . . does Father know?"

"Oh, yes. They did nothing but talk of it last night. Father seemed not to care for it, but Mr. Dawes seemed to want to make certain Cecila would not change her mind, and who can blame him? She has gone through, what, three gentlemen in almost as many days?"

Penelope frowned at that flippant comment, and then her mind began to turn. Perhaps she could ride after them, and . . .

No. She would not. This time she would leave Cecila to sort out her own life however she wished. And she would even allow herself to be happy for her sister. Yes, she would.

Sylvain had already gone off to her room, taking her fox, and so Penelope started downstairs, determined to have her breakfast in peace. Only the urge to do something still nagged.

Well, perhaps she could just go to the stables and at least learn from Peter when Bryn and Celia had set out—not that she would do anything more, mind.

However, as she turned the corner of the staircase and started down into the front hall, she caught sight of a familiar pair of shoulders.

He stood near the front door, his back to the stairs, and Penelope's heart turned over at the sight of him.

"Nevin."

He turned, and she realized then that she had spoken his name aloud.

He had left off his cravat, and his waistcoat lay unbuttoned. With his dusty boots and black coat, his buff breeches creased by dirt, he looked far more like a roguish Gypsy than a proper lord.

Straightening, she could not decide if he had yet had the news, for he looked in a rather uncertain temper, his dark eyes flashing and his mouth set in a hard line. She decided high fences were best taken fast. "I am afraid you have just missed your cousin. He left with Cecila this morning."

Nevin had already started toward the stairs. He had ridden all day yesterday, spending the night in a less than comfortable inn, and his patience had run thin. Seeing Penelope, that frown tight between her eyebrows, had left him wishing he had dragged Bryn with him to prevent this.

Taking the stairs two at a time, he strode toward her. "I know," he said. "For London. And I am sorry."

Puzzled, she stared down at him, one hand on the banister. "Sorry? Whatever for? And just how is it that you know?"

His mouth crooked. She had still not asked him why he had returned. "I had the news from Peter in the stable, and I could throttle my cousin just now for running off with your sister."

She seemed to find the worn banister of great interest, but then she glanced at him, and he thought at last she might be wondering why he had returned in such haste, looking like the Gypsy he was. However, she said instead, "Well, he did have Father's approval, and he . . . oh heavens, Bridges left you standing in the hall, did he not?"

He stopped before her, a step down from her so his eyes were level with hers. "That is of no matter."

She became interested in the banister again. "No. I suppose not." Then she glanced at him, pulled in a breath, and folded her hands before her. "We do, however, owe you a great apology, for your returning to find Cecila—well, her gone off with your cousin."

He studied her eyes, searching for some sign of distress, and his shoulders relaxed when he could not find it. He had risen yesterday, his dreams still clinging to him, leaving him with an unsettling dread long after the images faded. And that feeling had driven him as nothing ever had before. He had needed to come back, needed to see her again, to know that nothing was wrong, for he had had the worst feeling of his life.

When he had first glimpsed her on the stair, that feeling had at last faded. He had felt foolish to be so driven by a dream. He had never put any belief in them, but now he wondered if he had not been led back to her for a reason.

A very good one.

He kept his stare fixed on her as he answered, "Actually, I am relieved. And even more so to find that you do not seem overly distressed."

A smile began to brighten her eyes, but she shuttered it again. "Well, I was, on your behalf. But your cousin insisted you would not mind if he . . . if . . . is there something wrong?" she asked, frowning as he continued to gaze at her, unable to stop taking in his fill of her.

He shook his head, still staring at her, and then he said, his voice soft, his eyes locked on hers, "I had a dream of you. My mother swears dreams always mean something, but I never gave it any credit. Only the night before last, with the earth at my back, I found myself missing my bed, wanting my sheets, and aching for something else."

Her eyes widened, and Nevin hesitated. Was he foolish to push now? Should he wait and court her in a proper fashion? Only he did not feel proper. He had been away for but a day, time enough to show him the torture of staying away. Time enough to make him realize he had asked for the wrong Harwood sister. And that dream—that anguishing dream—had shown him his path.

He kept his stare fixed on her. If only he could look into her thoughts and know her desires. But he had only his feelings to guide him, and they drove him to risk everything. The relief that Bryn had taken Cecila away had filled him with a giddy hope that could not be denied.

He knew what he wanted—oh, how he knew. And now that he did know, he did not want to wait.

"I dreamed of my mother searching for me, only she could not find me," he told her, his voice low. "Not until I finally called out my name to her."

"Your name?" she said, her voice softening.

Afraid she might try to leave, he took her hand. She tugged to free it, but he closed his fingers, for he had no intention of releasing her—not until he had his answers. Rubbing his thumb across the inside of her wrist, he felt her pulse skitter at his touch. He could not be wrong about this.

Something had changed in him, a shift in his own view of himself. That dream had played a part. So had seeing his own people again. So had missing her, and so had his relief at the discovery that Bryn had run off with Cecila.

He knew now he would never make a proper lord. He actually had liked sleeping under the stars, though from the aches in his shoulders and back, he would not make a habit of it. But he had another habit he wanted.

"Christopher—but my family calls me Christo," he told her. "Will you also, Ella?"

The blush crept up her throat and into her cheeks. "Oh, I—what did you call me?"

"Ella. I heard your mother use it, and I like that name for you far better." He rubbed his thumb across her wrist again.

Eyes enormous, looking confused, she stared at him. "Yes, but . . . I . . . just why are you back so soon?"

He smiled now. He had been waiting for that question, to know she had been thinking of him. And wondering. "That dream brought me back. It was not just my mother I could not find. It became you."

Face scarlet, she jerked her hand away and turned, but he caught her by the waist. A half-choked 'please' came out, but he could not tell if she begged for release, or something else, so he said, "Ella, don't step away. I have something I must say to you."

She had lowered her chin, but from the stair below he could see into her eyes. He could glimpse the fear. And the need. They mirrored his own.

"It is time for both of us to stop running from ourselves. I know I may not be what you want, a half Gypsy who does not fit into your world."

She looked at him, and shook her head. "It is not that. It . . . oh, I am such a wretched coward. I thought I . . . well, I am terrified, and there is a very impolite honesty for you. I can tell others what to do, but I seem to be hopeless with myself."

"Then just tell me to go, and I shall. Or tell me to stay. Tell me what I must do. I have to hear that."

Biting her lower lip, Penelope glanced at him. Then he shifted his weight, and panic flared. *Oh, heavens, he is going to turn away and think I do not care because I am as tongue-tied as his cousin!*

And still the words caught in her chest. She had once been so bold with her heart, but for so long now she had done nothing but build walls between her and others. She knew the words lay in her, however, and they struggled for release. Only how did she say them?

Perhaps I could tell him in another fashion.

Hesitating, she lifted her hand, then touched it lightly to his shoulder to brush her palm along the strength encased there.

The smile started in his eyes. She watched his lips curve. Then his arms came around her, pulling her closer. One hand stole up her back, setting her tingling when he touched the soft hairs at the back of her neck. He drew her mouth to his.

Oh, this is going to be a disaster!

She braced herself, stiffening as his lips touched hers, but his kisses did not stop. His lips brushed hers again, then moved to the soft spot under her jaw. As his mouth came back to hers, asking for more this time, her sigh escaped.

I should not, she thought, then she smiled. *Oh, heavens!*

Scruples abandoned, she kissed him back, releasing the pent yearning, opening to herself and to him until he staggered and braced them both against the wall opposite the banister.

Opening his eyes, he stared down at her, then demanded, his voice rough, "Did that idiot who would not marry you ever kiss you like that?"

Dazed to discover that her arms had wound around his neck, she shook her head. "No—but you do know this is hardly proper. What if we both tumble down?"

"I think we already have." Slanting a smile at her, he swept her into his arms, startling a squeak.

"Heavens, I am far too large for this. Put me down!"

His smile widened to a grin. "I will—when I have you someplace less proper."

She frowned at him. "You are impossible!"

"Oh, I think you will find that a man in love is easy enough to manage."

"In love?" she asked, relaxing. How oddly pleasant to be carried as if she weighed no more than Sylvain's fox. "Really? You know, the day I found you in the paddock with the stallion and I was so terrified something would happen to you—I have been trying to think when I fell in love, and I think it might have been then."

He gave a chuckle, a warm sound that chased down her spine and curled into a ball inside her. "I think I loved you the moment I saw you. The moment I touched you."

She made a face. "Yes, and then I began to talk."

He had carried her down the stairs, and now he strode with her to the library, pausing only to bump open the half-ajar door. Putting her on her feet, he gripped her shoulders. "Yes, you talked—and I fell in love also with that sharp tongue, and the fierceness you use to protect those you love, so do not disparage yourself to me!"

She glanced up at him. "Is that true?"

"You know I never say polite lies."

The joy flooded her, as if something that had too long held her heart had broken loose. She cupped his face in her hands. "Oh, Christo, I do love you."

He took her into his arms. It had taken him a long time to find where he belonged. But the search had been worth it, for, looking into her eyes, he knew this was home for him—forever.

AUTHOR'S NOTE

Every book seems to have its own peculiar needs for research. While my information on Gypsies in England, which I'd done for *A Much Compromised Lady,* served me well in this book, I found an additional need to dig up details on libraries of the 1800s and on rare books. I have to thank Stephen Tabor, Curator of Early Printed Books at the Huntington Library, for pointing me in the right direction, and fellow author Ann Elizabeth Cree for sharing some of her information and some great resources.

As to the horse in this book, Whalebone actually was a noted offspring of the great racehorse Eclipse. That bloodline was famous not just for speed, but for bad tempers as well.

Readers can also look for future appearances of the 'wild Winslows' and others in *A Proper Mistress.*

As to any other questions or comments, write or e-mail, and don't forget to ask for a free bookmark: Shannon Donnelly, PO Box 3313, Burbank, CA 91508-3313, read@shannondonnelly.com.

Embrace the Romances of

Shannon Drake

More Zebra Regency Romances
